P9-CBD-978

Enter the

HORRIFYING
LYRICAL
POIGNANT
TERRIBLE
BEAUTIFUL
UNIQUE

World of
Zenna Henderson

where "a rare combination of energy,
sensitivity and imagination add up to
an exciting talent."

The Kirkus Service

Other Avon Books by
Zenna Henderson

HOLDING WONDER

THE PEOPLE: NO DIFFERENT FLESH

PILGRIMAGE

The Anything Box

ZENNA HENDERSON

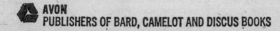
AVON
PUBLISHERS OF BARD, CAMELOT AND DISCUS BOOKS

All the characters in this book are fictitious,
and any resemblance to actual persons,
living or dead, is purely coincidental.

ACKNOWLEDGMENTS

The Magazine of Fantasy and Science Fiction:
  "The Anything Box" Copyright © 1956 by Mercury Press, Inc.
  "Subcommittee" Copyright © 1962 by Mercury Press, Inc.
  "Food to All Flesh" Copyright 1954 by Mercury Press, Inc.
  "Come On, Wagon!" Copyright 1951 by Mercury Press, Inc.
  "Walking Aunt Daid" Copyright © 1955 by Mercury Press, Inc.
  "Things" Copyright © 1960 by Mercury Press, Inc.
  "Turn the Page" Copyright © 1957 by Mercury Press, Inc.
  "And a Little Child—" Copyright © 1959 by Mercury Press, Inc.
  "The Last Step" Copyright © 1957 by Mercury Press, Inc.
Galaxy Magazine:
  "Something Bright" Copyright © 1959 by Galaxy Publishing Corporation
Beyond Fantasy Fiction:
  "Hush!" Copyright © 1953 by Galaxy Publishing Corporation
Imagination:
  "The Substitute" Copyright 1953 by Greenleaf Publishing Company
  "Stevie and The Dark" Copyright 1952 by Greenleaf Publishing Company
  "The Grunder" Copyright 1953 by Greenleaf Publishing Company

AVON BOOKS
A division of
The Hearst Corporation
959 Eighth Avenue
New York, New York 10019

Copyright © 1965 by Zenna Henderson
Published by arrangement with Doubleday & Co., Inc.
Library of Congress Catalog Card Number: 65-24001
ISBN: 0-380-01745-8

First Avon Printing, February, 1969
Sixth Printing

Cover illustration by Hector Garrido

AVON TRADEMARK REG. U.S. PAT. OFF. AND
FOREIGN COUNTRIES, REGISTERED TRADEMARK—
MARCA REGISTRADA, HECHO EN CHICAGO, U.S.A.

Printed in the U.S.A.

To all my friends who have spoken
for an Anything Box,
but especially for R. G.
who has no need of his now.

Contents

nearly burned out in her torment flared brightly again and she slept.

The Anything Box

The Anything Box

I suppose it was about the second week of school that I noticed Sue-lynn particularly. Of course, I'd noticed her name before and checked her out automatically for maturity and ability and probable performance the way most teachers do with their students during the first weeks of school. She had checked out mature and capable and no worry as to performance so I had pigeonholed her—setting aside for the moment the little nudge that said, "Too quiet"—with my other no-worrys until the fluster and flurry of the first days had died down a little.

I remember my noticing day. I had collapsed into my chair for a brief respite from guiding hot little hands through the intricacies of keeping a Crayola within reasonable bounds and the room was full of the relaxed, happy hum of a pleased class as they worked away, not realizing that they were rubbing "blue" into their memories as well as onto their papers. I was meditating on how individual personalities were beginning to emerge among the thirty-five or so heterogeneous first graders I had, when I noticed Sue-lynn—really noticed her—for the first time.

She had finished her paper—far ahead of the others as usual—and was sitting at her table facing me. She had her thumbs touching in front of her on the table and her fingers curving as though they held something between them—something large enough to keep her fingertips apart and angular enough to bend her fingers as if for corners. It was something pleasant that she held—pleasant and precious. You could tell that by the softness of her hold. She was leaning forward a little, her lower ribs pressed against the table, and she was looking, completely absorbed, at the table between her hands. Her face was relaxed and happy. Her mouth curved in a tender half-smile, and as I watched, her lashes lifted and she looked at me with a warm share-the-pleasure look. Then her

11

eyes blinked and the shutters came down inside them. Her hand flicked into the desk and out. She pressed her thumbs to her forefingers and rubbed them slowly together. Then she laid one hand over the other on the table and looked down at them with the air of complete denial and ignorance children can assume so devastatingly.

The incident caught my fancy and I began to notice Sue-lynn. As I consciously watched her, I saw that she spent most of her free time staring at the table between her hands, much too unobtrusively to catch my busy attention. She hurried through even the fun-est of fun papers and then lost herself in looking. When Davie pushed her down at recess, and blood streamed from her knee to her ankle, she took her bandages and her tear-smudged face to that comfort she had so readily—if you'll pardon the expression—at hand, and emerged minutes later, serene and dry-eyed. I think Davie pushed her down because of her Looking. I know the day before he had come up to me, red-faced and squirming.

"Teacher," he blurted. "She Looks!"

"Who looks?" I asked absently, checking the vocabulary list in my book, wondering how on earth I'd missed *where,* one of those annoying *wh* words that throw the children for a loss.

"Sue-lynn. She Looks and Looks!"

"At you?" I asked.

"Well—" He rubbed a forefinger below his nose, leaving a clean streak on his upper lip, accepted the proffered Kleenex and put it in his pocket. "She looks at her desk and tells lies. She says she can see—"

"Can see what?" My curiosity picked up its ears.

"Anything," said Davie. "It's her Anything Box. She can see anything she wants to."

"Does it hurt you for her to Look?"

"Well," he squirmed. Then he burst out. "She says she saw me with a dog biting me because I took her pencil— she said." He started a pell-mell verbal retreat. "She *thinks* I took her pencil. I only found—" His eyes dropped. "I'll give it back."

"I hope so," I smiled. "If you don't want her to look at you, then don't do things like that."

"Dern girls," he muttered, and clomped back to his seat.

So I think he pushed her down the next day to get back at her for the dogbite.

12

Several times after that I wandered to the back of the room, casually in her vicinity, but always she either saw or felt me coming and the quick sketch of her hand disposed of the evidence. Only once I thought I caught a glimmer of something—but her thumb and forefinger brushed in sunlight, and it must have been just that.

Children don't retreat for no reason at all, and though Sue-lynn did not follow any overt pattern of withdrawal, I started to wonder about her. I watched her on the playground, to see how she tracked there. That only confused me more.

She had a very regular pattern. When the avalanche of children first descended at recess, she avalanched along with them and nothing in the shrieking, running, dodging mass resolved itself into a withdrawn Sue-lynn. But after ten minutes or so, she emerged from the crowd, tousle-haired, rosy-cheeked, smutched with dust, one shoelace dangling, and through some alchemy that I coveted for myself, she suddenly became untousled, undusty and unsmutched.

And there she was, serene and composed on the narrow little step at the side of the flight of stairs just where they disappeared into the base of the pseudo-Corinthian column that graced Our Door and her cupped hands received whatever they received and her absorption in what she saw became so complete that the bell came as a shock every time.

And each time, before she joined the rush to Our Door, her hand would sketch a gesture to her pocket, if she had one, or to the tiny ledge that extended between the hedge and the building. Apparently she always had to put the Anything Box away, but never had to go back to get it.

I was so intrigued by her putting whatever it was on the ledge that once I actually went over and felt along the grimy little outset. I sheepishly followed my children into the hall, wiping the dust from my fingertips, and Sue-lynn's eyes brimmed amusement at me without her mouth's smiling. Her hands mischievously squared in front of her and her thumbs caressed a solidness as the line of children swept into the room.

I smiled too because she was so pleased with having outwitted me. This seemed to be such a gay withdrawal that I let my worry die down. Better this manifestation than any number of other ones that I could name.

13

Someday, perhaps, I'll learn to keep my mouth shut. I wish I had before that long afternoon when we primary teachers worked together in a heavy cloud of Ditto fumes, the acrid smell of India ink, drifting cigarette smoke and the constant current of chatter, and I let Alpha get me started on what to do with our behavior problems. She was all raunched up about the usual rowdy loudness of her boys and the eternal clack of her girls, and I—bless my stupidity—gave her Sue-lynn as an example of what should be our deepest concern rather than the outbursts from our active ones.

"You mean she just sits and looks at nothing?" Alpha's voice grated into her questioning tone.

"Well, I can't see anything," I admitted. "But apparently she can."

"But that's having hallucinations!" Her voice went up a notch. "I read a book once—"

"Yes." Marlene leaned across the desk to flick ashes in the ash tray. "So we have heard and heard and heard!"

"Well!" sniffed Alpha. "It's better than *never* reading a book."

"We're waiting," Marlene leaked smoke from her nostrils, "for the day when you read another book. This one must have been uncommonly long."

"Oh, I don't know." Alpha's forehead wrinkled with concentration. "It was only about—" Then she reddened and turned her face angrily away from Marlene.

"Apropos of *our* discussion—" she said pointedly. "It sounds to me like that child has a deep personality disturbance. Maybe even a psychotic—whatever—" Her eyes glistened faintly as she turned the thought over.

"Oh, I don't know," I said, surprised into echoing her words at my sudden need to defend Sue-lynn. "There's something about her. She doesn't have that apprehensive, hunched-shoulder, don't-hit-me-again air about her that so many withdrawn children have." And I thought achingly of one of mine from last year that Alpha had now and was verbally bludgeoning back into silence after all my work with him. "She seems to have a happy, adjusted personality, only with this odd little—*plus.*"

"Well, I'd be worried if she were mine," said Alpha. "I'm glad all my kids are so normal." She sighed complacently. "I guess I really haven't anything to kick about. I seldom ever have problem children except wigglers and

14

yakkers, and a holler and a smack can straighten them out."

Marlene caught my eye mockingly, tallying Alpha's class with me, and I turned away with a sigh. To be so happy—well, I suppose ignorance does help.

"You'd better do something about that girl," Alpha shrilled as she left the room. "She'll probably get worse and worse as time goes on. Deteriorating, I think the book said."

I had known Alpha a long time and I thought I knew how much of her talk to discount, but I began to worry about Sue-lynn. Maybe this *was* a disturbance that was more fundamental than the usual run of the mill that I had met up with. Maybe a child *can* smile a soft, contented smile and still have little maggots of madness flourishing somewhere inside.

Or, by gorry! I said to myself defiantly, maybe she *does* have an Anything Box. Maybe she *is* looking at something precious. Who am I to say no to anything like that?

An Anything Box! What could you see in an Anything Box? Heart's desire? I felt my own heart lurch—just a little—the next time Sue-lynn's hands curved. I breathed deeply to hold me in my chair. If it was *her* Anything Box, I wouldn't be able to see my heart's desire in it. Or would I? I propped my cheek up on my hand and doodled aimlessly on my time schedule sheet. How on earth, I wondered—not for the first time—do I manage to get myself off on these tangents?

Then I felt a small presence at my elbow and turned to meet Sue-lynn's wide eyes.

"Teacher?" The word was hardly more than a breath.

"Yes?" I could tell that for some reason Sue-lynn was loving me dearly at the moment. Maybe because her group had gone into new books that morning. Maybe because I had noticed her new dress, the ruffles of which made her feel very feminine and lovable, or maybe just because the late autumn sun lay so golden across her desk. Anyway, she was loving me to overflowing, and since, unlike most of the children, she had no casual hugs or easy moist kisses, she was bringing her love to me in her encompassing hands.

"See my box, Teacher? It's my Anything Box."

"Oh, my!" I said. "May I hold it?"

After all, I have held—tenderly or apprehensively or bravely—tiger magic, live rattlesnakes, dragon's teeth,

15

poor little dead butterflies and two ears and a nose that dropped off Sojie one cold morning—none of which I could see any more than I could the Anything Box. But I took the squareness from her carefully, my tenderness showing in my fingers and my face.

And I received weight and substance and actuality!

Almost I let it slip out of my surprised fingers, but Sue-lynn's apprehensive breath helped me catch it and I curved my fingers around the precious warmness and looked down, down, past a faint shimmering, down into Sue-lynn's Anything Box.

I was running barefoot through the whispering grass. The swirl of my skirts caught the daisies as I rounded the gnarled apple tree at the corner. The warm wind lay along each of my cheeks and chuckled in' my ears. My heart outstripped my flying feet and melted with a rush of delight into warmness as his arms—

I closed my eyes and swallowed hard, my palms tight against the Anything Box. "It's beautiful!" I whispered. "It's wonderful, Sue-lynn. Where did you get it?"

Her hands took it back hastily. "It's mine," she said defiantly. "It's mine."

"Of course," I said. "Be careful now. Don't drop it."

She smiled faintly as she sketched a motion to her pocket. "I won't." She patted the flat pocket on her way back to her seat.

Next day she was afraid to look at me at first for fear I might say something or look something or in some way remind her of what must seem like a betrayal to her now, but after I only smiled my usual smile, with no added secret knowledge, she relaxed.

A night or so later when I leaned over my moon-drenched window sill and let the shadow of my hair hide my face from such ebullient glory, I remembered the Anything Box. Could I make one for myself? Could I square off this aching waiting, this outreaching, this silent cry inside me, and make it into an Anything Box? I freed my hands and brought them together, thumb to thumb, framing a part of the horizon's darkness between my up-right forefingers. I stared into the empty square until my eyes watered. I sighed, and laughed a little, and let my hands frame my face as I leaned out into the night. To have magic so near—to feel it tingle off my fingertips and then to be so bound that I couldn't receive it. I turned away from the window—turning my back on brightness.

It wasn't long after this that Alpha succeeded in putting sharp points of worry back in my thoughts of Sue-lynn. We had ground duty together, and one morning when we shivered while the kids ran themselves rosy in the crisp air, she sizzed in my ear.

"Which one is it? The abnormal one, I mean."

"I don't have any abnormal children," I said, my voice sharpening before the sentence ended because I suddenly realized whom she meant.

"Well, I call it abnormal to stare at nothing." You could almost taste the acid in her words. "Who is it?"

"Sue-lynn," I said reluctantly. "She's playing on the bars now."

Alpha surveyed the upside-down Sue-lynn whose brief skirts were belled down from her bare pink legs and half covered her face as she swung from one of the bars by her knees. Alpha clutched her wizened, blue hands together and breathed on them. "She looks normal enough," she said.

"She *is* normal!" I snapped.

"*Well,* bite my head off!" cried Alpha. "You're the one that said she wasn't, not me—or is it 'not I'? I never could remember. Not me? Not I?"

The bell saved Alpha from a horrible end. I never knew a person so serenely unaware of essentials and so sensitive to trivia.

But she had succeeded in making me worry about Sue-lynn again, and the worry exploded into distress a few days later.

Sue-lynn came to school sleepy-eyed and quiet. She didn't finish any of her work and she fell asleep during rest time. I cussed TV and Drive-Ins and assumed a night's sleep would put it right. But next day Sue-lynn burst into tears and slapped Davie clear off his chair.

"Why Sue-lynn!" I gathered Davie up in all his astonishment and took Sue-lynn's hand. She jerked it away from me and flung herself at Davie again. She got two handfuls of his hair and had him out of my grasp before I knew it. She threw him bodily against the wall with a flip of her hands, then doubled up her fists and pressed them to her streaming eyes. In the shocked silence of the room, she stumbled over to Isolation and seating herself, back to the class, on the little chair, she leaned her head into the corner and sobbed quietly in big gulping sobs.

"What on earth goes on?" I asked the stupefied Davie

17

who sat spraddle-legged on the floor fingering a detached tuft of hair. "What did you do?"

"I only said 'Robber Daughter,'" said Davie. "It said so in the paper. My mama said her daddy's a robber. They put him in jail cause he robbered a gas station." His bewildered face was trying to decide whether or not to cry. Everything had happened so fast that he didn't know yet if he was hurt.

"It isn't nice to call names," I said weakly. "Get back into your seat. I'll take care of Sue-lynn later."

He got up and sat gingerly down in his chair, rubbing his ruffled hair, wanting to make more of a production of the situation but not knowing how. He twisted his face experimentally to see if he had tears available and had none.

"Dern girls," he muttered, and tried to shake his fingers free of a wisp of hair.

I kept my eye on Sue-lynn for the next half hour as I busied myself with the class. Her sobs soon stopped and her rigid shoulders relaxed. Her hands were softly in her lap and I knew she was taking comfort from her Anything Box. We had our talk together later, but she was so completely sealed off from me by her misery that there was no communication between us. She sat quietly watching me as I talked, her hands trembling in her lap. It shakes the heart, somehow, to see the hands of a little child quiver like that.

That afternoon I looked up from my reading group, startled, as though by a cry, to catch Sue-lynn's frightened eyes. She looked around bewildered and then down at her hands again—her empty hands. Then she darted to the Isolation corner and reached under the chair. She went back to her seat slowly, her hands squared to an unseen weight. For the first time, apparently, she had had to go get the Anything Box. It troubled me with a vague unease for the rest of the afternoon.

Through the days that followed while the trial hung fire, I had Sue-lynn in attendance bodily, but that was all. She sank into her Anything Box at every opportunity. And always, if she had put it away somewhere, she had to go back for it. She roused more and more reluctantly from these waking dreams, and there finally came a day when I had to shake her to waken her.

I went to her mother, but she couldn't or wouldn't

understand me, and made me feel like a frivolous gossipmonger taking her mind away from her husband, despite the fact that I didn't even mention him—or maybe because I didn't mention him.

"If she's being a bad girl, spank her," she finally said, wearily shifting the weight of a whining baby from one hip to another and pushing her tousled hair off her forehead. "Whatever you do is all right by me. My worrier is all used up. I haven't got any left for the kids right now."

Well, Sue-lynn's father was found guilty and sentenced to the State Penitentiary and school was less than an hour old the next day when Davie came up, clumsily a-tiptoe, braving my wrath for interrupting a reading group, and whispered hoarsely, "Sue-lynn's asleep with her eyes open again, Teacher."

We went back to the table and Davie slid into his chair next to a completely unaware Sue-lynn. He poked her with a warning finger. "I told you I'd tell on you."

And before our horrified eyes, she toppled, as rigidly as a doll, sideways off the chair. The thud of her landing relaxed her and she lay limp on the green asphalt tile—a thin paper doll of a girl, one hand still clenched open around something. I pried her fingers loose and almost wept to feel enchantment dissolve under my heavy touch. I carried her down to the nurse's room and we worked over her with wet towels and prayer and she finally opened her eyes.

"Teacher," she whispered weakly.

"Yes, Sue-lynn." I took her cold hands in mine.

"Teacher, I almost got in my Anything Box."

"No," I answered. "You couldn't. You're too big."

"Daddy's there," she said. "And where we used to live."

I took a long, long look at her wan face. I hope it was genuine concern for her that prompted my next words. I hope it wasn't envy or the memory of the niggling nagging of Alpha's voice that put firmness in my voice as I went on. "That's playlike," I said. "Just for fun."

Her hands jerked protestingly in mine. "Your Anything Box is just for fun. It's like Davie's cow pony that he keeps in his desk or Sojie's jet plane, or when the big bear chases all of you at recess. It's fun-for-play, but it's not for real. You mustn't think it's for real. It's only play."

"No!" she denied. "No!" she cried frantically, and hunching herself up on the cot, peering through her tear-

19

swollen eyes, she scrabbled under the pillow and down beneath the rough blanket that covered her.

"Where is it?" she cried. "Where is it? Give it back to me, Teacher!"

She flung herself toward me and pulled open both my clenched hands.

"Where did you put it? Where did you put it?"

"There is no Anything Box," I said flatly, trying to hold her to me and feeling my heart breaking along with hers.

"You took it!" she sobbed. "You took it away from me!" And she wrenched herself out of my arms.

"Can't you give it back to her?" whispered the nurse. "If it makes her feel so bad? Whatever it is—"

"It's just imagination," I said, almost sullenly. "I can't give her back something that doesn't exist."

Too young! I thought bitterly. Too young to learn that heart's desire is only play-like.

Of course the doctor found nothing wrong. Her mother dismissed the matter as a fainting spell and Sue-lynn came back to class next day, thin and listless, staring blankly out the window, her hands palm down on the desk. I swore by the pale hollow of her cheek that never, *never* again would I take any belief from anyone without replacing it with something better. What had I given Sue-lynn? What had she better than I had taken from her? How did I know but that her Anything Box was on purpose to tide her over rough spots in her life like this? And what now, now that I had taken it from her?

Well, after a time she began to work again, and later, to play. She came back to smiles, but not to laughter. She puttered along quite satisfactorily except that she was a candle blown out. The flame was gone wherever the brightness of belief goes. And she had no more sharing smiles for me, no overflowing love to bring to me. And her shoulder shrugged subtly away from my touch.

Then one day I suddenly realized that Sue-lynn was searching our classroom. Stealthily, casually, day by day she was searching, covering every inch of the room. She went through every puzzle box, every lump of clay, every shelf and cupboard, every box and bag. Methodically she checked behind every row of books and in every child's desk until finally, after almost a week, she had been through everything in the place except my desk. Then she began to materialize suddenly at my elbow every time I opened a drawer. And her eyes would probe quickly and sharply before I slid it shut again. But if I tried to intercept her looks, they slid away and she had some legitimate errand that had brought her up to the vicinity of the desk.

She believes it again, I thought hopefully. She won't accept the fact that her Anything Box is gone. She wants it again.

But it *is* gone, I thought drearily. It's really-for-true gone.

My head was heavy from troubled sleep, and sorrow was a weariness in all my movements. Waiting is sometimes a burden almost too heavy to carry. While my children hummed happily over their fun-stuff, I brooded silently out the window until I managed a laugh at myself. It was a shaky laugh that threatened to dissolve into something else, so I brisked back to my desk.

As good a time as any to throw out useless things, I thought, and to see if I can find that colored chalk I put away so carefully. I plunged my hands into the wilderness of the bottom right-hand drawer of my desk. It was deep with a huge accumulation of anything—just anything— that might need a temporary hiding place. I knelt to pull out leftover Jack Frost pictures, and a broken bean-shooter, a chewed red ribbon, a roll of cap gun ammunition, one striped sock, six Numbers papers, a rubber dagger, a copy of The Gospel According to St. Luke, a miniature coal shovel, patterns for jack-o'-lanterns, and a pink plastic pelican. I retrieved my Irish linen hankie I thought lost forever and Sojie's report card that he had told me solemnly had blown out of his hand and landed on a jet and broke the sound barrier so loud that it busted all to flitters. Under the welter of miscellany, I felt a squareness. Oh, happy! I thought, this *is* where I put the colored chalk! I cascaded papers off both sides of my lifting hands and shook the box free.

We were together again. Outside, the world was an enchanting wilderness of white, the wind shouting softly through the windows, tapping wet, white fingers against the warm light. Inside, all the worry and waiting, the apartness and loneliness were over and forgotten, their hugeness dwindled by the comfort of a shoulder, the warmth of clasping hands—and nowhere, nowhere was the fear of parting, nowhere the need to do without again. This was the happy ending. This was—

This was Sue-lynn's Anything Box!

My racing heart slowed as the dream faded—and rushed

21

again at the realization. I had it here! In my junk drawer! It had been here all the time!

I stood up shakily, concealing the invisible box in the flare of my skirts. I sat down and put the box carefully in the center of my desk, covering the top of it with my palms lest I should drown again in delight. I looked at Sue-lynn. She was finishing her fun paper, competently but unjoyously. Now would come her patient sitting with quiet hands until told to do something else.

Alpha would approve. And very possibly, I thought, Alpha would, for once in her limited life, be right. We may need "hallucinations" to keep us going—all of us but the Alphas—but when we go so far as to try to force ourselves, physically, into the Never-Neverland of heart's desire—

I remembered Sue-lynn's thin rigid body toppling doll-like off its chair. Out of her deep need she had found—or created? Who could tell?—something too dangerous for a child. I could so easily bring the brimming happiness back to her eyes—but at what a possible price!

No, I had a duty to protect Sue-lynn. Only maturity—the maturity born of the sorrow and loneliness that Sue-lynn was only beginning to know—could be trusted to use an Anything Box safely and wisely.

My heart thudded as I began to move my hands, letting the palms slip down from the top to shape the sides of—

I had moved them back again before I really saw, and I have now learned almost to forget that glimpse of what heart's desire is like when won at the cost of another's heart.

I sat there at the desk trembling and breathless, my palms moist, feeling as if I had been on a long journey away from the little schoolroom. Perhaps I had. Perhaps I had been shown all the kingdoms of the world in a moment of time.

"Sue-lynn," I called. "Will you come up here when you're through?"

She nodded unsmilingly and snipped off the last paper from the edge of Mistress Mary's dress. Without another look at her handiwork, she carried the scissors safely to the scissors box, crumpled the scraps of paper in her hand and came up to the wastebasket by the desk.

"I have something for you, Sue-lynn," I said, uncovering the box.

22

Her eyes dropped to the desk top. She looked indifferently up at me. "I did my fun paper already."

"Did you like it?"

"Yes." It was a flat lie.

"Good," I lied right back. "But look here." I squared my hands around the Anything Box.

She took a deep breath and the whole of her little body stiffened.

"I found it," I said hastily, fearing anger. "I found it in the bottom drawer."

She leaned her chest against my desk, her hands caught tightly between, her eyes intent on the box, her face white with the aching want you see on children's faces pressed to Christmas windows.

"Can I have it?" she whispered.

"It's yours," I said, holding it out. Still she leaned against her hands, her eyes searching my face.

"Can I have it?" she asked again.

"Yes!" I was impatient with this anti-climax. "But—"

Her eyes flickered. She had sensed my reservation before I had. "But you must never try to get into it again."

"Okay," she said, the word coming out on a long relieved sigh. "Okay, Teacher."

She took the box and tucked it lovingly into her small pocket. She turned from the desk and started back to her table. My mouth quirked with a small smile. It seemed to me that everything about her had suddenly turned upwards—even the ends of her straight taffy-colored hair. The subtle flame about her that made her Sue-lynn was there again. She scarcely touched the floor as she walked.

I sighed heavily and traced on the desk top with my finger a probable size for an Anything Box. What would Sue-lynn choose to see first? How like a drink after a drought it would seem to her.

I was startled as a small figure materialized at my elbow. It was Sue-lynn, her fingers carefully squared before her.

"Teacher," she said softly, all the flat emptiness gone from her voice. "Any time you want to take my Anything Box, you just say so."

I groped through my astonishment and incredulity for words. She couldn't possibly have had time to look into the Box yet.

"Why, thank you, Sue-lynn," I managed. "Thanks a lot. I would like very much to borrow it some time."

"Would you like it now?" she asked, proffering it.

"No, thank you," I said, around the lump in my throat. "I've had a turn already. You go ahead."

"Okay," she murmured. Then—"Teacher?"

"Yes?"

Shyly she leaned against me, her cheek on my shoulder. She looked up at me with her warm, unshuttered eyes, then both arms were suddenly around my neck in a brief awkward embrace.

"Watch out!" I whispered laughing into the collar of her blue dress. "You'll lose it again!"

"No I won't," she laughed back, patting the flat pocket of her dress. "Not ever, ever again!"

Subcommittee

First came the sleek black ships, falling out of the sky in patterned disorder, sowing fear as they settled like seeds on the broad landing field. After them, like bright butterflies, came the vividly colored slow ships that hovered and hesitated and came to rest scattered among the deadly dark ones.

"Beautiful!" sighed Serena, turning from the conference room window. "There should have been music to go with it."

"A funeral dirge," said Thorn. "Or a requiem. Or flutes before failure. Frankly, I'm frightened, Rena. If these conferences fail, all hell will break loose again. Imagine living another year like this past one."

"But the conference won't fail!" Serena protested. "If they're willing to consent to the conference, surely they'll be willing to work with us for peace."

"Their peace or ours?" asked Thorn, staring morosely out the window. "I'm afraid we're being entirely too naïve about this whole affair. It's been a long time since we finally were able to say, 'Ain't gonna study war no more,' and made it stick. We've lost a lot of the cunning that used to be necessary in dealing with other people. We can't, even now, be sure this isn't a trick to get all our high command together in one place for a grand massacre."

"Oh, no!" Serena pressed close to him and his arm went around her. "They couldn't possibly violate—"

"Couldn't they?" Thorn pressed his cheek to the top of her ear. "We don't know, Rena. We just don't know. We have so little information about them. We know practically nothing about their customs—even less about their values or from what frame of reference they look upon our suggestion of suspending hostilities."

"But surely they must be sincere. They brought their

families along with them. You did say those bright ships are family craft, didn't you?"

"Yes, they suggested we bring our families and they brought their families along with them, but it's nothing to give us comfort. They take them everywhere—even into battle."

"Into battle!"

"Yes. They mass the home craft off out of range during battles, but every time we disable or blast one of their fighters, one or more of the home craft spin away out of control or flare into nothingness. Apparently they're just glorified trailers, dependent on the fighters for motive power and everything else." The unhappy lines deepened in Thorn's face. "They don't know it, but even apart from their superior weapons, they practically forced us into this truce. How could we go on wiping out their war fleet when, with every black ship, those confounded posy-colored home craft fell too, like pulling petals off a flower. And each petal heavy with the lives of women and children."

Serena shivered and pressed closer to Thorn. "The conference must work. We just can't have war any more. You've got to get through to them. Surely, if we want peace and so do they—"

"We don't know what they want," said Thorn heavily. "Invaders, aggressors, strangers from hostile worlds—so completely alien to us—How can we ever hope to get together?"

They left the conference room in silence, snapping the button on the door knob before they closed it.

"Hey, lookit, Mommie! Here's a wall!" Splinter's five-year-old hands flattened themselves like grubby starfish against the greenish ripple of the ten-foot vitricrete fence that wound through the trees and slid down the gentle curve of the hill. "Where did it come from? What's it for? How come we can't go play in the go'fish pond any more?"

Serena leaned her hand against the wall. "The people who came in the pretty ships wanted a place to walk and play, too. So the Construction Corp put the fence up for them."

"Why won't they let me play in the go'fish pond?" Splinter's brows bent ominously.

"They don't know you want to," said Serena.

"I'll tell them, then," said Splinter. He threw his head

26

back. "Hey! Over there!" He yelled, his fists doubling and his whole body stiffening with the intensity of the shout. "Hey! I wanta play in the go'fish pond!"

Serena laughed. "Hush, Splinter. Even if they could hear you, they wouldn't understand. They're from far, far away. They don't talk the way we do."

"But maybe we could play," said Splinter wistfully.

"Yes," sighed Serena, "maybe you could play. If the fence weren't there. But you see, Splinter, we don't know what kind of—people—they are. Whether they would want to play. Whether they would be—nice."

"Well, how can we find out with that old wall there?"

"We can't, Splinter," said Serena. "Not with the fence there."

They walked on down the hill, Splinter's hand trailing along the wall.

"Maybe they're mean," he said finally. "Maybe they're so bad that the 'struction Corp had to build a cage for them—a big, big cage!" He stretched his arm as high as he could reach, up the wall. "Do you suppose they got tails?"

"Tails?" laughed Serena. "Whatever gave you that idea?"

"I dunno. They came from a long ways away. I'd like a tail—a long, curly one with fur on!" He swished his miniature behind energetically.

"Whatever for?" asked Serena.

"It'd come in handy," said Splinter solemnly. "For climbing and—and keeping my neck warm!"

"Why aren't there any other kids here?" he asked as they reached the bottom of the slope. "I'd like *somebody* to play with."

"Well, Splinter, it's kind of hard to explain," started Serena, sinking down on the narrow ledge shelving on the tiny dry watercourse at her feet.

"Don't esplain then," said Splinter. "Just tell me."

"Well, some Linjeni generals came in the big black ships to talk with General Worsham and some more of our generals. They brought their families with them in the fat, pretty ships. So our generals brought their families, too, but your daddy is the only one of our generals who has a little child. All the others are grown up. That's why there's no one for you to play with." I wish it were as simple as it sounds, thought Serena, suddenly weary again with the weeks of negotiation and waiting that had passed.

27

"Oh," said Splinter, thoughtfully. "Then there *are* kids on the other side of the wall, aren't there?"

"Yes, there must be young Linjeni," said Serena. "I guess you could call them children."

Splinter slid down to the bottom of the little watercourse and flopped down on his stomach. He pressed his cheek to the sand and peered through a tiny gap left under the fence where it crossed the stream bed. "I can't see anybody," he said, disappointed.

They started back up the hill toward their quarters, walking silently, Splinter's hand whispering along the wall.

"Mommie?" Splinter said as they neared the patio.

"Yes, Splinter?"

"That fence is to keep them in, isn't it?"

"Yes," said Serena.

"It doesn't feel like that to me," said Splinter. "It feels like it's to shut me out."

Serena suffered through the next days with Thorn. She lay wide-eyed beside him in the darkness of their bedroom, praying as he slept restlessly, struggling even in his sleep—groping for a way.

Tight-lipped, she cleared away untouched meals and brewed more coffee. Her thoughts went hopefully with him every time he started out with new hope and resolution, and her spirits flagged and fell as he brought back dead end, stalemate and growing despair. And in-between times, she tried to keep Splinter on as even a keel as possible, giving him the freedom of the Quarters Area during the long, sunlit days and playing with him as much as possible in the evenings.

One evening Serena was pinning up her hair and keeping half an eye on Splinter as he splashed in his bath. He was gathering up handsful of foaming soap bubbles and pressing them to his chin and cheeks.

"Now I hafta shave like Daddy," he hummed to himself. "Shave, shave, shave!" He flicked the suds off with his forefinger. Then he scooped up a big double handful of bubbles and pressed them all over his face. "Now I'm Doovie. I'm all over fuzzy like Doovie. Lookit, Mommie, I'm all over—" He opened his eyes and peered through the suds to see if she was watching. Consequently, Serena spent a busy next few minutes helping him get the soap out of his eyes. When the tears had finally washed away the trouble, Serena sat toweling Splinter's relaxed little body.

"I bet Doovie'd cry too, if he got soap in his eyes," he said with a sniff. "Wouldn't he, Mommie?"

"Doovie?" said Serena, "Probably. Almost anyone would. Who's Doovie?"

She felt Splinter stiffen on her lap. His eyes wandered away from hers. "Mommie, do you think Daddy will play with me a-morrow?"

"Perhaps." She captured one of his wet feet. "Who's Doovie?"

"Can we have pink cake for dessert tonight? I think I like pink—"

"Who's Doovie?" Serena's voice was firm. Splinter examined his thumbnail critically, then peered up at Serena out of the corner of his eye.

"Doovie," he began, "Doovie's a little boy."

"Oh?" said Serena. "A play-like little boy?"

"No," Splinter whispered, hanging his head. "A real little boy. A Linjeni little boy." Serena drew an astonished breath and Splinter hurried on, his eyes intent on hers. "He's nice people, Mommie, honest! He doesn't say bad words or tell lies or talk sassy to his mother. He can run as fast as I can—faster, if I stumble. He—he—," his eyes dropped again. "I like him—" His mouth quivered.

"Where did—how could—I mean, the fence—" Serena was horrified and completely at a loss for words.

"I dug a hole," confessed Splinter. "Under the fence where the sand is. You didn't say not to! Doovie came to play. His mommie came, too. She's pretty. Her fur is pink, but Doovie's is nice and green. All over!" Splinter got excited. "All over, even where his clothes are! All but his nose and eyes and ears and the front of his hands!"

"But Splinter, how could you! You might have got hurt! They might have—" Serena hugged him tight to hide her face from him.

Splinter squirmed out of her arms. "Doovie wouldn't hurt anyone. You know what, Mommie? He can shut his nose! Yes, he can! He can shut his nose and fold up his ears! I wish I could. It'd come in handy. But I'm bigger'n he is and I can sing and he can't. But he can whistle with his nose and when I try, I just blow mine. Doovie's nice!"

Serena's mind was churning as she helped Splinter get into his night clothes. She felt the chill of fear along her forearms and the back of her neck. What to do now? Forbid Splinter's crawling under the fence? Keep him from possible danger that might just be biding its time?

What would Thorn say? Should she tell him? This might precipitate an incident that—

"Splinter, how many times have you played with Doovie?"

"How many?" Splinter's chest swelled under his clean pajamas. "Let me count," he said importantly and murmured and mumbled over his fingers for a minute. "Four times!" he proclaimed triumphantly. "One, two, three, four whole times!"

"Weren't you scared?"

"Naw!" he said, adding hastily, "Well, maybe a little bit the first time. I thought maybe they might have tails that liked to curl around people's necks. But they haven't," disappointed, "only clothes on like us with fur on under."

"Did you say you saw Doovie's mother, too?"

"Sure," said Splinter. "She was there the first day. She was the one that sent all the others away when they all crowded around me. All grownups. Not any kids excepting Doovie. They kinda pushed and wanted to touch me, but she told them to go away, and they all did 'cepting her and Doovie."

"Oh Splinter!" cried Serena, overcome by the vision of his small self surrounded by pushing, crowding Linjeni grownups who wanted to "touch him."

"What's the matter, Mommie?" asked Splinter.

"Nothing, dear." She wet her lips. "May I go along with you the next time you go to see Doovie? I'd like to meet his mother."

"Sure, sure!" cried Splinter. "Let's go now. Let's go now!"

"Not now," said Serena, feeling the reaction of her fear in her knees and ankles. "It's too late. Tomorrow we'll go see them. And Splinter, let's not tell Daddy yet. Let's keep it a surprise for a while."

"Okay, Mommie," said Splinter. "It's a good surprise, isn't it? You were awful surprised, weren't you?"

"Yes, I was," said Serena. "Awful surprised."

Next day Splinter squatted down and inspected the hole under the fence. "It's kinda little," he said. "Maybe you'll get stuck."

Serena, her heart pounding in her throat, laughed. "That wouldn't be very dignified, would it?" she asked. "To go calling and get stuck in the door."

Splinter laughed. "It'd be funny," he said. "Maybe we better go find a really door for you."

30

"Oh, no," said Serena hastily. "We can make this one bigger."

"Sure," said Splinter. "I'll go get Doovie and he can help dig."

"Fine," said Serena, her throat tightening. *Afraid of a child,* she mocked herself. *Afraid of a Linjeni—aggressor —invader,* she defended.

Splinter flattened on the sand and slid under the fence. "You start digging," he called. "I'll be back!"

Serena knelt to the job, the loose sand coming away so readily that she circled her arms and dredged with them.

Then she heard Splinter scream.

For a brief second, she was paralyzed. Then he screamed again, closer, and Serena dragged the sand away in a frantic frenzy. She felt the sand scoop down the neck of her blouse and the skin scrape off her spine as she forced herself under the fence.

Then there was Splinter, catapulting out of the shrubbery, sobbing and screaming, "Doovie! Doovie's drowning! He's in the go'fish pond! All under the water! I can't get him out! Mommie, Mommie!"

Serena grabbed his hand as she shot past and towed him along, stumbling and dragging, as she ran for the goldfish pond. She leaned across the low wall and caught a glimpse, under the churning thrash of the water, of green mossy fur and staring eyes. With hardly a pause except to shove Splinter backward and start a deep breath, she plunged over into the pond. She felt the burning bite of water up her nostrils and grappled in the murky darkness for Doovie—feeling again and again the thrash of small limbs that slipped away before she could grasp them.

Then she was choking and sputtering on the edge of the pond, pushing the still-struggling Doovie up and over. Splinter grabbed him and pulled as Serena heaved herself over the edge of the pond and fell sprawling across Doovie.

Then she heard another higher, shriller scream and was shoved off Doovie viciously and Doovie was snatched up into rose pink arms. Serena pushed her lank, dripping hair out of her eyes and met the hostile glare of the rose pink eyes of Doovie's mother.

Serena edged over to Splinter and held him close, her eyes intent on the Linjeni. The pink mother felt the green child all over anxiously and Serena noticed with an odd

31

detachment that Splinter hadn't mentioned that Doovie's eyes matched his fur and that he had webbed feet.

Webbed feet! She began to laugh, almost hysterically. Oh Lordy! No wonder Doovie's mother was so alarmed.

"Can you talk to Doovie?" asked Serena of the sobbing Splinter.

"No!" wailed Splinter. "You don't have to talk to play."

"Stop crying, Splinter," said Serena. "Help me think. Doovie's mother thinks we were trying to hurt Doovie. He wouldn't drown in the water. Remember, he can close his nose and fold up his ears. How are we going to tell his mother we weren't trying to hurt him?"

"Well," Splinter scrubbed his cheeks with the back of his hand. "We could hug him—"

"That wouldn't do, Splinter," said Serena, noticing with near panic that other brightly colored figures were moving among the shrubs, drawing closer—"I'm afraid she won't let us touch him."

Briefly she toyed with the idea of turning and trying to get back to the fence, then she took a deep breath and tried to calm down.

"Let's play-like, Splinter," she said. "Let's show Doovie's mother that we thought he was drowning. You go fall in the pond and I'll pull you out. You play-like drowned and I'll—I'll cry."

"Gee, Mommie, you're crying already!" said Splinter, his face puckering.

"I'm just practicing," she said, steadying her voice. "Go on."

Splinter hesitated on the edge of the pond, shrinking away from the water that had fascinated him so many times before. Serena screamed suddenly, and Splinter, startled, lost his balance and fell in. Serena had hold of him almost before he went under water and pulled him out, cramming as much of fear and apprehension into her voice and actions as she could. "Be dead," she whispered fiercely. "Be dead all over!" And Splinter melted so completely in her arms that her moans and cries of sorrow were only partly make-believe. She bent over his still form and rocked to and fro in her grief.

A hand touched her arm and she looked up into the bright eyes of the Linjeni. The look held for a long moment and then the Linjeni smiled, showing even, white teeth, and a pink, furry hand patted Splinter on the shoulder. His eyes flew open and he sat up. Doovie

32

peered around from behind his mother and then he and Splinter were rolling and tumbling together, wrestling happily between the two hesitant mothers. Serena found a shaky laugh somewhere in among her alarms and Doovie's mother whistled softly with her nose.

That night, Thorn cried out in his sleep and woke Serena. She lay in the darkness, her constant prayer moving like a candle flame in her mind. She crept out of bed and checked Splinter in his shadowy room. Then she knelt and opened the bottom drawer of Splinter's chestrobe. She ran her hand over the gleaming folds of the length of Linjeni material that lay there—the material the Linjeni had found to wrap her in while her clothes dried. She had given them her lacy slip in exchange. Her fingers read the raised pattern in the dark, remembering how beautiful it was in the afternoon sun. Then the sun was gone and she saw a black ship destroyed, a home craft plunging to incandescent death, and the pink and green and yellow and all the other bright furs charring and crisping and the patterned materials curling before the last flare of flame. She leaned her head on her hand and shuddered.

But then she saw the glitter of a silver ship, blackening and fusing, dripping monstrously against the emptiness of space. And heard the wail of a fatherless Splinter so vividly that she shoved the drawer in hastily and went back to look at his quiet sleeping face and to tuck him unnecessarily in.

When she came back to bed, Thorn was awake, lying on his back, his elbows winging out.

"Awake?" she asked as she sat down on the edge of the bed.

"Yes." His voice was tense as the twang of a wire. "We're getting nowhere," he said. "Both sides keep holding up neat little hoops of ideas, but no one is jumping through, either way. We want peace, but we can't seem to convey anything to them. They want something, but they haven't said what, as though to tell us would betray them irrevocably into our hands, but they won't make peace unless they can get it. Where do we go from here?"

"If they'd just go away—" Rena swung her feet up onto the bed and clasped her slender ankles with both hands.

"That's one thing we've established." Thorn's voice was

33

bitter, "They *won't* go. They're here to stay—like it or not."

"Thorn—" Rena spoke impulsively into the shadowy silence. "Why don't we just make them welcome? Why can't we just say, 'Come on in!' They're travelers from afar. Can't we be hospitable—"

"You talk as though the afar was just the next county —or state!" Thorn tossed impatiently on the pillow.

"Don't tell me we're back to that old equation— Stranger equals Enemy," said Rena, her voice sharp with strain. "Can't we assume they're friendly? Go visit with them—talk with them casually—"

"Friendly!" Thorn shot upright from the tangled bed-clothes. "Go visit! Talk!" His voice choked off. Then carefully calmly he went on. "Would you care to visit with the widows of our men who went to visit the friendly Linjeni? Whose ships dripped out of the sky without warning—"

"Theirs did, too." Rena's voice was small but stubborn. "With no more warning than we had. Who shot first? You must admit no one knows for sure."

There was a tense silence; then Thorn lay down slowly, turned his back to Serena and spoke no more.

"Now I can't ever tell," mourned Serena into her crumpled pillow. "He'd die if he knew about the hole under the fence."

In the days that followed, Serena went every afternoon with Splinter and the hole under the fence got larger and larger.

Doovie's mother, whom Splinter called Mrs. Pink, was teaching Serena to embroider the rich materials like the length they had given her. In exchange, Serena was teaching Mrs. Pink how to knit. At least, she started to teach her. She got as far as purl and knit, decrease and increase, when Mrs. Pink took the work from her, and Serena sat widemouthed at the incredible speed and accuracy of Mrs. Pink's furry fingers. She felt a little silly for having assumed that the Linjeni didn't know about knitting. And yet, the other Linjeni crowded around and felt of the knitting and exclaimed over it in their soft, fluty voices as though they'd never seen any before. The little ball of wool Serena had brought was soon used up, but Mrs. Pink brought out hanks of heavy thread such as were split and used in their embroidery, and after a glance

34

through Serena's pattern book, settled down to knitting the shining brilliance of Linjeni thread.

Before long, smiles and gestures, laughter and whistling, were not enough. Serena sought out the available tapes—a scant handful—on Linjeni speech and learned them. They didn't help much since the vocabulary wasn't easily applied to the matters she wanted to discuss with Mrs. Pink and the others. But the day she voiced and whistled her first Linjeni sentence to Mrs. Pink, Mrs. Pink stumbled through her first English sentence. They laughed and whistled together and settled down to pointing and naming and guessing across areas of incommunication.

Serena felt guilty by the end of the week. She and Splinter were having so much fun and Thorn was wearier and wearier at each session's end.

"They're impossible," he said bitterly, one night, crouched forward tensely on the edge of his easy chair. "We can't pin them down to anything."

"What do they want?" asked Serena. "Haven't they said yet?"

"I shouldn't talk—" Thorn sank back in his chair. "Oh what does it matter?" he asked wearily. "It'll all come to nothing anyway!"

"Oh, no, Thorn!" cried Serena. "They're reasonable human—" she broke off at Thorn's surprised look. "Aren't they?" she stammered. "Aren't they?"

"Human? They're uncommunicative, hostile aliens," he said. "We talk ourselves blue in the face and they whistle at one another and say yes or no. Just that, flatly."

"Do they understand—" began Serena.

"We have interpreters, such as they are. None too good, but all we have."

"Well, what are they asking?" asked Serena.

Thorn laughed shortly. "So far as we've been able to ascertain, they just want all our oceans and the land contiguous thereto."

"Oh, Thorn, they couldn't be that unreasonable!"

"Well I'll admit we aren't even sure that's what they mean, but they keep coming back to the subject of the oceans, except they whistle rejection when we ask them point-blank if it's the oceans they want. There's just no communication." Thorn sighed heavily. "You don't know them like we do, Rena."

"No," said Serena, miserably. "Not like you do."

35

She took her disquiet, Splinter, and a picnic basket down the hill to the hole next day. Mrs. Pink had shared her lunch with them the day before, and now it was Serena's turn. They sat on the grass together, Serena crowding back her unhappiness to laugh at Mrs. Pink and her first olive with the same friendly amusement Mrs. Pink had shown when Serena had bit down on her first *pirwit* and had been afraid to swallow it and ashamed to spit it out.

Splinter and Doovie were agreeing over a thick meringued lemon pie that was supposed to be dessert.

"Leave the pie alone, Splinter," said Serena. "It's to top off on."

"We're only tasting the fluffy stuff," said Splinter, a blob of meringue on his upper lip bobbing as he spoke.

"Well, save your testing for later. Why don't you get out the eggs. I'll bet Doovie isn't familiar with them either."

Splinter rummaged in the basket, and Serena took out the huge camp salt shaker.

"Here they are, Mommie!" cried Splinter. "Lookit, Doovie, first you have to crack the shell—"

Serena began initiating Mrs. Pink into the mysteries of hard-boiled eggs and it was all very casual and matter of fact until she sprinkled the peeled egg with salt. Mrs. Pink held out her cupped hand and Serena sprinkled a little salt into it. Mrs. Pink tasted it.

She gave a low whistle of astonishment and tasted again. Then she reached tentatively for the shaker. Serena gave it to her, amused. Mrs. Pink shook more into her hand and peered through the holes in the cap of the shaker. Serena unscrewed the top and showed Mrs. Pink the salt inside it.

For a long minute Mrs. Pink stared at the white granules and then she whistled urgently, piercingly. Serena shrank back, bewildered, as every bush seemed to erupt Linjeni. They crowded around Mrs. Pink, staring into the shaker, jostling one another, whistling softly. One scurried away and brought back a tall jug of water. Mrs. Pink slowly and carefully emptied the salt from her hand into the water and then upended the shaker. She stirred the water with a branch someone snatched from a bush. After the salt was dissolved, all the Linjeni around them lined up with cupped hands. Each received—as though it were a sacrament—a handful of salt water. And they all, quickly, not to lose a drop, lifted the handful of water to their faces and inhaled, breathing deeply, deeply of the salty solution.

Mrs. Pink was last, and, as she raised her wet face from her cupped hands, the gratitude in her eyes almost made Serena cry. And the dozens of Linjeni crowded around, each eager to press a soft forefinger to Serena's cheek, a thank-you gesture Splinter was picking up already.

When the crowd melted into the shadows again, Mrs. Pink sat down, fondling the salt shaker.

"Salt," said Serena, indicating the shaker.

"Shreeprill," said Mrs. Pink.

"Shreeprill?" said Serena, her stumbling tongue robbing the word of its liquidness. Mrs. Pink nodded.

"Shreeprill good?" asked Serena, groping for an explanation for the just finished scene.

"Shreeprill good," said Mrs. Pink. "No *shreeprill,* no Linjeni baby. Doovie—Doovie—" she hesitated, groping. "One Doovie—no baby." She shook her head, unable to bridge the gap.

Serena groped after an idea she had almost caught from Mrs. Pink. She pulled up a handful of grass. "Grass," she said. She pulled another handful. "More grass. More. More." She added to the pile.

Mrs. Pink looked from the grass to Serena.

"No *more* Linjeni baby. Doovie—" She separated the grass into piles. "Baby, baby, baby—" she counted down to the last one, lingering tenderly over it. "Doovie."

"Oh," said Serena, "Doovie is the last Linjeni baby? No more?"

Mrs. Pink studied the words and then she nodded. "Yes, yes! No more. No *shreeprill,* no baby."

Serena felt a flutter of wonder. Maybe—maybe this is what the war was over. Maybe they just wanted salt. A world to them. Maybe—

"Salt, *shreeprill,"* she said. "More, more more *shreeprill,* Linjeni go home?"

"More more more *shreeprill,* yes," said Mrs. Pink. "Go home, no. No home. Home no good. No water, no *shreeprill."*

"Oh," said Serena. Then thoughtfully, "More Linjeni? More, more, more?"

Mrs. Pink looked at Serena and in the sudden silence

the realization that they were, after all, members of enemy camps flared between them. Serena tried to smile. Mrs. Pink looked over at Splinter and Doovie who were happily sampling everything in the picnic basket. Mrs. Pink relaxed, and then she said, "No more Linjeni." She gestured toward the crowded landing field. "Linjeni." She pressed her hands, palm to palm, her shoulders sagging. "No more Linjeni."

Serena sat dazed, thinking what this would mean to Earth's High Command. No more Linjeni of the terrible, devastating weapons. No more than those that had landed—no waiting alien world ready to send reinforcements when these ships were gone. When these were gone—no more Linjeni. All that Earth had to do now was wipe out these ships, taking the heavy losses that would be inevitable, and they would win the war—and wipe out a race.

The Linjeni must have come seeking asylum—or demanding it. Neighbors who were afraid to ask—or hadn't been given time to ask. How had the war started? Who fired upon whom? Did anyone know?

Serena took uncertainty home with her, along with the empty picnic basket. *Tell, tell, tell,* whispered her feet through the grass up the hill. *Tell and the war will end.* But how? she cried out to herself. By wiping them out or giving them a home? Which? Which?

Kill, kill, kill grated her feet across the graveled patio edge. *Kill the aliens—no common ground—not human —all our hallowed dead.*

But what about *their* hallowed dead? All falling, the flaming ships—the homeseekers—the dispossessed—the childless?

Serena settled Splinter with a new puzzle and a picture book and went into the bedroom. She sat on the bed and stared at herself in the mirror.

But give them salt water and they'll increase—all our oceans, even if they said they didn't want them. Increase and increase and take the world—push us out —trespass—oppress—

But their men—our men. They've been meeting for over a week and can't agree. Of course they can't! They're afraid of betraying themselves to each other. Neither knows anything about the other, really. They aren't trying to find out anything really important. I'll bet not one of our men know the Linjeni can close their noses and fold their ears. And not one of the Linjeni knows we sprinkle their life on our food.

Serena had no idea how long she sat there, but Splinter finally found her and insisted on supper and then Serena insisted on bed for him.

She was nearly mad with indecision when Thorn finally got home.

"Well," he said, dropping wearily into his chair. "It's almost over."

"Over!" cried Serena, hope flaring, "Then you've reached—"

"Stalemate, impasse," said Thorn heavily. "Our meeting tomorrow is the last. One final 'no' from each side and it's over. Back to bloodletting."

"Oh, Thorn, no!" Serena pressed her clenched fist to her mouth. "We can't kill any more of them! It's inhuman—it's—"

"It's self-defense," Thorn's voice was sharp with exasperated displeasure. "Please, not tonight, Rena. Spare me your idealistic ideas. Heaven knows we're inexperienced enough in warlike negotiations without having to cope with suggestions that we make cute pets out of our enemies. We're in a war and we've got it to win. Let the Linjeni get a wedge in and they'll swarm the Earth like flies!"

"No, no!" whispered Serena, her own secret fears sending the tears flooding down her face. "They wouldn't! They wouldn't! Would they?"

Long after Thorn's sleeping breath whispered in the darkness beside her, she lay awake, staring at the invisible ceiling. Carefully she put the words up before her on the slate of the darkness.

Tell—the war will end.
Either we will help the Linjeni—or wipe them out.
Don't tell. The conference will break up. The war will go on.
We will have heavy losses—and wipe the Linjeni out.
Mrs. Pink trusted me.
Splinter loves Doovie. Doovie loves him.

Then the little candle flame of prayer that had so

39

nearly burned out in her torment flared brightly again and she slept.

Next morning she sent Splinter to play with Doovie. "Play by the goldfish pond," she said. "I'll be along soon."

"Okay, Mommie," said Splinter. "Will you bring some cake?" Slyly, "Doovie isn't a-miliar with cake."

Serena laughed. "A certain little Splinter is a-miliar with cake, though! You run along, greedy!" And she boosted him out of the door with a slap on the rear.

" 'By, Mommie," he called back.

" 'By, dear. Be good."

"I will."

Serena watched until he disappeared down the slope of the hill, then she smoothed her hair and ran her tongue over her lips. She started for the bedroom, but turned suddenly and went to the front door. If she had to face even her own eyes, her resolution would waver and dissolve. She stood, hand on knob, watching the clock inch around until an interminable fifteen minutes had passed—Splinter safely gone—then she snatched the door open and left.

Her smile took her out of the Quarters Area to the Administration Building. Her brisk assumption of authority and destination took her to the conference wing and there her courage failed her. She lurked out of sight of the guards, almost wringing her hands in indecision. Then she straightened the set of her skirt, smoothed her hair, dredged a smile up from some hidden source of strength, and tiptoed out into the hall.

She felt like a butterfly pinned to the wall by the instant unwinking attention of the guards. She gestured silence with a finger to her lips and tiptoed up to them.

"Hello, Turner. Hi, Franiveri," she whispered.

The two exchanged looks and Turner said hoarsely, "You aren't supposed to be here, ma'am. Better go."

"I know I'm not," she said, looking guilty—with no effort at all. "But Turner, I—I just want to see a Linjeni." She hurried on before Turner's open mouth could form a word. "Oh, I've seen pictures of them, but I'd like awfully to see a real one. Can't I have even one little peek?" She slipped closer to the door. "Look!" she cried softly, "It's even ajar a little already!"

"Supposed to be," rasped Turner. "Orders. But ma'am, we can't—"

"Just one peek?" she pleaded, putting her thumb in the crack of the door. "I won't make a sound."

She coaxed the door open a little farther, her hand creeping inside, fumbling for the knob, the little button.

"But ma'am, you couldn't see 'em from here anyway."

Quicker than thought, Serena jerked the door open and darted in, pushing the little button and slamming the door to with what seemed to her a thunder that vibrated through the whole building. Breathlessly, afraid to think, she sped through the anteroom and into the conference room. She came to a scared skidding stop, her hands tight on the back of a chair, every eye in the room on her. Thorn, almost unrecognizable in his armor of authority and severity, stood up abruptly.

"Serena!" he said, his voice cracking with incredulity. Then he sat down again, hastily.

Serena circled the table, refusing to meet the eyes that bored into her—blue eyes, brown eyes, black eyes, yellow eyes, green eyes, lavender eyes. She turned at the foot of the table and looked fearfully up the shining expanse.

"Gentlemen," her voice was almost inaudible. She cleared her throat. "Gentlemen." She saw General Worsham getting ready to speak—his face harshly unfamiliar with the weight of his position. She pressed her hands to the polished table and leaned forward hastily.

"You're going to quit, aren't you? You're giving up!" The translators bent to their mikes and their lips moved to hers. "What have you been talking about all this time? Guns? Battles? Casualty lists? We'll-do-this-to-you-if-you-do-that-to-us? I don't know! . . ." she cried, shaking her head tightly, almost shuddering, ". . . I don't know what goes on at high level conference tables. All I know is that I've been teaching Mrs. Pink to knit, and how to cut a lemon pie . . ." she could see the bewildered interpreters thumbing their manuals ". . . and already I know why they're here and what they want!" Pursing her lips, she half-whistled, half-trilled in her halting Linjeni, "Doovie baby. No more Linjeni babies!"

One of the Linjeni started at Doovie's name and

stood up slowly, his lavender bulk towering over the table. Serena saw the interpreters thumbing frantically again. She knew they were looking for a translation of the Linjeni "baby." Babies had no place in a military conference.

The Linjeni spoke slowly, but Serena shook her head. "I don't know enough Linjeni."

There was a whisper at her shoulder. "What do you know of Doovie?" And a pair of earphones were pushed into her hands. She adjusted them with trembling fingers. Why were they letting her talk? Why was General Worsham sitting there letting her break into the conference like this?

"I know Doovie," she said breathlessly. "I know Doovie's mother, too. Doovie plays with Splinter, my son— my little son." She twisted her fingers, dropping her head at the murmur that arose around the table. The Linjeni spoke again and the metallic murmur of the earphones gave her the translation. "What is the color of Doovie's mother?"

"Pink," said Serena.

Again the scurry for a word—pink—pink. Finally Serena turned up the hem of her skirt and displayed the hem of her slip—rose pink. The Linjeni sat down again, nodding.

"Serena," General Worsham spoke as quietly as though it were just another lounging evening in the patio. "What do you want?"

Serena's eyes wavered and then her chin lifted.

"Thorn said today would be the last day. That it was to be 'no' on both sides. That we and the Linjeni have no common meeting ground, no basis for agreement on anything."

"And you think we have?" General Worsham's voice cut gently through the stir at the naked statement of thoughts and attitudes so carefully concealed.

"I know we do. Our alikenesses outweigh our differences so far that it's just foolish to sit here all this time, shaking our differences at each other and not finding out a thing about our likenesses. We are fundamentally the same—the same—" she faltered. "Under God we are all the same." And she knew with certainty that the translators wouldn't find God's name in their books. "I think we ought to let them eat our salt and bread and make them welcome!" She half smiled and said, "The word for salt is *shreeprill.*"

There was a smothered rush of whistling from the Linjeni, and the lavender Linjeni half rose from his chair but subsided.

General Worsham glanced at the Linjeni speculatively and pursed his lips. "But there are ramifications—" he began.

"Ramifications!" spat Serena. "There are no ramifications that can't resolve themselves if two peoples really know each other!"

She glanced around the table, noting with sharp relief that Thorn's face had softened.

"Come with me!" she urged. "Come and see Doovie and Splinter together—Linjeni young and ours, who haven't learned suspicion and fear and hate and prejudice yet. Declare a—a—recess or a truce or whatever is necessary and come with me. After you see the children and see Mrs. Pink knitting and we talk this matter over like members of a family—Well, if you still think you have to fight after that, then—" she spread her hands.

Her knees shook so as they started downhill that Thorn had to help her walk.

"Oh, Thorn," she whispered, almost sobbing. "I didn't think they would. I thought they'd shoot me or lock me up or—"

"We don't want war. I told you that," he murmured. "We're ready to grab at straws, even in the guise of snippy females who barge in on solemn councils and display their slips!" Then his lips tightened. "How long has this been going on?"

"For Splinter, a couple of weeks. For me, a little more than a week."

"Why didn't you tell me?"

"I tried—twice. You wouldn't listen. I was too scared to insist. Besides, you know what your reaction would have been."

Thorn had no words until they neared the foot of the hill, then he said, "How come you know so much? What makes you think you can solve—"

Serena choked back a hysterical laugh. "I took eggs to a picnic!"

43

And then they were standing, looking down at the hole under the fence.

"Splinter found the way," Serena defended. "I made it bigger, but you'll have to get down—flat."

She dropped to the sand and wiggled under. She crouched on the other side, her knees against her chest, her clasped hands pressed against her mouth, and waited. There was a long minute of silence and then a creak and a grunt and Serena bit her lips as General Worsham inched under the fence, flat on the sand, catching and jerking free halfway through. But her amusement changed to admiration as she realized that even covered with dust, scrambling awkwardly to his feet and beating his rumpled clothing, he possessed dignity and strength that made her deeply thankful that he was the voice of Earth in this time of crisis.

One by one the others crawled under, the Linjeni sandwiched between the other men and Thorn bringing up the rear. Motioning silence, she led them to the thicket of bushes that screened one side of the goldfish pond.

Doovie and Splinter were leaning over the edge of the pond.

"There it is!" cried Splinter, leaning perilously and pointing. "Way down there on the bottom and it's my best marble. Would your Mommie care if you got it for me?"

Doovie peered down. "Marble go in water."

"That's what I said," cried Splinter impatiently. "And you can shut your nose . . ." he put his finger to the black, glistening button ". . . and fold your ears," he flicked them with his forefinger and watched them fold. "Gee!" he said admiringly. "I wish I could do that."

"Doovie go in water?" asked Doovie.

"Yes," nodded Splinter. "It's my good taw, and you won't even have to put on swimming trunks—you got fur."

Doovie shucked out of his brief clothing and slid down into the pond. He bobbed back up, his hand clenched.

"Gee, thanks." Splinter held out his hand and Doovie carefully turned his hand over and Splinter closed his. Then he shrieked and flung his hand out. "You mean old thing!" yelled Splinter. "Give me my marble! That was a slippy old fish!" he leaned over, scuffling, trying to reach Doovie's other hand. There was a slither and a splash and Splinter and Doovie disappeared under the water.

Serena caught her breath and had started forward when

44

Doovie's anxious face bobbed to the surface again. He yanked and tugged at the sputtering, coughing Splinter and tumbled him out onto the grass. Doovie squatted by Splinter, patting his back and alternately whistling dolefully through his nose and talking apologetic-sounding Linjeni.

Splinter coughed and dug his fists into his eyes.

"Golly, golly!" he said, spatting his hands against his wet jersey. "Mommie'll sure be mad. My clean clothes all wet. Where's my marble, Doovie?"

Doovie scrambled to his feet and went back to the pond. Splinter started to follow, then he cried. "Oh, Doovie, where did that poor little fish go? It'll die if it's out of the water. My guppy did."

"Fish?" asked Doovie.

"Yes," said Splinter, holding out his hand as he searched the grass with intent eyes. "The slippy little fish that wasn't my marble."

The two youngsters scrambled around in the grass until Doovie whistled and cried out triumphantly, "Fish!" and scooped it up in his hands and rushed it back to the pond.

"There," said Splinter. "Now it won't die. Looky, it's swimming away!"

Doovie slid into the pond again and retrieved the lost marble.

"Now," said Splinter. "Watch me and I'll show you how to shoot."

The bushes beyond the two absorbed boys parted and Mrs. Pink stepped out. She smiled at the children and then she saw the silent group on the other side of the clearing. Her eyes widened and she gave an astonished whistle. The two boys looked up and followed the direction of her eyes.

"Daddy!" yelled Splinter. "Did you come to play?" And he sped, arms outstretched, to Thorn, arriving only a couple of steps ahead of Doovie who was whistling excitedly and rushing to greet the tall lavender Linjeni.

Serena felt a sudden choke of laughter at how alike Thorn and the Linjeni looked, trying to greet their offspring adequately and still retain their dignity.

Mrs. Pink came hesitantly to the group to stand in the circle of Serena's arm. Splinter had swarmed up Thorn, hugged him with thoroughness and slid down again. "Hi, General Worsham!" he said, extending a muddy hand in a belated remembrance of his manners. "Hey, Daddy, I'm

45

showing Doovie how to play marbles, but you can shoot better'n I can. You come show him how."

"Well—" said Thorn, glancing uncomfortably at General Worsham.

General Worsham was watching the Linjeni as Doovie whistled and fluted over a handful of bright-colored glassies. He quirked an eyebrow at Thorn and then at the rest of the group.

"I suggest a recess," he said. "In order that we may examine new matters that have been brought to our attention."

Serena felt herself getting all hollow inside, and she turned her face away so Mrs. Pink wouldn't see her cry. But Mrs. Pink was too interested in the colorful marbles to see Serena's gathering, hopeful tears.

Something Bright

Do you remember the Depression? That black shadow across time? That hurting place in the consciousness of the world? Maybe not. Maybe it's like asking do you remember the Dark Ages. Except what would I know about the price of eggs in the Dark Ages? I knew plenty about prices in the Depression.

If you had a quarter—*first find your quarter*—and five hungry kids, you could supper them on two cans of soup and a loaf of day-old bread, or two quarts of milk and a loaf of day-old bread. It was filling—in an afterthoughty kind of way—nourishing. But if you were one of the hungry five, you eventually began to feel erosion set in, and your teeth ached for substance.

But to go back to eggs. Those were a precious commodity. You savored them slowly or gulped them eagerly —unmistakably as eggs—boiled or fried. That's one reason why I remember Mrs. Klevity. She had eggs for *breakfast!* And *every day!* That's one reason why I remember Mrs. Klevity.

I didn't know about the eggs the time she came over to see Mom, who had just got home from a twelve-hour day, cleaning up after other people at thirty cents an hour. Mrs. Klevity lived in the same court as we did. Courtesy called it a court because we were all dependent on the same shower house and two toilets that occupied the shack square in the middle of the court.

All of us except the Big House, of course. It had a bathroom of its own and even a radio blaring "Nobody's Business" and "Should I Reveal" and had ceiling lights that didn't dangle nakedly at the end of a cord. But then it really wasn't a part of the court. Only its back door shared our area, and even that was different. It had *two* back doors in the same frame—a screen one and a wooden one!

Our own two-room place had a distinction, too. It had

47

an upstairs. One room the size of our two. The Man Upstairs lived up there. He was mostly only the sound of footsteps overhead and an occasional cookie for Danna.

Anyway, Mrs. Klevity came over before Mom had time to put her shopping bag of work clothes down or even to unpleat the folds of fatigue that dragged her face down ten years or more of time to come. I didn't much like Mrs. Klevity. She made me uncomfortable. She was so solid and slow-moving and so nearly blind that she peered frighteningly wherever she went. She stood in the doorway as though she had been stacked there like bricks and a dress drawn hastily down over the stack and a face sketched on beneath a fuzz of hair. Us kids all gathered around to watch, except Danna who snuffled wearily into my neck. Day nursery or not, it was a long, hard day for a four-year-old.

"I wondered if one of your girls could sleep at my house this week." Her voice was as slow as her steps.

"At your house?" Mom massaged her hand where the shopping bag handles had crisscrossed it. "Come in. Sit down." We had two chairs and a bench and two apple boxes. The boxes scratched bare legs, but surely they couldn't scratch a stack of bricks.

"No, thanks." Maybe she couldn't bend! "My husband will be away several days and I don't like to be in the house alone at night."

"Of course," said Mom. "You must feel awfully alone."

The only aloneness she knew, what with five kids and two rooms, was the taut secretness of her inward thoughts as she mopped and swept and ironed in other houses. "Sure, one of the girls would be glad to keep you company." There was a darting squirm and LaNell was safely hidden behind the swaying of our clothes in the diagonally curtained corner of the Other room, and Kathy knelt swiftly just beyond the dresser, out of sight.

"Anna is eleven." I had no place to hide, burdened as I was with Danna. "She's old enough. What time do you want her to come over?"

"Oh, bedtime will do." Mrs. Klevity peered out the door at the darkening sky. "Nine o'clock. Only it gets dark before then—" Bricks can look anxious, I guess.

"As soon as she has supper, she can come," said Mom, handling my hours as though they had no value to me. "Of course she has to go to school tomorrow."

48

"Only when it's dark," said Mrs. Klevity. "Day is all right. How much should I pay you?"

"Pay?" Mom gestured with one hand. "She has to sleep anyway. It doesn't matter to her where, once she's asleep. A favor for a friend."

I wanted to cry out: Whose favor for what friend? We hardly passed the time of day with Mrs. Klevity. I couldn't even remember Mr. Klevity except that he was straight and old and wrinkled. Uproot me and make me lie in a strange house, a strange dark, listening to a strange breathing, feeling a strange warmth making itself part of me for all night long, seeping into me—

"Mom—" I said.

"I'll give her breakfast," said Mrs. Klevity. "And lunch money for each night she comes."

I resigned myself without a struggle. Lunch money each day—a whole dime! Mom couldn't afford to pass up such a blessing, such a gift from God, who unerringly could be trusted to ease the pinch just before it became intolerable.

"Thank you, God," I whispered as I went to get the can opener to open supper. For a night or two I could stand it.

I felt all naked and unprotected as I stood in my flimsy crinkle cotton pajamas, one bare foot atop the other, waiting for Mrs. Klevity to turn the bed down.

"We have to check the house first," she said thickly. "We can't go to bed until we check the house."

"Check the house?" I forgot my starchy stiff shyness enough to question. "What for?"

Mrs. Klevity peered at me in the dim light of the bedroom. They had *three* rooms for only the two of them! Even if there was no door to shut between the bedroom and the kitchen.

"I couldn't sleep," she said, "unless I looked first. I have to."

So we looked. Behind the closet curtain, under the table—Mrs. Klevity even looked in the portable oven that sat near the two-burner stove in the kitchen.

When we came to the bed, I was moved to words again. "But we've been in here with the doors locked ever since I got here. What could possibly—"

"A prowler?" said Mrs. Klevity nervously, after a brief pause for thought. "A criminal?"

Mrs. Klevity pointed her face at me. I doubt if she

49

could see me from that distance. "Doors make no difference," she said. "It might be when you least expect, so you have to expect all the time."

"I'll look," I said humbly. She was older than Mom. She was nearly blind. She was one of God's *Also Unto Me's*.

"No," she said. "I have to. I couldn't be sure, else."

So I waited until she grunted and groaned to her knees, then bent stiffly to lift the limp spread. Her fingers hesitated briefly, then flicked the spread up. Her breath came out flat and finished. Almost disappointed, it seemed to me.

She turned the bed down and I crept across the gray, wrinkled sheets, and turning my back to the room, I huddled one ear on the flat, tobacco-smelling pillow and lay tense and uncomfortable in the dark, as her weight shaped and reshaped the bed around me. There was a brief silence before I heard the soundless breathy shape of her words, "How long, O God, how long?"

I wondered through my automatic *bless Papa and Mama*—and the automatic backup, because Papa had abdicated from my specific prayers, *bless Mama and my brother and sisters*—what it was that Mrs. Klevity was finding too long to bear.

After a restless waking, dozing sort of night that strange sleeping places held for me, I awoke to a thin chilly morning and the sound of Mrs. Klevity moving around. She had set the table for breakfast, a formality we never had time for at home. I scrambled out of bed and into my clothes with only my skinny, goose-fleshed back between Mrs. Klevity and me for modesty. I felt uncomfortable and unfinished because I hadn't brought our comb over with me.

I would have preferred to run home to our usual breakfast of canned milk and Shredded Wheat, but instead I watched, fascinated, as Mrs. Klevity struggled with lighting the kerosene stove. She bent so close, peering at the burners with the match flaring in her hand that I was sure the frowzy brush of her hair would catch fire, but finally the burner caught instead and she turned her face toward me.

"One egg or two?" she asked.

"Eggs! Two!" Surprise wrung the exclamation from me. Her hand hesitated over the crumpled brown bag on the table. "No, no!" I corrected her thought hastily. "One.

50

One is plenty," and sat on the edge of a chair watching as she broke an egg into the sizzling frying pan.

"Hard or soft?" she asked.

"Hard," I said casually, feeling very woman-of-the-worldish, dining out—well, practically—and for breakfast, too! I watched Mrs. Klevity spoon the fat over the egg, her hair swinging stiffly forward when she peered. Once it even dabbled briefly in the fat, but she didn't notice, and as it swung back, it made a little shiny curve on her cheek.

"Aren't you afraid of the fire?" I asked as she turned away from the stove with the frying pan. "What if you caught on fire?"

"I did once." She slid the egg out onto my plate. "See?" She brushed her hair back on the left side and I could see the mottled pucker of a large old scar. "It was before I got used to Here," she said, making Here more than the house, it seemed to me.

"That's awful," I said, hesitating with my fork.

"Go ahead and eat," she said. "Your egg will get cold." She turned back to the stove and I hesitated a minute more. Meals at a table you were supposed to ask a blessing, but—I ducked my head quickly and had a mouthful of egg before my soundless amen was finished.

After breakfast I hurried back to our house, my lunch-money dime clutched securely, my stomach not quite sure it liked fried eggs so early in the morning. Mom was ready to leave, her shopping bag in one hand, Danna swinging from the other, singing one of her baby songs. She *liked* the day nursery.

"I won't be back until late tonight," Mom said. "There's a quarter in the corner of the dresser drawer. You get supper for the kids and try to clean up this messy place. We don't have to be pigs just because we live in a place like this."

"Okay, Mom." I struggled with a snarl in my hair, the pulling making my eyes water. "Where you working today?" I spoke over the clatter in the Other room where the kids were getting ready for school.

She sighed, weary before the day began. "I have three places today, but the last is Mrs. Paddington." Her face lightened. Mrs. Paddington sometimes paid a little extra or gave Mom discarded clothes or leftover food she didn't want. She was nice.

51

"You get along all right with Mrs. Klevity?" asked Mom as she checked her shopping bag for her work shoes.

"Yeah," I said. "But she's funny. She looks under the bed before she goes to bed."

Mom smiled. "I've heard of people like that, but it's usually old maids they're talking about."

"But, Mom, nothing coulda got in. She locked the door after I got there."

"People who look under beds don't always think straight," she said. "Besides, maybe she'd *like* to find something under there."

"But she's *got* a husband," I cried after her as she herded Danna across the court.

"There are other things to look for besides husbands," she called back.

"Anna wants a husband! Anna wants a husband!" Deet and LaNell were dancing around me, teasing me singsong. Kathy smiled slowly behind them.

"Shut up," I said. "You don't even know what you're talking about. Go on to school."

"It's too early," said Deet, digging his bare toes in the dust of the front yard. "Teacher says we get there too early."

"Then stay here and start cleaning house," I said.

They left in a hurry. After they were gone, Deet's feet reminded me I'd better wash my own feet before I went to school. So I got a washpan of water from the tap in the middle of the court, and sitting on the side of the bed, I eased my feet into the icy water. I scrubbed with the hard, gray, abrasive soap we used and wiped quickly on the tattered towel. I threw the water out the door and watched it run like dust-covered snakes across the hard-packed front yard.

I went back to put my shoes on and get my sweater. I looked at the bed. I got down on my stomach and peered under. *Other things to look for.* There was the familiar huddle of cardboard cartons we kept things in and the familiar dust fluffs and one green sock LaNell had lost last week, but nothing else.

I dusted my front off. I tied my lunch-money dime in the corner of a handkerchief, and putting my sweater on, left for school.

I peered out into the windy wet semi-twilight. "Do I have to?"

"You said you would," said Mom. "Keep your promises. You should have gone before this. She's probably been waiting for you."

"I wanted to see what you brought from Mrs. Paddington's." LaNell and Kathy were playing in the corner with a lavender hug-me-tight and a hat with green grapes on it. Deet was rolling an orange on the floor, softening it preliminary to poking a hole in it to suck the juice out.

"She cleaned a trunk out today," said Mom. "Mostly old things that belonged to her mother, but these two coats are nice and heavy. They'll be good covers tonight. It's going to be cold. Someday when I get time, I'll cut them up and make quilts." She sighed. Time was what she never had enough of. "Better take a newspaper to hold over your head."

"Oh, Mom!" I huddled into my sweater. "It isn't raining now. I'd feel silly!"

"Well, then, scoot!" she said, her hand pressing my shoulder warmly, briefly.

I scooted, skimming quickly the flood of light from our doorway, and splishing through the shallow runoff stream that swept across the court. There was a sudden wild swirl of wind and a vindictive splatter of heavy, cold raindrops that swept me, exhilarated, the rest of the way to Mrs. Klevity's house and under the shallow little roof that was just big enough to cover the back step. I knocked quickly, brushing my disordered hair back from my eyes. The door swung open and I was in the shadowy, warm kitchen, almost in Mrs. Klevity's arms.

"Oh!" I backed up, laughing breathlessly. "The wind blew—"

"I was afraid you weren't coming." She turned away to the stove. "I fixed some hot cocoa."

I sat cuddling the warm cup in my hands, savoring the chocolate sip by sip. She had made it with milk instead of water, and it tasted rich and wonderful. But Mrs. Klevity was sharing my thoughts with the cocoa. In that brief moment when I had been so close to her, I had looked deep into her dim eyes and was feeling a vast astonishment. The dimness was only on top. Underneath—underneath—

I took another sip of cocoa. Her eyes—almost I could have walked into them, it seemed like. Slip past the gray film, run down the shiny bright corridor, into the live young sparkle at the far end.

I looked deep into my cup of cocoa. Were all grown-ups like that? If you could get behind their eyes, were they different too? Behind Mom's eyes, was there a corridor leading back to youth and sparkle?

I finished the cocoa drowsily. It was still early, but the rain was drumming on the roof and it was the kind of night you curl up to if you're warm and fed. Sometimes you feel thin and cold on such nights, but I was feeling curl-uppy. So I groped under the bed for the paper bag that had my jamas in it. I couldn't find it.

"I swept today," said Mrs. Klevity, coming back from some far country of her thoughts. "I musta pushed it farther under the bed."

I got down on my hands and knees and peered under the bed. "Ooo!" I said. "What's shiny?"

Something snatched me away from the bed and flung me to one side. By the time I had gathered myself up off the floor and was rubbing a banged elbow, Mrs. Klevity's bulk was pressed against the bed, her head under it.

"Hey!" I cried indignantly, and then remembered I wasn't at home. I heard an odd whimpering sob and then Mrs. Klevity backed slowly away, still kneeling on the floor.

"Only the lock on the suitcase," she said. "Here's your jamas." She handed me the bag and ponderously pulled herself upright again.

We went silently to bed after she had limped around and checked the house, even under the bed again. I heard that odd breathy whisper of a prayer and lay awake, trying to add up something shiny and the odd eyes and the whispering sob. Finally I shrugged in the dark and wondered what I'd pick for funny when I grew up. All grownups had some kind of funny.

The next night Mrs. Klevity couldn't get down on her knees to look under the bed. She'd hurt herself when she plumped down on the floor after yanking me away from the bed.

"You'll have to look for me tonight," she said slowly, nursing her knees. "Look good. Oh, Anna, look good!"

I looked as good as I could, not knowing what I was looking for.

"It should be under the bed," she said, her palms tight on her knees as she rocked back and forth. "But you can't be sure. It might miss completely."

"What might?" I asked, hunkering down by the bed.

She turned her face blindly toward me. "The way out," she said. "The way back again—"

"Back again?" I pressed my cheek to the floor again. "Well, I don't see anything. Only dark and suitcases."

"Nothing bright? Nothing? Nothing—" She tried to lay her face on her knees, but she was too unbendy to manage it, so she put her hands over her face instead. Grownups aren't supposed to cry. She didn't quite, but her hands looked wet when she reached for the clock to wind it.

I lay in the dark, one strand of her hair tickling my hand where it lay on the pillow. Maybe she was crazy. I felt a thrill of terror fan out on my spine. I carefully moved my hand from under the lock of hair. How can you find a way *out* under a bed? I'd be glad when Mr. Klevity got home, eggs or no eggs, dime or no dime.

Somewhere in the darkness of the night, I was suddenly swimming to wakefulness, not knowing what was waking me but feeling that Mrs. Klevity was awake too.

"Anna." Her voice was small and light and silver. "Anna—"

"Hummm?" I murmured, my voice still drowsy.

"Anna, have you ever been away from home?" I turned toward her, trying in the dark to make sure it was Mrs. Klevity. She sounded so different.

"Yes," I said. "Once I visited Aunt Katie at Rocky Butte for a week."

"Anna . . ." I don't know whether she was even hearing my answers; her voice was almost a chant ". . . Anna, have you ever been in prison?"

"No! Of course not!" I recoiled indignantly. "You have to be awfully bad to be in prison."

"Oh, no. Oh, no!" she sighed. "Not jail, Anna. Prison—prison. The weight of the flesh—bound about—"

"Oh," I said, smoothing my hands across my eyes. She was talking to a something deep in me that never got talked to, that hardly even had words. "Like when the wind blows the clouds across the moon and the grass whispers along the road and all the trees pull like

55

balloons at their trunks and one star comes out and says 'Come' and the ground says 'Stay' and part of you tries to go and it hurts—" I could feel the slender roundness of my ribs under my pressing hands. "And it hurts—"

"Oh Anna, Anna!" The soft, light voice broke. "You feel that way and you *belong* Here. You won't ever—"

The voice stopped and Mrs. Klevity rolled over. Her next words came thickly, as though a gray film were over them as over her eyes. "Are you awake, Anna? Go to sleep, child. Morning isn't yet."

I heard the heavy sigh of her breathing as she slept. And finally I slept too, trying to visualize what Mrs. Klevity would look like if she looked like the silvery voice in the dark.

I sat savoring my egg the next morning, letting thoughts slip in and out of my mind to the rhythm of my jaws. What a funny dream to have, to talk with a silver-voiced someone. To talk about the way blowing clouds and windy moonlight felt. But it wasn't a dream! I paused with my fork raised. At least not my dream. But how can you tell? If you're part of someone else's dream, can it still be real for you?

"Is something wrong with the egg?" Mrs. Klevity peered at me.

"No—no—" I said, hastily snatching the bite on my fork. "Mrs. Klevity—"

"Yes." Her voice was thick and heavy-footed.

"Why did you ask me about being in prison?"

"Prison?" Mrs. Klevity blinked blindly. "Did I ask you about prison?"

"Someone did—I thought—" I faltered, shyness shutting down on me again.

"Dreams." Mrs. Klevity stacked her knife and fork on her plate. "Dreams."

I wasn't quite sure I was to be at Klevity's the next evening. Mr. Klevity was supposed to get back sometime during the evening. But Mrs. Klevity welcomed me.

"Don't know when he'll get home," she said. "Maybe not until morning. If he comes early, you can go home to sleep and I'll give you your dime anyway."

56

"Oh, no," I said, Mom's teachings solidly behind me. "I couldn't take it if I didn't stay."

"A gift," said Mrs. Klevity.

We sat opposite one another until the silence stretched too thin for me to bear.

"In olden times," I said, snatching at the magic that drew stories from Mom, "when you were a little girl—"

"When I was a girl—" Mrs. Klevity rubbed her knees with reflective hands. "The other Where. The other When."

"In olden times," I persisted, "things were different then."

"Yes." I settled down comfortably, recognizing the reminiscent tone of voice. "You do crazy things when you are young." Mrs. Klevity leaned heavily on the table. "Things you have no business doing. You volunteer when you're young." I jerked as she lunged across the table and grabbed both my arms. "But I *am* young! Three years isn't an eternity. I *am* young!"

I twisted one arm free and pried at her steely fingers that clamped the other one.

"Oh." She let go. "I'm sorry. I didn't mean to hurt you."

She pushed back the tousled brush of her hair.

"Look," she said, her voice almost silver again. "Under all this—this grossness, I'm still me. I thought I could adjust to anything, but I had no idea that they'd put me in such—" She tugged at her sagging dress. "Not the clothes!" she cried. "Clothes you can take off. But this—" Her fingers dug into her heavy shoulder and I could see the bulge of flesh between them.

"If I knew *anything* about the setup maybe I could locate it. Maybe I could call. Maybe—"

Her shoulders sagged and her eyelids dropped down over her dull eyes.

"It doesn't make any sense to you," she said, her voice heavy and thick again. "To you I'd be old even There. At the time it seemed like a perfect way to have an odd holiday and help out with research, too. But we got caught."

She began to count her fingers, mumbling to herself. "Three years There, but Here that's—eight threes

57

are—" She traced on the table with a blunt forefinger, her eyes close to the old, worn-out cloth.

"Mrs. Klevity." My voice scared me in the silence, but I was feeling the same sort of upsurge that catches you sometimes when you're playing-like and it gets so real. "Mrs. Klevity, if you've lost something, maybe I could look for it for you."

"You didn't find it last night," she said.

"Find what?"

She lumbered to her feet. "Let's look again. Everywhere. They'd surely be able to locate the house."

"What are we looking for?" I asked, searching the portable oven.

"You'll know it when we see it," she said.

And we searched the whole house. Oh, such nice things! Blankets, not tattered and worn, and even an extra one they didn't need. And towels with washrags that matched—and weren't rags. And uncracked dishes that matched! And glasses that weren't jars. And books. And money. Crisp new-looking bills in the little box in the bottom drawer—pushed back under some *extra* pillowcases. And clothes—lots and lots of clothes. All too big for any of us, of course, but my practiced eye had already visualized this, that, and the other cut down to dress us all like rich people.

I sighed as we sat wearily looking at one another. Imagine having so much and still looking for something else! It was bedtime and all we had for our pains were dirty hands and tired backs.

I scooted out to the bath house before I undressed. I gingerly washed the dirt off my hands under the cold of the shower and shook them dry on the way back to the house. Well, we had moved everything in the place, but nothing was what Mrs. Klevity looked for.

Back in the bedroom, I groped under the bed for my jamas and again had to lie flat and burrow under the bed for the tattered bag. Our moving around had wedged it back between two cardboard cartons. I squirmed under farther and tried to ease it out after shoving the two cartons a little farther apart. The bag tore, spilling out my jamas, so I grasped them in the bend of my elbow and started to back out.

Then the whole world seemed to explode into brightness that pulsated and dazzled, that splashed brilliance into my astonished eyes until I winced them shut to rest their seeing and saw the dark inversions of the radiance behind my eyelids.

I forced my eyes open again and looked sideways so the edge of my seeing was all I used until I got more accustomed to the glory.

Between the two cartons was an opening like a window would be, but little, little, into a wonderland of things I could never tell. Colors that had no names. Feelings that made windy moonlight a puddle of dust. I felt tears burn out of my eyes and start down my cheeks, whether from brightness or wonder, I don't know. I blinked them away and looked again.

Someone was in the brightness, several someones. They were leaning out of the squareness, beckoning and calling—silver signals and silver sounds.

"Mrs. Klevity," I thought. "Something bright."

I took another good look at the shining people and the tree things that were like music bordering a road, and grass that was the song my evening grass hummed in the wind—a last, last look, and began to back out.

I scrambled to my feet, clutching my jamas. "Mrs. Klevity." She was still sitting at the table, as solid as a pile of bricks, the sketched face under the wild hair a sad, sad one.

"Yes, child." She hardly heard herself.

"Something bright—" I said.

Her heavy head lifted slowly, her blind face turned to me. "What, child?"

I felt my fingers bite into my jamas and the cords in my neck getting tight and my stomach clenching itself. "Something bright!" I thought I screamed. She didn't move. I grabbed her arm and dragged her off balance in her chair. "Something bright!"

"Anna." She righted herself on the chair. "Don't be mean."

I grabbed the bedspread and yanked it up. The light sprayed out like a sprinkler on a lawn.

Then *she* screamed. She put both hands up her heavy face and screamed, "Leolienn! It's here! Hurry, hurry!"

"Mr. Klevity isn't here," I said. "He hasn't got back."

"I can't go without him! Leolienn!"

"Leave a note!" I cried. "If you're there, you can make them come back again and I can show him the right place!" The upsurge had passed make-believe and everything was realer than real.

Then, quicker than I thought she ever could move, she got paper and a pencil. She was scribbling away at the table as I stood there holding the spread. So I dropped to my knees and then to my stomach and crawled under the bed again. I filled my eyes with the brightness and beauty and saw, beyond it, serenity and orderliness and—and uncluttered cleanness. The miniature landscape was like a stage setting for a fairy tale— so small, so small—so lovely.

And then Mrs. Klevity tugged at my ankle and I slid out, reluctantly, stretching my sight of the bright square until the falling of the spread broke it. Mrs. Klevity worked her way under the bed, her breath coming pantingly, her big, ungainly body inching along awkwardly.

She crawled and crawled and crawled until she should have come up short against the wall, and I knew she must be funnelling down into the brightness, her face, head and shoulders, so small, so lovely, like her silvery voice. But the rest of her, still gross and ugly, like a butterfly trying to skin out of its cocoon.

Finally only her feet were sticking out from under the bed and they thrashed and waved and didn't go anywhere, so I got down on the floor and put my feet against hers and braced myself against the dresser and pushed. And pushed and pushed. Suddenly there was a going, a finishing, and my feet dropped to the floor.

There, almost under the bed, lay Mrs. Klevity's shabby old-lady black shoes, toes pointing away from each other. I picked them up in my hands, wanting, somehow, to cry. Her saggy lisle ·stockings were still in the shoes.

Slowly I pulled all the clothes of Mrs. Klevity out from under the bed. They were held together by a thin skin, a sloughed-off leftover of Mrs. Klevity that only showed, gray and lifeless, where her bare hands and face would have been, and her dull gray filmed eyes.

I let it crumple to the floor and sat there, holding one of her old shoes in my hand.

The door rattled, and it was gray, old, wrinkled Mr. Klevity.

"Hello, child," he said. "Where's my wife?"

"She's gone," I said, not looking at him. "She left you a note there on the table."

"Gone—?" He left the word stranded in mid-air as he read Mrs. Klevity's note.

The paper fluttered down. He yanked a dresser drawer open and snatched out spool-looking things, both hands full. Then he practically dived under the bed, his elbows thudding on the floor, to hurt hard. And there was only a wiggle or two, and *his* shoes slumped away from each other.

I pulled his cast aside from under the bed and crawled under it myself. I saw the tiny picture frame—bright, bright, but so small.

I crept close to it, knowing I couldn't go in. I saw the tiny perfection of the road, the landscape, the people—the laughing people who crowded around the two new rejoicing figures—the two silvery, lovely young creatures who cried out in tiny voices as they danced. The girl one threw a kiss outward before they all turned away and ran up the winding white road together.

The frame began to shrink, faster, faster, until it squeezed to a single bright bead and then blinked out.

All at once the house was empty and cold. The upsurge was gone. Nothing was real any more. All at once the faint ghost of the smell of eggs was frightening. All at once I whimpered, "My lunch money!"

I scrambled to my feet, tumbling Mrs. Klevity's clothes into a disconnected pile. I gathered up my jamas and leaned across the table to get my sweater. I saw my name on a piece of paper. I picked it up and read it.

Everything that is ours in this house now belongs to Anna-across-the-court, the little girl that's been staying with me at night.

Ahvlaree Klevity

I looked from the paper around the room. All for me? All for us? All this richness and wonder of good things? All this and the box in the bottom drawer, too? And a paper that said so, so that nobody could take them away from us.

A fluttering wonder filled my chest and I walked stiffly around the three rooms, visualizing everything without opening a drawer or door. I stood by the stove and looked at the frying pan hanging above it. I opened the cupboard door. The paper bag of eggs was on the shelf. I reached for it, looking back over my shoulder almost guiltily.

The wonder drained out of me with a gulp. I ran back over to the bed and yanked up the spread. I knelt and hammered on the edge of the bed with my clenched fists. Then I leaned my forehead on my tight hands and felt my knuckles bruise me. My hands went limply to my lap, my head drooping.

I got up slowly and took the paper from the table, bundled my jamas under my arm and got the eggs from the cupboard. I turned the lights out and left.

I felt tears wash down from my eyes as I stumbled across the familiar yard in the dark. I don't know why I was crying—unless it was because I was homesick for something bright that I knew I would never have, and because I knew I could never tell Mom what really had happened.

Then the pale trail of light from our door caught me and I swept in on an astonished Mom, calling softly, because of the sleeping kids, "Mom! Mom! Guess what!"

Yes, I remember Mrs. Klevity because she had eggs for *breakfast! Every day!* That's one of the reasons I remember her.

Hush!

June sighed and brushed her hair back from her eyes automatically as she marked her place in her geometry book with one finger and looked through the dining-room door at Dubby lying on the front-room couch. "Dubby, *please*," she pleaded. "You promised your mother that you'd be quiet tonight. How can you get over your cold if you bounce around making so much noise?"

Dubby's fever-bright eyes peered from behind his tented knees where he was holding a tin truck which he hammered with a toy guitar.

"I am quiet, June. It's the truck that made the noise. See?" And he banged on it again. The guitar splintered explosively and Dubby blinked in surprise. He was wavering between tears at the destruction and pleased laughter for the awful noise it made. Before he could decide, he began to cough, a deep-chested pounding cough that shook his small body unmercifully.

"That's just about enough out of you, Dubby," said June firmly, clearing the couch of toys and twitching the covers straight with a practiced hand. "You have to go to your room in just fifteen minutes anyway—or right now if you don't settle down. Your mother will be calling at seven to see if you're okay. I don't want to have to tell her you're worse because you wouldn't be good. Now read your book and keep quiet. I've got work to do."

There was a brief silence broken by Dubby's sniffling and June's scurrying pencil. Then Dubby began to chant:

"Shrimp boatses running a dancer tonight
Shrimp boatses running a dancer tonight
Shrimp boatses *running* a *dancer tonight*

"Dub-by!" called June, frowning over her paper at
him.

"That's not noise," protested Dubby. "It's singing.
Shrimp boatses—" The cough caught him in mid-phrase
and June busied herself providing Kleenexes and comfort until the spasm spent itself.

"See?" she said. "Your cough thinks it's noise."

"Well, what can I do then?" fretted Dubby, bored by
four days in bed and worn out by the racking cough
that still shook him. "I can't sing and I can't play. I want
something to do."

"Well," June searched the fertile pigeonholes of her
baby sitter's repertoire and came up with an idea that
Dubby had once originated himself and dearly loved.

"Why not play-like? Play-like a zoo. I think a green
giraffe with a mop for a tail and roller skates for feet
would be nice, don't you?"

Dubby considered the suggestion solemnly. "If he had
egg beaters for ears," he said, overly conscious as always of ears, because of the trouble he so often had
with his own.

"Of course he does," said June. "Now you play-like
one."

"Mine's a lion," said Dubby, after mock consideration. "Only he has a flag for a tail—a pirate flag—and
he wears yellow pajamas and airplane wings sticking
out of his back and his ears turn like propellers."

"That's a good one," applauded June. "Now mine is
an eagle with rainbow wings and roses growing around
his neck. And the only thing he ever eats is the song of
birds, but the birds are scared of him and so he's
hungry nearly all the time—pore ol' iggle!"

Dubby giggled. "Play-like some more," he said, settling back against the pillows.

"No, it's your turn. Why don't you play-like by yourself now? I've just got to get my geometry done."

Dubby's face shadowed and then he grinned. "Okay."

June went back to the table, thankful that Dubby was
a nice kid and not like some of the brats she had met
in her time. She twined both legs around the legs of
her chair, running both hands up through her hair. She
paused before tackling the next problem to glance in at

Dubby. A worry nudged at her heart as she saw how pale and fine-drawn his features were. It seemed, every time she came over, he was more nearly transparent.

She shivered a little as she remembered her mother saying, "Poor child. He'll never have to worry about old age. Have you noticed his eyes, June? He has wisdom in them now that no child should have. He has looked too often into the Valley."

June sighed and turned to her work.

The heating system hummed softly and the out-of-joint day settled into a comfortable accustomed evening.

Mrs. Warren rarely ever left Dubby because he was ill so much of the time, and she practically never left him until he was settled for the night. But today when June got home from school, her mother had told her to call Mrs. Warren.

"Oh, June," Mrs. Warren had appealed over the phone, "could you possibly come over right now?"

"Now?" asked June, dismayed, thinking of her hair and nails she'd planned to do, and the tentative date with Larryanne to hear her new album.

"I hate to ask it," said Mrs. Warren. "I have no patience with people who make last minute arrangements, but Mr. Warren's mother is very ill again and we just have to go over to her house. We wouldn't trust Dubby with anyone but you. He's got that nasty bronchitis again, so we can't take him with us. I'll get home as soon as I can, even if Orin has to stay. He's home from work right now, waiting for me. So please come, June!"

"Well," June melted to the tears in Mrs. Warren's voice. She could let her hair and nails and album go and she could get her geometry done at the Warrens' place. "Well, okay. I'll be right over."

"Oh, bless you, child," cried Mrs. Warren. Her voice faded away from the phone. "Orin, she's coming—" and the receiver clicked.

"June!" He must have called several times before June began to swim back up through the gloomy haze of the new theorem.

"Joo-un!" Dubby's plaintive voice reached down to

her and she sighed in exasperation. She had nearly figured out how to work the problem.

"Yes, Dubby." The exaggerated patience in her voice signaled her displeasure to him.

"Well," he faltered, "I don't want to play-like anymore. I've used up all my thinkings. Can I make something now? Something for true?"

"Without getting off the couch?" asked June cautiously, wise from past experience.

"Yes," grinned Dubby.

"Without my to-ing and fro-ing to bring you stuff?" she questioned, still wary.

"Uh-huh," giggled Dubby.

"What can you make for true without anything to make it with?" June asked skeptically.

Dubby laughed. "I just thought it up." Then all in one breath, unable to restrain his delight: "It's-really-kinda-like-play-like, but-I'm going-to-make-something-that-isn't-like-anything-real-so it'll-be-for-true, cause-it-won't-be-play-like-anything-that's-real!"

"Huh? Say that again," June challenged. "I bet you can't do it."

Dubby was squirming with excitement. He coughed tentatively, found it wasn't a prelude to a full production and said: "I can't say it again, but I can do it, I betcha. Last time I was sick, I made up some new magic words. They're real good. I betcha they'll work real good like anything."

"Okay, go ahead and make something," said June. "Just so it's quiet."

"Oh, it's *real* quiet," said Dubby in a hushed voice. "Exter quiet. I'm going to make a Noise-eater."

"A Noise-eater?"

"Uh-huh!" Dubby's eyes were shining. "It'll eat up all the noises. I can make lotsa racket then, 'cause it'll eat it all up and make it real quiet for you so's you can do your jommety."

"Now that's right thunkful of you, podner," drawled June. "Make it a good one, because little boys make a lot of noise."

"Okay." And Dubby finally calmed down and settled back against his pillows.

The heating system hummed. The old refrigerator in the kitchen cleared its throat and added its chirking throb to the voice of the house. The mantel clock tocked firmly to itself in the front room. June was absorbed in her homework when a flutter of movement at her elbow jerked her head up.

"Dubby!" she began indignantly.

"Shh!" Dubby pantomimed, finger to lips, his eyes wide with excitement. He leaned against June, his fever radiating like a small stove through his pajamas and robe. His breath was heavy with the odor of illness as he put his mouth close to her ear and barely whispered.

"I made it. The Noise-eater. He's asleep now. Don't make a noise or he'll get you."

"I'll get you, too," said June. "Play-like is play-like, but you get right back on that couch!"

"I'm too scared," breathed Dubby. "What if I cough?"

"You will cough if you—" June started in a normal tone, but Dubby threw himself into her lap and muffled her mouth with his small hot hand. He was trembling.

"Don't! Don't!" he begged frantically. "I'm scared. How do you un-play-like? I didn't know it'd work so good!"

There was a *choonk* and a slither in the front room. June strained her ears, alarm stirring in her chest.

"Don't be silly," she whispered. "Play-like isn't for true. There's nothing in there to hurt you."

A sudden succession of musical pings startled June and threw Dubby back into her arms until she recognized Mrs. Warren's bedroom clock striking seven o'clock—early as usual. There was a soft, drawn-out slither in the front room and then silence.

"Go on, Dubby. Get back on the couch like a nice child. We've played long enough."

"You take me."

June herded him ahead of her, her knees bumping his reluctant back at every step until he got a good look at the whole front room. Then he sighed and relaxed.

"He's gone," he said normally.

"Sure he is," replied June. "Play-like stuff always goes away." She tucked him under his covers. Then, as if hoping to brush his fears—and hers—away, by calmly discussing it, "What did he look like?"

"Well, he had a body like Mother's vacuum cleaner —the one that lies down on the floor—and his legs

67

were like my sled, so he could slide on the floor, and had a nose like the hose on the cleaner only he was able to make it long or short when he wanted to."

Dubby, overstrained, leaned back against his pillows. The mantel clock began to boom the hour deliberately.

"And he had little eyes like the light inside the refrigerator—"

June heard a *choonk* at the hall door and glanced up. Then with fear-stiffened lips, she continued for him, "And ears like TV antennae because he needs good ears to find the noises." And watched, stunned, as the round metallic body glided across the floor on shiny runners and paused in front of the clock that was deliberating on the sixth stroke.

The long, wrinkly trunk-like nose on the front of the thing flashed upward. The end of it shimmered, then melted into the case of the clock. And the seventh stroke never began. There was a soft sucking sound and the nose dropped free. On the mantel, the hands of the clock dropped soundlessly to the bottom of the dial.

In the tight circle of June's arms, Dubby whimpered. June clapped her hand over his mouth. But his shoulders began to shake and he rolled frantic imploring eyes at her as another coughing spell began. He couldn't control it.

June tried to muffle the sound with her shoulder, but over the deep, hawking convulsions, she heard the *choonk* and slither of the creature and screamed as she felt it nudge her knee. Then the long snout nuzzled against her shoulder and she heard a soft hiss as it touched the straining throat of the coughing child. She grabbed the horribly vibrating thing and tried to pull it away, but Dubby's cough cut off in mid-spasm.

In the sudden quiet that followed she heard a gurgle like a straw in the bottom of a soda glass and Dubby folded into himself like an empty laundry bag. June tried to straighten him against the pillows, but he slid laxly down.

June stood up slowly. Her dazed eyes wandered trance-like to the clock, then to the couch, then to the horrible thing that lay beside it. Its glowing eyes were blinking and its ears shifting planes—probably to locate sound.

Her mouth opened to let out the terror that was constricting her lungs, and her frantic scream coincided with the shrill clamor of the telephone. The Eater hesitated, then slid swiftly toward the repeated ring. In the pause after the party line's four identifying rings, it stopped and June clapped both hands over her mouth, her eyes dilated with paralyzed terror.

The ring began again. June caught Dubby up into her arms and backed slowly toward the front door. The Eater's snout darted out to the telephone and the ring stilled without even an after-resonance.

The latch of the front door gave a rasping click under June's trembling hand. Behind her, she heard the *choonk* and horrible slither as the Eater lost interest in the silenced telephone. She whirled away from the door, staggering off balance under the limp load of Dubby's body. She slipped to one knee, spilling the child to the floor with a thump. The Eater slid toward her, pausing at the hall door, its ears tilting and moving.

June crouched on her knees, staring, one hand caught under Dubby. She swallowed convulsively, then cautiously withdrew her hand. She touched Dubby's bony little chest. There was no movement. She hesitated indecisively, then backed away, eyes intent on the Eater.

Her heart drummed in her burning throat. Her blood roared in her ears. The starchy *krunkle* of her wide skirt rattled in the stillness. The fibers of the rug murmured under her knees and toes. She circled wider, wider, the noise only loud enough to hold the Eater's attention—not to attract him to her. She backed guardedly into the corner by the radio. Calculatingly, she reached over and clicked it on, turning the volume dial as far as it would go.

The Eater slid tentatively toward her at the click of the switch. June backed slowly away, eyes intent on the creature. The sudden insane blare of the radio hit her an almost physical blow. The Eater glided up close against the vibrating cabinet, its snout lifting and drinking in the horrible cacophony of sound.

June lurched for the front door, wrenching frantically at the door knob. She stumbled outside, slamming the door behind her. Trembling, she sank to the top step, wiping the cold sweat from her face with the under side of her skirt. She shivered in the sharp cold, listening to the raucous outpouring from the radio that boomed so loud it was no longer intelligible.

She dragged herself to her feet, pausing irresolutely, looking around at the huddled houses, each set on its own acre of weeds and lawn. They were all dark in the early winter evening.

June gave a little moan and sank on the step again, hugging herself desperately against the penetrating chill. It seemed an eternity that she crouched there before the radio cut off in mid-note.

Fearfully, she roused and pressed her face to one of the door panes. Dimly through the glass curtains she could see the Eater, sluggish and swollen, lying quietly by the radio. Hysteria was rising for a moment, but she resolutely knuckled the tears from her eyes.

The headlights scythed around the corner, glittering swiftly across the blank windows next door as the car crunched into the Warrens' driveway and came to a gravel-skittering stop.

June pressed her hands to her mouth, sure that even through the closed door she could hear the *choonk* and slither of the thing inside as it slid to and fro, seeking sound.

The car door slammed and hurried footsteps echoed along the path. June made wild shushing motions with her hands as Mrs. Warren scurried around the corner of the house.

"June!" Mrs. Warren's voice was ragged with worry. "Is Dubby all right? What are you doing out here? What's wrong with the phone?" She fumbled for the door knob.

"No, no!" June shouldered her roughly aside. "Don't go in! It'll get you, too!"

She heard a thud just inside the door. Dimly through the glass she saw the flicker of movement as the snout of the Eater raised and wavered toward them.

"June!" Mrs. Warren jerked her away from the door. "Let me in! What's the matter? Have you gone crazy?"

Mrs. Warren stopped suddenly, her face whitening. *"What have you done to Dubby, June?"*

The girl gulped with the shock of the accusation. "I haven't done anything, Mrs. Warren. He made a Noise-

70

eater and it—it—" June winced away from the sudden blaze of Mrs. Warren's eyes.

"Get away from that door!" Mrs. Warren's face was that of a stranger, her words icy and clipped. "I trusted you with my child. If anything has happened to him—"

"Don't go in—oh, don't go in!" June grabbed at her coat hysterically. "Please, please wait! Let's get—"

"Let go!" Mrs. Warren's voice grated between her tightly clenched teeth. "Let me go, you—you—" Her hand flashed out and the crack of her palm against June's cheek was echoed by a *choonk* inside the house. June was staggered by the blow, but she clung to the coat until Mrs. Warren pushed her sprawling down the front steps and fumbled at the knob, crying, "Dubby! Dubby!"

June, scrambling up the steps on hands and knees, caught a glimpse of a hovering something that lifted and swayed like a waiting cobra. It was slapped aside by the violent opening of the door as Mrs. Warren stumbled into the house, her cries suddenly stilling on her slack lips as she saw her crumpled son by the couch.

She gasped and whispered, "Dubby!" She lifted him into her arms. His head rolled loosely against her shoulder. Her protesting, "No, no, no!" merged into half-articulate screams as she hugged him to her.

And from behind the front door there was a *choonk* and a slither.

June lunged forward and grabbed the reaching thing that was homing in on Mrs. Warren's hysterical grief. Her hands closed around it convulsively, her whole weight dragging backward, but it had a strength she couldn't match. Desperately then, her fists clenched, her eyes tight shut, she screamed and screamed and screamed.

The snout looped almost lazily around her straining throat, but she fought her way almost to the front door before the thing held her, feet on the floor, body at an impossible angle and stilled her frantic screams, quieted her straining lungs and sipped the last of her heartbeats, and let her drop.

Mrs. Warren stared incredulously at June's crumpled body and the horrible creature that blinked its lights and shifted its antennae questingly. With a muffled gasp, she sagged, knees and waist and neck, and fell soundlessly to the floor.

The refrigerator in the kitchen cleared its throat and the Eater turned from June with a *choonk* and slid away, crossing to the kitchen.

The Eater retracted its snout and slid back from the refrigerator. It lay quietly, its ears shifting from quarter to quarter.

The thermostat in the dining room clicked and the hot air furnace began to hum. The Eater slid to the wall under the register that was set just below the ceiling. Its snout extended and lifted and narrowed until the end of it slipped through one of the register openings. The furnace hum choked off abruptly and the snout end flipped back into sight.

Then there was quiet, deep and unbroken until the Eater tilted its ears and slid up to Mrs. Warren.

In such silence, even a pulse was noise.

There was a sound like a straw in the bottom of a soda glass.

A stillness was broken by the shrilling of a siren on the main highway four blocks away.

A *choonk* and a slither and the metallic bump of runners down the three front steps.

And a quiet, quiet house on a quiet side street.

Hush.

Food to All Flesh

O give thanks unto the LORD . . . who giveth food
to all flesh: for his mercy endureth for ever.
Psalm 136

Padre Manuel sighed with pleasure as he stepped into
the heavy shade of the salt cedars. It was a welcome
relief from the downpouring sun that drenched the
whole valley and seemed today to press down especially
hard on the little adobe church and its cluster of
smaller buildings. Padre Manuel sighed again with regret that they could manage so little greenery around
the church, but it was above the irrigation canal, huddled against the foot of the bleak Estrellas.

But it was pleasant here in the shade at the foot of
the alfalfa field, and across the pasture was the old fig
tree with the mourning dove nest that Padre Manuel
had been watching.

Well! Padre Manuel let the leaves conceal the nest
again. Two eggs now! And soon the little birds—little
live things. How long did it take? He sat down in the
grass at the foot of the hill, grateful for this leisure
time. He opened his breviary, his lips moving silently
as the pages turned.

And so it was that Padre Manuel was in the south
pasture when the thing came down. It sagged and rippled as if it were made of something soft instead of
metal as you'd expect a spaceship to be. Because that's
what Padre Manuel, after his first blank amazement,
figured it must be.

It didn't act like a spaceship, though. At least not like
the ones that were in the comics that Sor Concepción
brought, clucking disapprovingly, to him when she con-
fiscated them from the big boys who found them so
much more interesting than the catechism class on
drowsy summer afternoons. There was no burned grass,
no big noise, none of the signs of radiation that made
the comic pages so vivid that, most regrettably, Padre
Manuel usually managed a quick read-through before
restoring them at the day's end. The thing just fluttered

on the grass and scooted ahead of a gust of wind until it came up against a tree.

Padre Manuel waited to see what would happen. That was his way. If anything new came along, he'd sit for a while, figuring it all out—but slowly, carefully—and usually he came out right. This time, when he had finished thinking it over, he got a thrill up and down his back, knowing that God had seen fit to let him be the first man on earth to see a spaceship land. At least the first to land in this quiet oasis of cottonwood and salt cedar held in a fold of the desert.

Well, after nothing happened for a long time, he decided he'd go over and get a closer look at the ship. Apparently it wasn't going to do anything more at the moment.

There weren't any doors or windows or peepholes. The thing was bigger than you'd think, standing back from it. Padre Manuel figured it might be thirty feet through, and it looked rather like a wine-colored balloon except that it flattened where it touched the ground, like a low tire. He leaned a hand against it and it had a give to it and a feeling that was like nothing he ever felt before. It even had a smell—a pretty good smell—and Padre Manuel was about to lick it to see if it tasted as good as it smelled, when it opened a hole. One minute no hole. Next minute a little tiny hole, opening bigger and bigger like a round mouth without lips. Nothing swung back or folded up. The ball just opened a hole, about a yard across.

Padre Manuel's heart jumped and he crossed himself swiftly, but when nothing else happened, he edged over to the hole, wondering if he dared stick his head in and take a look. But then he had a sort of vision of the hole shutting again with his head in there and all at once his Adam's apple felt too tight and he swallowed hard.

Then a head stuck out through the hole and Padre Manuel got almost dizzy, thinking about being the first man on earth to see something alive from another world. Then he blinked and squared his shoulders and took stock of what it was that he was seeing for the first time.

It was a head all right, about as big as his, only with the hair tight and fuzzy. It looked as if it had been shaved into patterns though it could have grown that way. And there were two eyes that looked like nice round

gray eyes until they blinked, and then—*Madre de Dios!*
—the lids slid over from the outside edges toward the nose
and flipped back again like a sliding door. And the nose
was a nose, only with stuff growing in the nostrils that
was tight and fuzzy like the hair. It was hard to see how
the thing could breathe through it.

Then the mouth. Padre Manuel felt creepy when
he looked at the mouth. There was no particular reason
why, though. It was just a mouth with the eyeteeth lapped
sharply over the bottom lip. He'd seen people like that
in his time, though maybe not quite so long in the
tooth.

Padre Manuel smiled at the creature and almost dodged
when it smiled back, because those teeth looked as if
they jumped right out at him, white and shiny.

"*Buenos dias,*" said Padre Manuel.

"*Buenos dias,*" said the creature, like an echo.

"Hello," said Padre Manuel, almost exhausting his English.

"Hello," said the creature, like an echo.

Then the conversation lagged. After a while Padre
Manuel said, "Won't you get out and stay for a while?"
He waved his hand and stepped back.

Well, the space man slid his eyelids a couple of times,
then the hole got bigger downwards and he got out and
got out and got out.

Padre Manuel backed away pretty fast when all that
long longness crawled out of the hole, but he came
back wide-eyed when the space creature began to push
himself together, shorter and shorter and ended up about
a head taller than Padre Manuel and about twice as big
around. He was almost man-looking except that his hands
were round pad things with a row of fingers clear around
them that he could put out or pull in when he wanted
to. His hide was stretchy looking and beautifully striped,
silver and black. All tight together the way he was now,
it was mostly black with silver flashing when he moved
and he had funny looking knobs hanging along his ribs,
but all in all he wasn't anything to put fear into anyone.

Padre Manuel wished he could talk with the creature,
to make him welcome to this world, but words seemed
to make only echoes. He fingered his breviary, then on
impulse, handed it to the creature. The creature turned
it over in his silvery tipped hands. It flared open at one
of the well-worn pages and the creature ran a finger

over the print. Then he flipped the book shut. He ran his finger over the cross on the cover and then he reached over and lifted the heavy crucifix that swung from Padre Manuel's waist. He traced its shape with his fingertip and then the cross on the book. He smiled at Padre Manuel and gave the book back to him.

Padre Manuel was as pleased as if he'd spoken to him. The creature was a noticing thing anyway. He ran his own hand over the book, feeling with a warm glow (which he hoped was not too much of pride) that he had the only breviary in the whole world that had been handled by someone from another world.

The space creature had reached inside the ship and now he handed Padre Manuel a stack of metallic disks, fastened together near the top. Each disk was covered with raised marks that tried to speak to Padre Manuel's fingertips like writing for the blind. And some of the disks had raised pictures of strange wheels and machinery-looking things.

Padre Manuel found one that looked like the ship. He touched the ship and then the disk. He smiled at the creature and pushed the plates back together and re-turned them to the creature. *He* was a noticing thing too.

The space creature ran his fingers lightly down Padre Manuel's face and smiled. Padre Manuel thought with immense gratification, "He likes me!"

The creature turned from Padre Manuel, lifted his face, his nose flaring, and waddled on short, heavy legs over to a greasewood bush and took a bite, his two long teeth flashing white in the sun. He chewed—leaves, stems and all—and swallowed. He squatted down and kind of sat without bending, and waited.

Padre Manuel sat, too. Then the creature unswal-lowed. Just opened his mouth and out came the bite of greasewood, chewed up and wet. Well, he went from tree to tree and bush to bush and tried the same thing and unswallowed every mouthful. He even tried a mouth-ful of Johnson grass, but nothing stayed down.

By this time, Padre Manuel had figured out that the poor creature must be hungry. Often on these walks to the pasture, he would take an apple or some crackers or something else to eat that he could have offered him, but it so happened that this time he had nothing to

76

offer. He was feeling sorry when the creature shrugged himself so the knobs on his ribs waggled, and turned back to the ship, scratching as though the knobs itched him. He crawled back into the ship.

Padre Manuel went over cautiously, and almost got a look inside, but the creature's face, teeth and all, pushed out of the hole right at him. Padre Manuel backed away and the creature climbed out with a big box thing under his arm. He scoonched himself all up together again and put the box down. He motioned Padre Manuel to come closer and pointed at one side of the box and said something that ended questiony. Padre Manuel looked at the box. There was a hole in the top and some glittery stuff on the side of it just above a big slot and the glittery stuff was broken. Only a few little pieces were hanging by reddish wire things.

"What is it for?" he asked, making his voice as questiony as he could.

The creature looked at him and slid his eyelids a couple of times, then he picked up a branch of greasewood and pushed it in the top of the box. Then he waggled one hand in the slot and stuck a few of his fingers in his mouth. Padre Manuel considered for a moment. It must be that the box was some kind of food-making thing that had broken. That was why the poor creature was acting so hungry. *Que lástima!*

"I'll get you something to eat, my son," said Padre Manuel. "You wait here." And he hurried away, cutting across the corner of the alfalfa field in his hurry, his cassock whispering through the purply blue flowers.

He was afraid someone might start asking questions and he wasn't one to talk much about what he was doing until it was done, but Sor Concepción and Sor Esperanza had taken the old buckboard and driven over to Gastelum's to see if Chenchita would like to take a job at the Dude Ranch during the vacation that had just begun. She had graduated from the tiny school at the mission and something had to be found to occupy the time she was all too willing to devote to the boys. Padre Manuel sighed and laid the note aside. God be thanked that this offer of a job had come just now. The Gastelums could use the money and Chenchita would have a chance to see that there was something more in the world than boys.

Padre Manuel raided the kitchen and filled a box with all kinds of things and went back out to the pasture.

Well, the creature tried everything. Most of it he un-swallowed almost as soon as it went down. Padre Manuel thought they had it for sure when he tried the pork roast, but just as they were heaving a sigh of relief, up it came—all that beautiful roast, mustard and all. The creature must have been pretty upset, because he grabbed Padre Manuel and shook him, yelling something at him. Padre Manuel recoiled, but his hand went to the band of tight fingers that circled his arm. He laid his hand upon the cool smoothness of the fingers.

"My child!" he rebuked. "My son!" He looked up into the blazing silvery gray of the eyes above him. In the tight silence that followed, Padre Manuel realized, with a pleasurable pang, that he had touched a creature from another world.

The creature stepped back and looked at Padre Manuel. Then he picked up a pinch of dirt and sprinkled it on his head and smiled.

Padre Manuel bowed gravely. Then he, too, smiled.

It was almost dark before Padre Manuel gave up going around the pasture with the creature, trying to find something he could stomach. He was careful to avoid the tree where the dove's nest was. Surely if the creature couldn't eat the egg from the kitchen, he wouldn't be able to eat a dove's egg. He sighed and started home.

Gonzales' bull was stretching his neck through the barb-wire fence, trying to reach the lush green alfalfa just beyond his tongue's reach. "You tell Nacio to plant his own alfalfa," said Padre Manuel. "And don't break the fence down again. To die of bloat is unpleasant and be-sides, there is a hungry thing in the pasture tonight."

He glanced back across the field. The trees hid the ship from here. Good. It was pleasant to have a little secret for a while. Then he began to worry about the creature. This matter was too big to keep to himself too long. It might be very important to others. Maybe the sheriff should be told. Maybe even the government. And the scientists. They would go mad over a ship and a creature from another world. There was Professor Whiting at the Dude Ranch. True, he was an archaeologist. He looked for Indian ruins and people long dead, but he would know names. He would know whom to tell and what to do. But unless Padre Manuel found something that the creature could eat, it would be a dead creature long before letters could go and come. But what was it to be?

The matter was in his prayers that night and after he turned out the light, he stood at the window and looked up at the stars. He knew nothing of them except that they were far, far, but perhaps one of those he could see was the creature's home. He wondered what God's name was, in that world.

Next morning, as soon as Mass was over, Padre Manuel started out to the pasture again. He was carrying a bushel basket full of all kinds of things that might perhaps be eatable for the creature. There were two bars of soap and a sack of sugar. A length of mesquite wood and a half-dozen tortillas. There were four dried chili peppers and a bouquet of paper roses. There were two candles that regrettably had been left in the sun and were now flat dusty curlicues. There was a little bit of most anything Padre Manuel could think of, including half a can of Prince Albert and a pair of canvas gloves. A tin cup rattled against a canteen of water on top of the load. Irrigation wasn't due in the pasture for three days yet and the ditch was dry.

Padre Manuel was just fastening the pasture gate when he heard a terrible bellering, and there was Gonzales' bull, the meanest one in the valley, running like a deer and bellering every time he hit the ground.

"The fence!" gasped Padre Manuel. "He broke in again!"

Behind the bull came the space creature, his short, stubby legs running like the wind. But the wildest, most astonishing thing was how the rest of him came. His legs were running all the time, but the rest of him would shoot out like a rattler striking, flashing silver lightning in the sun and then he'd have to wait for his short legs to catch up.

Well, the bull and the creature went out of sight around the salt cedars and there was one last beller and then lots of silence. Padre Manuel hurried as fast as he could, with the basket bumping him every step, and there, right in front of the spaceship, was the bull, very dead, with its neck folded back and a big hole torn in its flank.

Padre Manuel was slow to anger, but he felt his temper beginning to rise. To destroy the property of others! And Gonzales could so little afford—But he didn't say anything. He looked around quickly while he waited for the creature to make a move. He could see all kinds of unswallowed stuff around the ship. Stuff that probably had been a rabbit and a gopher and an owl and even a bull snake. Then the poor thing gave a groan and unswallowed the piece of bull he had eaten.

"Hello," said the creature.

"Hello," said Padre Manuel, then he uncapped the canteen and poured out a cup of water. He held it out to the creature, thinking as the cup was taken, "A cup of cold water in Thy Name," and blinked as the creature lifted the cup and emptied it on his head, his hide fairly crawling up to meet the water. Padre Manuel filled the cup again and again until the canteen was empty, reproaching himself for not having thought of water the night before. The creature's hide rippled luxuriously as Padre Manuel indicated the basket he'd put down by the ship.

The creature looked at it hopelessly and went back, with sagging shoulders, to the ship. He reached inside and lifted out something and held it out to Padre Manuel. The Padre took it—and almost dropped it when he saw what it was. It was another space creature, no bigger than a kitten, mewling and pushing its nose against Padre Manuel's thumb.

"*Madre de Dios!*" gasped Padre Manuel. "A little one! A baby! Where—?" He turned in astonishment to the space creature. The creature ran his hand down his ribs and Padre Manuel saw that all the waggly knobs were gone. The creature reached into the ship again and brought out two more of the little creatures. He held one of them up to a round silver spot on his ribs.

Padre Manuel stared at the creature and then at the kitteny thing.

"Why, why!" he said, wide-eyed with amazement. "Why *Señora, Señora!*" And he could hear some more mewling coming from the ship.

Well, the space *lady* put down the little ones and so did the Padre and they crawled around on their hands and feet, stretching and pushing together for all the world like little inch worms, taking bites of anything they could find. But everything unswallowed almost as fast as it swallowed.

The space lady was going through the bushel basket, biting and waiting and unswallowing. Pretty soon she'd tried everything in the basket, and she and Padre Manuel sat there looking kind of hopeless at all the unswallowed stuff. Padre Manuel was feeling especially bad about the little kitten things. They were so little, and so hungry.

He picked one up in his hand and patted its nudging little head with his finger. *"Pobrecito,"* he said, "Poor little one—"

Then he let out a yell and dropped the thing. The space lady snarled.

"It bit me!" gasped Padre Manuel. "It took a chunk out of me!"

He pulled out his bandana and tried to tie it over the bleeding place on the ball of his thumb.

All at once he was conscious of a big silence and he looked at the space lady. She was looking down at the little space creature. It was curling up in her hand like a kitten and purring to itself. Its little silver tongue came out and licked around happily and it went to sleep. Fed.

Padre Manuel stared hard. It hadn't unswallowed! It had eaten a chunk of him and hadn't unswallowed! He looked up at the space lady. She stared back. Her eyes slid shut a couple of times. In the quiet you could hear the other little ones mewling. She put the space kitten down.

Padre Manuel stood, one hand clasped over the crude bandage, his eyes dark and questioning in his quiet face. The space lady started toward him, her many-fingered hands reaching. They closed around his arms, above his elbows. Padre Manuel looked up into the silver gray eyes, long, long, and then closed his eyes against the nearness.

Suddenly the fingers were gone. Padre Manuel's eyes opened. He saw the space creature scoop up her little ones, the quiet one, the crying ones, and hurry them into the spaceship. She slid in after them and the hole began to close. Padre Manuel caught a last glimpse of silver and black and a last glint of the white pointed teeth and the hole was closed.

He watched the wine-colored ship dwindle away above the Estrellas until it was gone, back into space. He waved his hand at the empty sky.

81

Then he sighed and picked up the canteen and cup and put them into the basket. He shooed away the flies that swarmed around him and, lifting the basket, started back across the pasture.

Come On, Wagon!

I don't like kids—never have. They're too uncanny. For one thing, there's no bottom to their eyes. They haven't learned to pull down their mental curtains the way adults have. For another thing, there's so much they don't know. And not knowing things makes them know lots of other things grownups can't know. That sounds confusing and it is. But look at it this way. Every time you teach a kid something, you teach him a hundred things that are impossible because that one thing is so. By the time we grow up, our world is so hedged around by impossibilities that it's a wonder we ever try anything new.

Anyway, I don't like kids, so I guess it's just as well that I've stayed a bachelor.

Now take Thaddeus. I don't like Thaddeus. Oh, he's a fine kid, smarter than most—he's my nephew—but he's too young. I'll start liking him one of these days when he's ten or eleven. No, that's still too young. I guess when his voice starts cracking and he begins to slick his hair down, I'll get to liking him fine. Adolescence ends lots more than it begins.

The first time I ever really got acquainted with Thaddeus was the Christmas he was three. He was a solemn little fellow, hardly a smile out of him all day, even with the avalanche of everything to thrill a kid. Starting first thing Christmas Day, he made me feel uneasy. He stood still in the middle of the excited squealing bunch of kids that crowded around the Christmas tree in the front room at the folks' place. He was holding a big rubber ball with both hands and looking at the tree with his eyes wide with wonder. I was sitting right by him in the big chair and I said, "How do you like it, Thaddeus?"

He turned his big solemn eyes to me, and for a long time, all I could see was the deep, deep reflections in his eyes of the glitter and glory of the tree and a special

83

shiningness that originated far back in his own eyes. Then he blinked slowly and said solemnly, "Fine."

Then the mob of kids swept him away as they all charged forward to claim their Grampa-gift from under the tree. When the crowd finally dissolved and scattered all over the place with their play-toys, there was Thaddeus squatting solemnly by the little red wagon that had fallen to him. He was examining it intently, inch by inch, but only with his eyes. His hands were pressed between his knees and his chest as he squatted.

"Well, Thaddeus." His mother's voice was a little provoked. "Go play with your wagon. Don't you like it?"

Thaddeus turned his face up to her in that blind, unseeing way little children have.

"Sure," he said, and standing up, tried to take the wagon in his arms.

"Oh for pity sakes," his mother laughed. "You don't carry a wagon, Thaddeus." And aside to us, "Sometimes I wonder. Do you suppose he's got all his buttons?"

"Now, Jean." Our brother Clyde leaned back in his chair. "Don't heckle the kid. Go on, Thaddeus. Take the wagon outside."

So what does Thaddeus do but start for the door, saying over his shoulder, "Come on, Wagon."

Clyde laughed. "It's not that easy, Punkin-Yaller, you've gotta have pull to get along in this world."

So Jean showed Thaddeus how and he pulled the wagon outdoors, looking down at the handle in a puzzled way, absorbing this latest rule for acting like a big boy.

Jean was embarrassed the way parents are when their kids act normal around other people.

"Honest. You'd think he never saw a wagon before."

"He never did," I said idly. "Not his own, anyway." And had the feeling that I had said something profound, but wasn't quite sure what.

The whole deal would have gone completely out of my mind if it hadn't been for one more little incident. I was out by the barn waiting for Dad. Mom was making him change his pants before he demonstrated his new tractor for me. I saw Thaddeus loading rocks into his little red wagon. Beyond the rock pile, I could see that he had started a playhouse or ranch of some kind, laying the rocks out to make rooms or corrals or whatever. He finished loading the wagon and picked up another rock that took both arms to carry, then he looked down at the wagon.

"Come on, Wagon." And he walked over to his play place.

And the wagon went with him, trundling along over the uneven ground, following at his heels like a puppy.

I blinked and inventoried rapidly the Christmas cheer I had imbibed. It wasn't enough for an explanation. I felt a kind of cold grue creep over me.

Then Thaddeus emptied the wagon and the two of them went back for more rocks. He was just going to pull the same thing again when a big boy-cousin came by and laughed at him.

"Hey, Thaddeus, how you going to pull your wagon with both hands full? It won't go unless you pull it."

"Oh," said Thaddeus and looked off after the cousin who was headed for the back porch and some pie.

So Thaddeus dropped the big rock he had in his arms and looked at the wagon. After struggling with some profound thinking, he picked the rock up again and hooked a little finger over the handle of the wagon.

"Come on, Wagon," he said, and they trundled off together, the handle of the wagon still slanting back over the load while Thaddeus grunted along by it with his heavy armload.

I was glad Dad came just then, hooking the last strap of his striped overalls. We started into the barn together. I looked back at Thaddeus. He apparently figured he'd need his little finger on the next load, so he was squatting by the wagon, absorbed with a piece of flimsy red Christmas string. He had twisted one end around his wrist and was intent on tying the other to the handle of the little red wagon.

It wasn't so much that I avoided Thaddeus after that. It isn't hard for grownups to keep from mingling with kids. After all, they do live in two different worlds. Anyway, I didn't have much to do with Thaddeus for several years after that Christmas. There was the matter of a side trip to the South Pacific where even I learned that there are some grown-up impossibilities that are not always absolute. Then there was a hitch in the hospital where I waited for my legs to put themselves together again. I was luckier than most of the guys. The folks wrote often and regularly and kept me posted on all the home talk. Nothing spectacular, nothing special, just the

85

old familiar stuff that makes home, home and folks, folks.

I hadn't thought of Thaddeus in a long time. I hadn't been around kids much and unless you deal with them, you soon forget them. But I remembered him plenty when I got the letter from Dad about Jean's new baby. The kid was a couple of weeks overdue and when it did come—a girl—Jean's husband, Bert, was out at the farm checking with Dad on a land deal he had cooking. The baby came so quickly that Jean couldn't even make it to the hospital and when Mom called Bert, he and Dad headed for town together, but fast.

"Derned if I didn't have to hold my hair on," wrote Dad. "I don't think we hit the ground but twice all the way to town. Dern near overshot the gate when we finally tore up the hill to their house. Thaddeus was playing out front and we dang near ran him down. Smashed his trike to flinders. I saw the handle bars sticking out from under the front wheel when I followed Bert in. Then I got to thinking that he'd get a flat parking on all that metal so I went out to move the car. Lucky I did. Bert musta forgot to set the brakes. Derned if that car wasn't headed straight for Thaddeus. He was walking right in front of it. Even had his hand on the bumper and the dern thing rolling right after him. I yelled and hit out for the car. But by the time I got there, it had stopped and Thaddeus was squatting by his wrecked trike. What do you suppose the little cuss said? 'Old car broke my trike. I made him get off.'

"Can you beat it? Kids get the dernedest ideas. Lucky it wasn't much down hill, though. He'd have been hurt sure."

I lay with the letter on my chest and felt cold. Dad had forgotten that they "tore up the hill" and that the car must have rolled up the slope to get off Thaddeus' trike.

That night I woke up the ward yelling, "Come on, Wagon!"

It was some months later when I saw Thaddeus again. He and half a dozen other nephews—and the one persistent niece—were in a tearing hurry to be somewhere else and nearly mobbed Dad and me on the front porch as they boiled out of the house with mouths and hands full of cookies. They all stopped long enough to give me the once-over and fire a machine gun volley with my crutches, then they disappeared down the land on their bikes, heads low, rear ends high, and every one of them being bombers at the tops of their voices.

I only had time enough to notice that Thaddeus had lanked out and was just one of the kids as he grinned engagingly at me with the two-tooth gap in his front teeth.

"Did you ever notice anything odd about Thaddeus?" I pulled out the makin's.

"Thaddeus?" Dad glanced up at me from firing up his battered old corncob pipe. "Not particularly. Why?"

"Oh, nothing." I ran my tongue along the paper and rolled the cigarette shut. "He just always seemed kinda different."

"Well, he's always been kinda slow about some things. Not that he's dumb. Once he catches on, he's as smart as anyone, but he's sure pulled some funny ones."

"Give me a fer-instance," I said, wondering if he'd remember the trike deal.

"Well, coupla years ago at a wienie roast he was toting something around wrapped in a paper napkin. Jean saw him put it in his pocket and she thought it was probably a dead frog or a beetle or something like that, so she made him fork it over. She unfolded the napkin and derned if there wasn't a big live coal in it. Dern thing flamed right up in her hand. Thaddeus bellered like a bull calf. Said he wanted to take it home cause it was pretty. How he ever carried it around that long without setting himself afire is what got me."

"That's Thaddeus," I said, "odd."

"Yeah." Dad was firing his pipe again, flicking the burned match down, to join the dozen or so others by the porch railing. "I guess you might call him odd. But he'll outgrow it. He hasn't pulled anything like that in a long time."

"They do outgrow it," I said. "Thank God." And I think it was a real prayer. I don't like kids. "By the way, where's Clyde?"

"Down in the East Pasture, plowing. Say, that tractor I got that last Christmas you were here is a bear cat. It's lasted me all this time and I've never had to do a lick of work on it. Clyde's using it today."

"When you get a good tractor you got a good one," I said. "Guess I'll go down and see the old son-of-a-gun

—Clyde, I mean. Haven't seen him in a coon's age." I gathered up my crutches.

Dad scrambled to his feet. "Better let me run you down in the pickup. I've gotta go over to Jesperson's anyway."

"Okay," I said. "Won't be long till I can throw these things away." So we piled in the pickup and headed for the East Pasture.

We were ambushed at the pump corner by the kids and were killed variously by P-38s, atomic bombs, ackack, and the Lone Ranger's six-guns. Then we lowered our hands which had been raised all this time and Dad reached out and collared the nearest nephew.

"Come along, Punkin-Yaller. That blasted Holstein has busted out again. You get her out of the alfalfa and see if you can find where she got through this time."

"Aw, gee whiz!" The kid—and of course it was Thaddeus—climbed into the back of the pickup. "That dern cow."

We started up with a jerk and I turned half around in the seat to look back at Thaddeus.

"Remember your little red wagon?" I yelled over the clatter.

"Red wagon?" Thaddeus yelled back. His face lighted. "Red wagon?"

I could tell he had remembered and then, as plainly as the drawing of a shade, his eyes went shadowy and he yelled, "Yeah, kinda." And turned around to wave violently at the unnoticing kids behind us.

So, I thought, he is outgrowing it. Then spent the rest of the short drive trying to figure just what it was he was outgrowing.

Dad dumped Thaddeus out at the alfalfa field and took me on across the canal and let me out by the pasture gate.

"I'll be back in about an hour if you want to wait. Might as well ride home."

"I might start back afoot," I said. "It'd feel good to stretch my legs again."

"I'll keep a look out for you on my way back." And he rattled away in the ever present cloud of dust.

I had trouble managing the gate. It's one of those wire affairs that open by slipping a loop off the end post and lifting the bottom of it out of another loop. This one was taut and hard to handle. I just got it opened when Clyde turned the far corner and started back toward me, the plow behind the tractor curling up red-brown ribbons in its wake. It was the last go-round to complete the field.

I yelled, "Hi!" and waved a crutch at him.

He yelled, "Hi!" back at me. What came next was too fast and too far away for me to be sure what actually happened. All I remember was a snort and roar and the tractor bucked and bowed. There was a short yell from Clyde and the shriek of wires pulling loose from a fence post followed by a choking smothering silence.

Next thing I knew, I was panting halfway to the tractor, my crutches sinking exasperatingly into the soft plowed earth. A nightmare year later I knelt by the stalled tractor and called, "Hey, Clyde!"

Clyde looked up at me, a half grin, half grimace on his muddy face.

"Hi. Get this thing off me, will you. I need that leg." Then his eyes turned up white and he passed out.

The tractor had toppled him from the seat and then run over top of him, turning into the fence and coming to rest with one huge wheel half burying his leg in the soft dirt and pinning him against a fence post. The far wheel was on the edge of the irrigation ditch that bordered the field just beyond the fence. The huge bulk of the machine was balanced on the raw edge of nothing and it looked like a breath would send it on over—then God have mercy on Clyde. It didn't help much to notice that the red-brown dirt was steadily becoming redder around the imprisoned leg.

I knelt there paralyzed with panic. There was nothing I could do. I didn't dare to try to start the tractor. If I touched it, it might go over. Dad was gone for an hour. I couldn't make it by foot to the house in time.

Then all at once out of nowhere I heard a startled "Gee whiz!" and there was Thaddeus standing goggle-eyed on the ditch bank.

Something exploded with a flash of light inside my head and I whispered to myself, *Now take it easy. Don't scare the kid, don't startle him.*

"Gee whiz!" said Thaddeus again. "What happened?"

I took a deep breath. "Old Tractor ran over Uncle Clyde. Make it get off."

Thaddeus didn't seem to hear me. He was intent on taking in the whole shebang.

"Thaddeus," I said, "make Tractor get off."

Thaddeus looked at me with that blind, unseeing stare he used to have. I prayed silently, *Don't let him be too old. O God, don't let him be too old.* And Thaddeus jumped across the ditch. He climbed gingerly through the barbwire fence and squatted down by the tractor, his hands caught between his chest and knees. He bent his head forward and I stared urgently at the soft vulnerable nape of his neck. Then he turned his blind eyes to me again.

"Tractor doesn't want to."

I felt a yell ball up in my throat, but I caught it in time. *Don't scare the kid,* I thought. *Don't scare him.*

"Make Tractor get off anyway," I said as matter-of-factly as I could manage. "He's hurting Uncle Clyde."

Thaddeus turned and looked at Clyde.

"He isn't hollering."

"He can't. He's unconscious." Sweat was making my palms slippery.

"Oh." Thaddeus examined Clyde's quiet face curiously. "I never saw anybody unconscious before."

"Thaddeus." My voice was sharp. "Make—Tractor—get—off."

Maybe I talked too loud. Maybe I used the wrong words, but Thaddeus looked up at me and I saw the shutters close in his eyes. They looked up at me, blue and shallow and bright.

"You mean start the tractor?" His voice was brisk as he stood up. "Gee whiz! Grampa told us kids to leave the tractor alone. It's dangerous for kids. I don't know whether I know how—"

"That's not what I meant," I snapped, my voice whetted on the edge of my despair. "Make it get off Uncle Clyde. He's dying."

"But I can't! You can't just make a tractor do something. You gotta run it." His face was twisting with approaching tears.

"You could if you wanted to," I argued, knowing how useless it was. "Uncle Clyde will die if you don't."

"But I can't! I don't know how! Honest I don't." Thaddeus scrubbed one bare foot in the plowed dirt, sniffing miserably.

I knelt beside Clyde and slipped my hand inside his dirt-smeared shirt. I pulled my hand out and rubbed the stained palm against my thigh. "Never mind," I said bluntly, "it doesn't matter now. He's dead."

Thaddeus started to bawl, not from grief but bewilderment. He knew I was put out with him and he didn't know why. He crooked his arm over his eyes and leaned against a fence post, sobbing noisily. I shifted myself over in the dark furrow until my shadow sheltered Clyde's quiet face from the hot afternoon sun. I clasped my hands palm to palm between my knees and waited for Dad.

I knew as well as anything that *once* Thaddeus could have helped. Why couldn't he then, when the need was so urgent? Well, maybe he really *had* outgrown his strangeness. Or it might be that he actually couldn't do anything just because Clyde and I were grownups. Maybe if it had been another kid—

Sometimes my mind gets cold trying to figure it out. Especially when I get the answer that kids and grownups live in two worlds so alien and separate that the gap can't be bridged even to save a life. Whatever the answer is—I still don't like kids.

Walking Aunt Daid

I looked up in surprise and so did Ma. And so did Pa. Aunt Daid was moving. Her hands were coming together and moving upward till the light from the fireplace had a rest from flickering on that cracked, wrinkled wreck that was her face. But the hands didn't stay long. They dropped back to her saggy lap like two dead bats, and the sunken old mouth that had fallen in on its lips years before I was born puckered and worked and let Aunt Daid's tongue out a little ways before it pulled it back in again. I swallowed hard. There was something alive about that tongue and *alive* wasn't a word I'd associate with Aunt Daid.

Ma let out a sigh that was almost a snort and took up her fancy work again. "Guess it's about time," she said over a sudden thrum of rain against the darkening parlor windows.

"Naw," said Pa. "Too soon. Years yet."

"Don't know 'bout that," said Ma. "Paul here's going on twenty. Count back to the last time. Remember that, Dev?"

"Aw!" Pa squirmed in his chair. Then he rattled the *Weekly Wadrow* open and snapped it back to the state news. "Better watch out," he warned, his eyes answering hers. "I might learn more this time and decide I need some other woman."

"Can't scare me," said Ma over the strand of embroidery thread she was holding between her teeth to separate it into strands. " 'Twon't be your place this time anyhow. Once for each generation, hasn't it been? It's Paul this time."

"He's too young," protested Pa. "Some things younguns should be sheltered from." He was stern.

"Paul's oldern'n you were at his age," said Ma. "Schooling does that to you, I guess."

"Sheltered from what?" I asked. "What about last time?

92

What's all this just 'cause Aunt Daid moved without anyone telling her to?"

"You'll find out," said Ma, and she shivered a little. "We make jokes about it—but only in the family," she warned. "This is strictly family business. But it isn't any joking matter. I wish the good Lord would take Aunt Daid. It's creepy. It's not healthy."

"Aw, simmer down, Mayleen," said Pa. "It's not all that bad. Every family's got its problems. Ours just happens to be Aunt Daid. It could be worse. At least she's quiet and clean and biddable and that's more than you can say for some other people's old folks."

"*Old* folks is right," said Ma. "We hit the jackpot there."

"How old *is* Aunt Daid?" I asked, wondering just how many years it had taken to suck so much sap out of her that you wondered that the husk of her didn't rustle when she walked.

"No one rightly knows," said Ma, folding away her fancy work. She went over to Aunt Daid and put her hand on the sagging shoulder.

"Bedtime, Aunt Daid," she called, loud and clear. "Time for bed."

I counted to myself. ". . . three, four, *five*, six, seven, eight, nine, *ten*," and Aunt Daid was on her feet, her bent old knees wavering to hold her scanty weight.

I shook my head wonderingly and half grinned. Never failed. Up at the count of ten, which was pretty good, seeing as she never started stirring until the count of five. It took that long for Ma's words to sink in.

I watched Aunt Daid follow Ma out. You couldn't push her to go anywhere, but she followed real good. Then I said to Pa, "What's Aunt Daid's whole name? How's she kin to us?"

"Don't rightly know," said Pa. "I could maybe figger it out—how she's kin to us, I mean—if I took the time— a lot of it. Great-great-grampa started calling her Aunt Daid. Other folks thought it was kinda disrespectful but it stuck to her." He stood up and stretched and yawned. "Morning comes early," he said. "Better hit the hay." He pitched the paper at the woodbox and went off toward the kitchen for his bed snack.

"What'd he call her Aunt Daid for?" I hollered after him.

"Well," yelled Pa, his voice muffled, most likely from

coming out of the icebox. "He said she shoulda been 'daid' a long time ago, so he called her Aunt Daid."

I figured on the edge of the *Hog Breeder's Gazette.* "Let's see. Around thirty years to a generation. Me, Pa, Grampa, great-grampa, great-great-grampa—and let's see for me that'd be another great. That makes six generations. That's 180 years—" I chewed on the end of my pencil, a funny flutter inside me.

" 'Course, that's just guessing," I told myself. "Maybe Pa just piled it on for devilment. Minus a generation— that's 150." I put my pencil down real careful. *Shoulda been dead a long time ago.* How old *was* Aunt Daid that they said that about her a century and a half ago?

Next morning the whole world was fresh and clean. Last night's spell of rain had washed the trees and the skies and settled the dust. I stretched in the early morning cool and felt like life was a pretty good thing. Vacation before me and nothing much to be done on the farm for a while.

Ma called breakfast and I followed my nose to the buttermilk pancakes and sausages and coffee and outate Pa by a stack and a half of pancakes.

"Well, son, looks like you're finally a man," said Pa. "When you can outeat your pa—"

Ma scurried in from the other room. "Aunt Daid's sitting on the edge of her bed," she said anxiously. "And I didn't get her up."

"Um," said Pa. "Begins to look that way doesn't it?"

"Think I'll go up to Honan's Lake," I said, tilting my chair back, only half hearing what they were saying. "Feel like a coupla days fishing."

"Better hang around, son," said Pa. "We might be needing you in a day or so."

"Oh?" I said, a little put out. "I had my mouth all set for Honan's Lake."

"Well, unset it for a spell," said Pa. "There's a whole summer ahead."

"But what for?" I asked. "What's cooking?"

Pa and Ma looked at each other and Ma crumpled the corner of her apron in her hand. "We're going to need you," she said.

"How come?" I asked.

"To walk Aunt Daid," said Ma.

"To walk Aunt Daid?" I thumped my chair back on four legs. "But my gosh, Ma, you always do for Aunt Daid."

"Not for this," said Ma, smoothing at the wrinkles in her apron. "Aunt Daid won't walk this walk with a woman. It has to be you."

I took a good look at Aunt Daid that night at supper. I'd never really looked at her before. She'd been around ever since I could remember. She was as much a part of the house as the furniture.

Aunt Daid was just soso sized. If she'd been fleshed out, she'd be about Ma for bigness. She had a wisp of hair twisted into a walnut-sized knob at the back of her head. The ends of the hair sprayed out stiffly from the knob like a worn-out brush. Her face looked like wrinkles had wrinkled on wrinkles and all collapsed into the emptiness of no teeth and no meat on her skull bones. Her tiny eyes, almost hidden under the crepe of her eyelids, were empty. They just stared across the table through me and on out into nothingness while her lips sucked open at the tap of the spoon Ma held, inhaled the soft stuff Ma had to feed her on, and then shut, working silently until her skinny neck bobbed with swallowing.

"Doesn't she ever say anything?" I finally asked.

Pa looked quick at Ma and then back down at his plate.

"Never heard a word out of her," said Ma.

"Doesn't she ever *do* anything?" I asked.

"Why sure," said Ma. "She shells peas real good when I get her started."

"Yeah." I felt my spine crinkle, remembering once when I was little. I sat on the porch and passed the peapods to Aunt Daid. I was remembering how, after I ran out of peas, her withered old hands had kept reaching and taking and shelling and throwing away with nothing but emptiness in them.

"And she tears rug rags good. And she can pull weeds if nothing else is growing where they are."

"Why—" I started—and stopped.

"Why do we keep her?" asked Ma. "She doesn't die. She's alive. What should we do? She's no trouble. Not much, anyway."

"Put her in a home somewhere," I suggested.

"She's in a home now," said Ma, spooning up custard

95

for Aunt Daid. "And we don't have to put out cash for her and no telling what'd happen to her."

"What is this walking business anyway? Walking where?"

"Down hollow," said Pa, cutting a quarter of a cherry pie. "Down to the oak—" he drew a deep breath and let it out— "and back again."

"Why down there?" I asked. "Hollow's full of weeds and mosquitoes. Besides it's—it's—"

"Spooky," said Ma, smiling at me.

"Well, yes, spooky," I said. "There's always a quiet down there when the wind's blowing everywhere else, or else a wind when everything's still. Why down there?"

"There's where she wants to walk," said Pa. "You walk her down there."

"Well." I stood up. "Let's get it over with. Come on, Aunt Daid."

"She ain't ready yet," said Ma. "She won't go till she's ready."

"Well, Pa, why can't you walk her then?" I asked. "You did it once—"

"Once is enough," said Pa, his face shut and still. "It's your job this time. You be here when you're needed. It's a family duty. Them fish will wait."

"Okay, okay," I said. "But at least tell me what the deal is. It sounds like a lot of hogwash to me."

There wasn't much to tell. Aunt Daid was a family heirloom, like, but Pa never heard exactly who she was to the family. She had always been like this—just as old and so dried up she wasn't even repulsive. I guess it's only when there's enough juice for rotting that a body is repulsive and Aunt Daid was years and years past that. That must be why the sight of her wet tongue jarred me.

Seems like once in every twenty-thirty years, Aunt Daid gets an awful craving to go walking. And always someone has to go with her. A man. She won't go with a woman. And the man comes back changed.

"You can't help being changed," said Pa, "when your eyes look on things your mind can't—" Pa swallowed.

"Only time there was any real trouble with Aunt Daid," said Pa, "was when the family came west. That was back in your great-great-grampa's time. They left the old place and came out here in covered wagons and Aunt Daid didn't even notice until time for her to walk again. Then she got violent. Great-grampa tried to walk her down the road, but she dragged him all over the place, coursing like a hunting dog that's lost the trail only with her eyes blind-like, all through the dark. Great-grampa finally brought her back almost at sunrise. He was pert nigh a broken man, what with cuts and bruises and scratches —and walking Aunt Daid. She'd finally settled on down hollow."

"What does she walk for?" I asked. "What goes on?"

"You'll see, son," said Pa, "Words wouldn't tell anything, but you'll see."

That evening Aunt Daid covered her face again with her hands. Later she stood up by herself, teetering by her chair a minute, one withered old hand pawing at the air, till Ma, with a look at Pa, set her down again.

All next day Aunt Daid was quiet, but come evening she got restless. She went to the door three or four times, just waiting there like a puppy asking to go out, but after my heart had started pounding and I had hurried to her and opened the door, she just waved her face blindly at the darkness outside and went back to her chair.

Next night was the same until along about ten o'clock, just as Ma was thinking of putting Aunt Daid to bed. First thing we knew, Aunt Daid was by the door again, her feet tramping up and down impatiently, her dry hands whispering over the door.

"It's time," said Pa quiet-like, and I got all cold inside.

"But it's blacker'n pitch tonight," I protested. "It's as dark as the inside of a cat. No moon."

Aunt Daid whimpered. I nearly dropped. It was the first sound I'd ever heard from her.

"It's time," said Pa again, his face bleak. "Walk her, son. And, Paul—bring her back."

"Down hollow's bad enough by day," I said, watching, half sick, as Aunt Daid spread her skinny arms out against the door, her face pushed up against it hard, her saggy black dress looking like spilled ink dripped down, "but on a moonless night—"

"Walk her somewhere else, then," said Pa, his voice getting thin. "If you can. But get going, son, and don't come back without her."

And I was outside, feeling the shifting of Aunt Daid's hand bones inside my hand as she set off through the dark, dragging me along with her, scared half to death, wondering if the rustling I heard was her skin or her clothes, wondering on the edge of screaming where she was dragging me to—*what* she was dragging me to.

I tried to head her off from down hollow, steering her toward the lane or the road or across lots or out into the pasture, but it was like being a dog on a leash. I went my way the length of our two arms, then I went her way. Finally I gave up and let her drag me, my eyes opened to aching, trying to see in the dark so heavy that only a less dark showed where the sky was. There wasn't a sound except the thud of our feet in the dust and a thin straining hiss that was Aunt Daid's breath and a gulping gasp that was mine. I'd've cried if I hadn't been so scared.

Aunt Daid stopped so quick that I plowed into her, breathing in a sudden puff of a smell like a stack of old newspapers that have been a long time in a dusty shed. And there we stood, so close I could touch her but I couldn't even see a glimmer of her face in the darkness that was so thick it seemed like the whole night had poured itself down into the hollow. But between one blink and another, I could see Aunt Daid. Not because there was any more light, but because my eyes seemed to get more seeing to them.

She was yawning—a soft little yawn that she covered with a quick hand—and then she laughed. My throat squeezed my breath. The yawn and the hand movement and the laugh were all young and graceful and—and beautiful—but the hand and the face were still withered-up old Aunt Daid.

"I'm waking up." The voice sent shivers up me—pleasure shivers. "I'm waking up," said Aunt Daid again, her soft, light voice surprised and delighted. "And I *know* I'm waking up!"

She held her hands up and looked at them. "They look so horribly real," she marveled. "Don't they?"

She held them out to me and in my surprise I croaked, "Yeah, they sure do."

At the sound of my voice, she jerked all over and got shimmery all around the edges.

"He said," she whispered, her lips firming and coloring as she talked, "he said if ever I could know in my dream that I was just dreaming, I'd be on the way to a cure. I *know* this is the same recurrent nightmare. I *know*

98

I'm asleep, but I'm talking to one of the creatures—"
she looked at me a minute "—one of the *people* in
my dream. And he's talking to me—for the first time!"

Aunt Daid was changing. Her face was filling out and
her eyes widening, her body was straining at the old
black dress that wasn't saggy any more. Before I could
draw a breath, the old dress rustled to the ground and
Aunt Daid—I mean *she* was standing there, light rippling
around her like silk—a light that cast no shadows nor
even flickered on the tangled growth in the hollow.

It seemed to me that I could see into that light, farther
than any human eyes ought to see, and all at once the
world that had always been absolute bedrock to me became a shimmering edge of something, a path between
places or a brief stopping place. And the wonder that
was the existence of mankind wasn't unique any more.

"Oh, if only I *am* cured!" she cried. "If only I don't
ever have to go through this nightmare again!" She lifted
her arms and drew herself up into a slim growing exclamation point.

"For the first time I really know I'm dreaming," she
said. "And I know this isn't real!" Her feet danced across
the hollow and she took both my numb hands. "You
aren't real, are you?" she asked. "None of this is, is it?
All this ugly, old, dragging—" She put her arms around
me and hugged me tight.

My hands tingled to the icy fire of her back and my
breath was tangled in the heavy silvery gleam of her
hair.

"Bless you for being unreal!" she said. "And may I
never dream you again!"

And there I was, all alone in the dark hollow, staring
at hands I couldn't see, trying to see the ice and fire
that still tingled on my fingertips. I took a deep shuddery
breath and stopped to grope for Aunt Daid's dress that
caught at my feet. Fear melted my knees and they
wouldn't straighten up again. I could feel terror knocking
at my brain and I knew as soon as it could break
through I'd go screaming up the hollow like a crazy
man, squeezing the black dress like a rattlesnake in my
hands. But I heard Pa saying, "Bring her back," and I
thought, "All my grampas saw it, too. All of them brought
her back. It's happened before." And I crouched there,
squinching my eyes tight shut, holding my breath, my
fingers digging into my palms, clutching the dress.

It might have been a minute, it might have been an hour, or a lifetime before the dress stirred in my hands. My knees jerked me upright and I dropped the dress like a live coal.

She was there again, her eyes dreaming-shut, her hair swinging like the start of music, her face like every tender thing a heart could ever know. Then her eyes opened slowly and she looked around her.

"Oh, *no!*" she cried, the back of her hand muffling her words. "Not again! Not after all this time! I thought I was over it!"

And I had her crying in my arms—all that wonderfulness against me. All that softness and sorrow.

But she pulled away and looked up at me. "Well, I'll say it again so I won't forget it," she said, her tears slipping from her face and glittering down through the dark. "And this time it'll work. This is only a dream. My own special nightmare. This will surely be the last one. I have just this one night to live through and never again, never again. You are my dream—this is all a dream—" Her hands touched the wrinkles that started across her forehead. The old black dress was creeping like a devouring snake up her and her flesh was sagging away before it as it crept. Her hair was dwindling and tarnishing out of its silvery shining, her eyes shrinking and blanking out.

"No, no!" I cried, sick to the marrow to see Aunt Daid coming back over all that wonder. I rubbed my hand over her face to erase the lines that were cracking across it, but the skin under my fingers stiffened and crumpled and stiffened and hardened, and before I could wipe the feel of dried oldness from the palm of my hand, all of Aunt Daid was there and the hollow was fading as my eyes lost their seeing.

I felt the drag and snag of weeds and briars as I brought Aunt Daid back—a sobbing Aunt Daid, tottering and weak. I finally had to carry her, all match-sticky and musty in my arms.

As I struggled up out of the hollow that was stirring behind me in a wind that left the rest of the world silent, I heard singing in my head, *Life is but a dream . . . Life is but a dream.* But before I stumbled blindly into the blare of light from the kitchen door, I shook

100

the sobbing bundle of bones in my arms—the withered cocoon, the wrinkled seed of such a flowering—and whispered,

"Wake up, Aunt Daid! Wake up, *you!*"

The Substitute

"But I tell you, Mr. Bennett, he's disrupting my whole room! We've got to do something!" Miss Amberly's thin, classroom-grimed fingers brushed back the strand of soft brown hair that habitually escaped from her otherwise neatly disciplined waves.

Mr. Bennett, twiddling a pencil between his fingers, wondered, as he sometimes did at ten-after-four of a weekday, if being a principal was a sign of achievement or of softening of the brain, and quite irrelevantly, how Miss Amberly would look with all of her hair softly loose around her face.

"What has he done now, Miss Amberly? I mean other than just be himself?"

Miss Amberly flushed and crossed her ankles, her feet pushed back under the chair. "I know I'm always bothering you about him, but Mr. Bennett, he's the first student in all my teaching career that I haven't been able to reach. I heard about him from the other teachers as he came up through the grades, but I thought . . . Well, a child can get a reputation, and if each teacher expects it of him, he can live up to it good or bad. When you put him in my class this fall, I was quite confident that I'd be able to get through to him—somehow." She flushed again. "I don't mean to sound conceited."

"I know," Mr. Bennett pried the eraser out of the pencil and tried to push it back in. "I've always depended on you to help straighten out problem children. In fact I won't deny that I've deliberately given you more than your share, because you do have a knack with them. That's why I thought that Keeley . . ." He tapped the pencil against his lower lip and then absently tried to widen the metal eraser band with his teeth. The metal split and bruised against his upper lip. He rubbed a thumb across his mouth and put the pencil down.

"So the new desk didn't work?"

"You ought to see it! It's worse than the old one—ink marks, gum, wax, old wire!" Miss Amberly's voice was hot with indignation. "He has no pride to appeal to. Besides that, the child isn't normal, Mr. Bennett. We shouldn't have him in class with the others!"

"Hasn't he been doing any work at all?" Bennett's quiet voice broke in.

"Practically none. Here. I brought today's papers to show you. His spelling. I gave him fourth grade words since he barely reads on that level and would be lost completely on seventh grade words. Look. *beecuss*. That's because. *liby*. That's library. Well, just look at it!"

Bennett took the dirty, tattered piece of paper and tried to decipher the words. "Pretty poor showing," he murmured. "What's this on the bottom. *Vector, Mare Imbrium, velocity*. Hm, fourth grade spelling?"

"Of course not!" said Miss Amberly, exasperation sharpening her voice. "That's what makes me so blistering mad. He can't spell *cat* twice the same way, but he can spend all spelling period writing down nonsense like that. It proves he's got *something* behind that empty look on his face. And that makes me madder. Stupidity I can make allowances for, but a child who *can* and won't—!"

The slam of a door down the emptying hall was an echoing period to her outburst.

"Well!" Bennett slid down in his chair and locked his fingers around one bent knee. "So you think he really has brains? Mrs. Ensign assured me last year that he was a low-grade moron, incapable of learning."

"Look." Miss Amberly pushed another crumpled exhibit across the desk. "His arithmetic. Fifth grade problems. Two and two is two. Every subtraction problem added—wrong. Every division problem with stars for answers. But look here. Multiplication with three numbers top and bottom. All the answers there without benefit of intermediate steps—and every one of them right!"

"Co-operation?" Bennett's eyebrows lifted.

"No. Positively not. I stood and watched him do them. Watched him make a mess of the others and when he got to the multiplication, he grinned that engaging grin he has occasionally and wrote out the answers as fast as he could read the problems. Tomorrow he won't be

103

able to multiply three and one and get a right answer! He skipped the fractions. Just sat and doodled these funny eights lying on their sides and all these quadratic equation-looking things that have no sense."

"Odd," said Bennett. Then he laid the papers aside. "But was it something besides his school work today? Is he getting out of hand disciplinewise again?"

"Of course, he's always a bad influence on the other children," said Miss Amberly. "He won't work and I can't keep him in every recess and every lunch hour. He might be able to take it, but I can't. Anyway, lately he's begun to be quite impudent. That isn't the problem either. I don't think he realizes how impudent he sounds. But this afternoon he—well, I thought he was going to hit me." Miss Amberly shivered in recollection, clasping her hands.

"Hit you?" Bennett jerked upright, the chair complaining loudly. "Hit *you?*"

"I thought so," she nodded, twisting her hands. "And I'm afraid the other children—"

"What happened?"

"Well, you remember, we just gave him that brand new desk last week, hoping that it would give him a feeling of importance and foster some sort of pride in him to make him want to keep it clean and unmarred. I was frankly very disappointed in his reaction—and almost scared. I didn't tell you when it happened." The faint flush returned to her thin face. "I—I—the others think I run to you too much and . . ." Her voice fluttered and died.

"Not at all," he reassured her, taking up the pencil again and eying it intently as he rolled it between his fingers. "A good administrator must keep in close touch with his teachers. Go on."

"Oh, yes. Well, when he walked in and saw his new desk, he ran over to it and groped down the side of it, then he said, 'Where is it?' and whirled on me like a wildcat. 'Where's my desk?'

"I told him this was to be his desk now. That the old one was too messy. He acted as if he didn't even hear me.

" 'Where's all my stuff?' and he was actually shaking, with his eyes blazing at me. I told him we had put his books and things in the desk. He yanked the drawer clear out onto the floor and pawed through the books. Then he must have found something because he relaxed all at once. He put whatever it was in his pocket and put the drawer back in the desk. I asked him how he liked it and he said 'Okay' with his face as empty . . ."

Miss Amberly tucked her hair back again.

"It didn't do any good—giving him a new desk, I mean. You should see it now."

"What's this about his trying to hit you this afternoon?"

"He didn't really *try* to," said Miss Amberly. "But he did act like he was going to. Anyway, he raised his fist and—well, the children thought he was going to. They were shocked. So it must have been obvious.

"He was putting the English work books on my desk, so I could grade today's exercise. I was getting the art supplies from the cupboard just in back of his desk. It just made me sick to see how he's marked it all up with ink and stuck gum and stuff on it. I noticed some of the ink was still wet, so I wiped it off with a Kleenex. And the first thing I knew, he was standing over me—he's so tall!" She shivered. "And he had his fist lifted up. 'Leave it alone!' he shouted at me. 'You messed it up good once already. Leave it alone, can't you!'

"I just looked at him and said, 'Keeley!' and he sat down, still muttering.

"Mr. Bennett, he looked crazy when he came at me. And he's so big now. I'm afraid for the other children. If he ever hurt one of them—" She pressed a Kleenex to her mouth. "I'm sorry," she said brokenly. And two tears slid furtively down from her closed eyes.

"Now, now," muttered Bennett, terribly embarrassed, hoping no one would come in, and quite irrelevantly, wondering how it would seem to lift Miss Amberly's chin and wipe her tears away himself.

"I'm afraid there isn't much we can do about Keeley," he said, looking out the window at the ragged vine that swayed in the wind. "By law he has to be in school until he is sixteen. Until he actually does something criminal or nearly so, the juvenile division can't take a hand.

"You know his background, of course, living in a cardboard shack down between Tent Town and the dump, with that withered old—is it aunt or grandmother?"

"I don't know," Miss Amberly's voice was very crisp and decisive to contradict her late emotion. "Keeley doesn't seem to know either. He calls her Aunt sometimes, but I doubt if they're even related. People down there think she's a witch. The time we tried to get some of them to testify that he was a neglected child and should become a ward of the court, not a one would say a word against her. She has them all terrified. After all, what would she do if he were taken away from her? She's past cotton picking age. Keeley can do that much and he actually supports her along with his ADC check from the Welfare. We did manage to get that for him."

"So—what can't be cured must be endured." Bennett felt a Friday yawn coming on and stood up briskly. "This desk business. Let's go see it. I'm curious about what makes him mark it all up. He hasn't done any carving on it, has he?"

"No," said Miss Amberly, leading the way out of the office. "No. All he seems to do is draw ink lines all over it, and stick blobs of stuff around. It seems almost to be a fetish or a compulsion of some kind. It's only developed over the last two or three years. It isn't that he likes art. He doesn't like anything."

"Isn't there a subject he's responded to at all? If we could get a wedge in anywhere . . ." said Bennett as they rounded the deserted corner of the building.

"No. Well, at the beginning of school, he actually paid attention during science period when we were having the Solar System." Miss Amberly half skipped, trying to match her steps with his strides. "The first day or so he leafed through that section a dozen times a day. Just looking, I guess, because apparently nothing sank in. On the test over the unit he filled in all the blanks with *baby* and *green cheese* misspelled, of course."

They paused at the closed door of the classroom. "Here, I'll unlock it," said Miss Amberly. She bent to the keyhole, put the key in, lifted hard on the knob and turned the key. "There's a trick to it. This new foundation is still settling."

They went into the classroom which seemed lonely and full of echoes with no students in it. Bennett nodded approval of the plants on the window sills and the neatness of the library table.

"I have him sitting clear in back, so he won't disrupt any more of the children than absolutely necessary."

"Disrupt? Miss Amberly, just exactly what does he *do?* Poke, punch, talk, tear up papers?"

Miss Amberly looked startled as she thought it over. "No. Between his wild silent rages when he's practically impossible—you know those, he spends most of them sitting in the corner of your office—he doesn't actually *do* anything out of the way. At the very most he occasionally mutters to himself. He just sits there, either with his elbows on the desk and both hands over his ears, or he leans on one hand or the other and stares at nothing—apparently bored to death. Yet any child who sits near him, gets restless and talkative and kind of—well, what-does-it-matter-ish. *They* won't work. *They* disturb others. *They* create disturbances. They think that because Keeley gets along without doing any work, that they can too. Why didn't they pass him on a long time ago and get rid of him? He could stay in school a hundred years and never learn anything." Her voice was bitter.

Bennett looked at Keeley's desk. The whole table was spiderwebbed with lines drawn in a silvery ink that betrayed a sort of bas-relief to his inquiring fingers. At irregular intervals, blobs of gum or wax or some such stuff was stuck, mostly at junctions of lines. There were two circles on the desk, about elbow-sized and spaced about right to accommodate two leaning elbows. Each circle was a network of lines. Bennett traced with his finger two fine coppery wires that were stuck to the side of the desk. Following them down into the desk drawer, he rummaged through an unsightly mass of papers and fished out two little metallic disks, one on each wire.

"Why those must be what he was looking for when he was so worked up last week," said Miss Amberly. "They look a little bit like a couple of bottle caps stuck together, don't they?"

Bennett turned them over in his hands, then he ran his fingers over the marked-up desk, nothing that the lines ran together at the edge of the desk and ended at the metal table support.

Bennett laughed, "Looks like Keeley has been bitten by the radio bug. I'd guess these for earphones." He tossed the disks in his hand. "And all these mysterious lines are probably his interpretation of a schematic diagram. I suppose he gets so bored doing nothing that he dreamed this little game up for himself. Where did he get this

107

ink, though? It's not school ink." He ran his fingers over the raised lines again.

"I don't know. He brings it to school in a little pill bottle," said Miss Amberly. "I tried to confiscate it when he started marking things up again, but he seemed inclined to make an issue of it and it wasn't worth running the risk of another of his wild ones. The janitor says he can't wash the stuff off and the only time I've seen any rub off was when I wiped away the wet marks today."

Bennett examined the metal disks. "Let's try this out," he said, half joking. He slid into the desk and leaned his elbows in the circles. He pressed the disks to his ears. A look of astonishment flicked across his face.

"Hey! I hear something! Listen!"

He gestured Miss Amberly down to him and pressed the earphones to her ears. She closed her eyes against his nearness and could hear nothing but the tumultuous roar of her heart in her ears. She shook her head.

"I don't hear anything."

"Why sure! Some odd sort of . . ." He listened again. "Well, no. I guess you're right," he said ruefully.

He put the earphones back in the desk.

"Harmless enough, I suppose. Let him have his radio if it gives him any satisfaction. He certainly isn't getting any out of his schoolwork. This might be a way to reach him though. Next week I'll check with a friend of mine and see if I can get any equipment for Keeley. It might be an answer to our problem."

But next week Mr. Bennett had no time to do any checking with his friend. The school found itself suddenly in the middle of a virus epidemic.

Monday he stared aghast at the attendance report. Tuesday he started grimly down his substitute list. Wednesday he reached the bottom of it. Thursday he groaned and taught a third grade himself. Friday he dragged himself to the phone and told his secretary to carry on as best she could and went shaking back to bed. He was cheered a little by the report that the third grade teacher had returned, but he had a sick, sunken feeling inside occasioned by the news that for the first time Miss Amberly was going to be absent.

"But don't worry, Mr. Bennett," the secretary had said, "we have a good substitute. A *man* substitute. He just got here from back east and he hasn't filed his certificate yet, but he came well recommended."

So Mr. Bennett pulled the covers up to his chin and wondered, quite irrelevantly, if Miss Amberly had a sunken feeling too, because *he* was absent.

Miss Amberly's seventh grade buzzed and hummed when at eight-thirty Miss Amberly was nowhere to be seen. When the nine o'clock bell pulled all the students in from the playfield, they tumbled into their seats, eyes wide, as they surveyed the substitute. Glory May took one look at the broad shoulders and black hair and began to fish the bobby pins out of her curls that were supposed to stay up until evening so they would be perfect for the date tonight—with a seventeen-year-old high school man. The other girls stared at him covertly from behind books or openly with slack-jawed wonder.

The boys, with practiced eyes, looked him over and decided that even if old lady Amberly was absent, they had better behave.

And of course, at ten past nine, Keeley sauntered in, carrying his arithmetic book by one corner, the pages fluttering and fanning as he came. The substitute took little notice of him beyond asking his name and waiting for him to slump into his desk before going on with the opening exercises.

Keeley arranged himself in his usual pose, the metal disks pressed to his ears, his elbows in the webbed circles. He sat for a minute blank-faced, and then he began to frown. He pressed his hands tighter to his ears. He traced the lengths of the coppery wire with inquiring fingers. He checked the blobs and chunks of stuff stuck on the lines. He reamed his ears out with his little finger and listened again. Finally his squirming and wiggling called forth a "Please settle down, Keeley, you're disturbing the class," from the substitute.

"Go soak your head," muttered Keeley, half audibly. He pushed the earphones back into the drawer and slouched sullenly staring at the ceiling.

By noon, Keeley, the blank-faced, no-doer, had become Keeley, the disrupting Demon. He pulled hair and tore papers. He swaggered up the aisle to the pencil sharpener, shoving books off every desk as he went. He shot paper clips with rubber bands and scraped his thumb nail down the blackboard, a half-dozen times. By some wild contortion, he got both his feet up on top of his desk, and when the impossible happened and he jackknifed under the desk with his heels caught on the edge, it took the substitute and the two biggest boys to extract him.

By the time he got out of the cafeteria, leaving behind him a trail of broken milk bottles, spilled plates and streaked clothes, Miss Ensign was gasping in the teachers' room, "And last year I prayed he'd wake up and begin to function. Lor-dee! I hope he goes back to sleep again!"

Keeley simmered down a little after lunch until he tried the earphones again and then he sat sullenly glowering at his desk, muttering threateningly, a continuous annoying stream of disturbance. Finally the substitute said placidly, "Keeley, you're disturbing the class again."

"Aw shaddup! You meathead, you!" said Keeley.

There was a stricken silence in the room as everyone stared aghast at Keeley.

The substitute looked at him dispassionately. "Keeley, come here."

"Come and get me if you think you can!" snarled Keeley.

A horrified gasp swept the room and Angie began to sob in terror.

The substitute spoke again, something nobody caught, but the result was unmistakable. Keeley jerked as though he had been stabbed and his eyes widened in blank astonishment. The substitute wet his lips and spoke again, "Come here, Keeley."

And Keeley came, stumbling blindly down the aisle, to spend the rest of the afternoon until Physical Ed hunched over his open book in the seat in the front corner, face to wall.

At PE period, he stumbled out and stood lankly by the basketball court, digging a hole in the ground with the flapping sole of one worn shoe. The coach, knowing Keeley in such moods, passed him by with a snort of exasperation and turned to the clamoring wildness of the rest of the boys.

When the three fifty-five bell rang, the seventh grade readied itself for home by shoving everything into the drawers and slamming them resoundingly. As usual, the worn one shot out the other side of the desk and it and its contents had to be scrambled back into place before a wholly unnatural silence fell over the room, a silence through which could be felt almost tangibly, the straining to be first out the door, first to the bus line, first in the bus—just to be first.

The substitute stood quietly by his desk. "Keeley, you will stay after school."

The announcement went almost unnoticed. Keeley had spent a good many half hours after school this year with Miss Amberly sweating out page after page in his tattered books.

Keeley sat in his own desk, his hands pressed tightly together, his heart fluttering wildly in his throat as he listened to the receding clatter of hurried feet across the patio. Something inside him cried. "Wait! Wait for me!" as the sounds died away.

The substitute came down the aisle and turned one of the desks so he could sit facing Keeley. He ran a calculating eye over Keeley's desk.

"Not bad," he said. "You have done well with what materials you had. But why here at school where everyone could see?"

Keeley gulped. "Have you seen where I live? Couldn't keep nothing there. Come a rain, wouldn't be no house left. Besides Aunt Mo's too dang nosey. She'd ask questions. She know I ain't as dumb as I look. Ever body at school thinks I'm a dope."

"You certainly have been a stinker today," grinned the substitute. "Your usual behavior?"

Keeley squirmed. "Naw. I kinda like old lady Amberly. I was mad because I couldn't get nothing on my radio. I thought it was busted. I didn't know you was here."

"Well, I am. Ready to take you with me. Our preliminary training period shows you to be the kind of material we want."

"Gee!" Keeley ran his tongue across his lips. "That's swell. Where's your ship?"

"It's down by the county dump. Just beyond the hill in back of the tin can section. Think you can find it tonight?"

"Sure. I know that dump like my hand, but . . ."

"Good. We'll leave Earth tonight. Be there by dark." The substitute stood up. So did Keeley, slowly.

"Leave Earth?"

"Of course," impatiently. "You knew we weren't from Earth when we first made contact."

"When will I get to come back?"

111

"There's no reason for you to, ever. We have work geared to your capabilities to keep you busy and happy from here on out."

"But," Keeley sat down slowly, "leave Earth forever?"

"What has Earth done for you, that you should feel any ties to it?" The substitute sat down again.

"I was born here."

"To live like an animal in a cardboard hut that the next rain will melt away. To wear ragged clothes and live on beans and scrap vegetables except for free lunch at school."

"I don't get no free lunch!" retorted Keeley, "I work ever morning in the Cafeteria for my lunch. I ain't no charity case."

"But Keeley, you'll have whole clothes and good quarters and splendid food in our training center."

"Food and clothes ain't all there is to living."

"No, I grant you that," admitted the substitute. "But the world calls you stupid and useless. We can give you the opportunity to work to your full capacity, to develop your mind and abilities to the level you're capable of achieving instead of sitting day after day droning out kindergarten pap with a roomful of stupid . . ."

"I won't have to do that all my life. When I get to high school . . ."

"With marks like yours? No one's going to *ask* you how smart you are. They're going to see all the 4s and 5s and all the minuses on the citizenship side of your card and you'll never make it into high school. Besides, Keeley, you don't need all these petty little steps. Right now, you're trained in math and physics past college level. You'll go crazy marking time."

"There's other stuff to learn besides them things."

"Granted, but are you learning them? Spell *because.*"

"Bee—that's not important!"

"To this earth it is. What has changed you, Keeley? You were wild to go . . ."

"I got to thinking," said Keeley. "All afternoon I been thinking. How come you guys pick brains off of Earth? What's the matter with your world, where ever it is? You guys ain't leveling with me somewhere."

The substitute met Keeley's eyes. "There's nothing sinister about us," he said. "We do need brains. Our world is —different. We don't range from imbeciles to geniuses

112

like you do. The people are either geniuses on your scale or just vegetables, capable of little more than keeping themselves alive. And yet, from the vegetable ranks come the brains, but too seldom for our present needs. We're trying to find ways to smooth out that gap between the haves and the have-nots, and some years ago we lost a lot of our 'brains' in an experiment that got out of hand. We need help in keeping civilization going for us until more of the native-born fill in the vacancy. So we recruit."

"Why not pick on grownups then? There's plenty of big bugs who'd probably give an arm to even look at your ship."

"That's true," nodded the substitute, "but we like them young so we can train them to our ways. Besides, we don't want to attract attention. Few grownups could step out of the world without questions being asked, especially highly trained specialists. So we seek out kids like you who are too smart for their own good in the environments where they happen to be. Sometimes they know they're smart. Sometimes we have to prove it to them. And they're never missed for long when we take them. Who is there to ask questions if you should leave with me?"

"Aunt Mo," snapped Keeley, "And—and—"

"A half-crazy old hag—no one else!"

"You shut up about Aunt Mo. She's mine. I found her. And there is too someone else—Miss Amberly. She'd care!"

"Dried up old maid school teacher!" the substitute returned bitingly.

"For a genius, you're pretty dumb!" retorted Keeley. "She ain't so very old and she ain't dried up and as soon as her and Mr. Bennett stop batting so many words around, she won't be an old maid no more neither!"

"But two out of a world! That's not many to hold a fellow back from all we could give you."

"Two's two," replied Keeley. "How many you got that will care if you get back from here or not?"

The substitute stood up abruptly, his face expressionless. "Are you coming with me, Keeley?"

"If I did, why couldn't I come back sometime?" Keeley's voice was pleading. "I bet you know a lot of stuff that'd help Earth."

"And we should give it to Earth, just like that?" asked the substitute coldly.

"As much as I should leave Earth, just like that," Keeley's voice was just as icy.

"We could argue all night, Keeley," said the substitute. "Maybe it'd help if I told you that Earth is in for a pretty sticky time of it and this is your chance to get out of it."

"Can you guys time-travel too?" asked Keeley.

"Well, no. But we can take into consideration the past and the present and postulate the future."

"Sounds kind of guessy to me. The future ain't an already built road. We're making some of it right now that I betcha wasn't in your figgering. Nope. If we're in for a sticky time, I'll get stuck too, and maybe do some of the unsticking."

"That's your decision?"

"Yep." Keeley stood up and began to stack his books.

The substitute watched him silently, then he said, "Suppose I should insist?"

Keeley grinned at him. "I can be awful dumb. Ask anybody."

"Very well. It has to be voluntary or not at all. You might as well give me those earphones." He held out his hand. "They'll be of no use to you with our training ship gone."

Keeley snapped the wires and hefted the disks in his hand. Then he put them in his pocket.

"I'll keep them. Someday I'll figure out how come this setup works without words. If I can't, we've got men who can take stuff like this and figger out the other end of it."

"You're not so dumb, Keeley," the substitute smiled suddenly.

"No, I'm not," said Keeley. "And I'm gonna prove it. Starting Monday, I'm gonna set my mind to school. By then I oughta be up with the class. I only have to look a coupla times at a page to get it."

The substitute paused at the door. "Your last chance, Keeley. Coming or staying?"

"Staying. Thanks for the help you gave me."

"It was just an investment that didn't pay off," said the substitute. "But Keeley . . ."

"Yeah?"

"I'm glad you're staying. I was born on Earth."

The Grunder

Almost before Crae brought the car to a gravel-spraying stop in front of the Murmuring Pines Store and Station, Ellena had the door open and was out and around the corner marked His and Hers. Crae stared angrily after her, his jaw set and his lips moving half-audibly. Anger burned brightly in his brain and the tight, swollen sickness inside him throbbed like a boil. It was all her fault—all because she had to smile at every man—she had to entice every male—she always—! And then the fire was gone and Crae slumped down into the ashes of despair. It was no use. No matter how hard he tried—no matter what he did, it always ended this way.

This was to have been it. This trip into the White Mountains—a long happy fishing trip for the two of them to celebrate because he was learning to curb his jealousy, his blind, unreasoning, unfounded jealousy that was wrecking everything he and Ellena had planned for a life together. It had gone so well. The shadowy early morning beginning, the sweep up the hills from the baking, blistering valley, the sudden return to spring as they reached pine country, the incredible greenness of everything after the dust and dryness of the desert.

And then they had stopped at Lakeside.

She said she had only asked how the fishing was. *She* said they had known the same old-timers. *She* said—! Crae slid lower in the car seat, writhing inside as he remembered his icy return to the car, his abrupt backing away from the laughing group that clustered around Ellena's window, his measured, insane accusations and the light slowly dying out of Ellena's eyes, the quiet, miserable turning away of her white face and her silence as the car roared on—through hell as far as the two of them were concerned—through the rolling timberland to Murmuring Pines.

Crae wrenched himself up out of his futile rememberings and slid out of the car, slamming the door resoundingly. He climbed the three steps up to the sagging store porch and stopped, fumbling for a cigarette.

"Wife trouble?"

Crae started as the wheezy old voice from the creaking rocking chair broke through his misery. He stared over his half-raised cigarette into the faded blue eyes that peered through dirty bifocals at him. Then he put the cigarette in his mouth and cupped his palms around his light.

"What's it to you?" he half snapped, but even his hair-triggered temper seemed to have deserted him.

"Nothing, son, nothing." The chair rocked violently, then slowed down. "Only thing is, I kinda wondered, seeing her kite outa the car like that and you standing there, sulling up. Sit down a spell. I'm Eli. Old Eli."

Inexplicably, Crae sat down on the top step and said, "You're right, Eli. Plenty of trouble, but it's me—not my wife."

"Oh, that-a-way." The frowsy old head nodded.

"Yeah," muttered Crae, wondering dismally why he should be spilling his guts to a busted-down old coot like this one. "Jealous, crazy jealous."

"Can't trust her, huh?" The chair rocked madly a moment, then slowed again.

"I can too!" flared Crae.

"Then what's the kick?" The old man spat toward the porch railing. "Way I see it, it takes a certain amount of co-operation from a woman before she can go far wrong. If you can trust your wife, whatcha got to worry about?"

"Nothing," muttered Crae. "I know I've got nothing to worry about. But," his hand clenched on his knee, "if only I could be *sure!* I know there's no logical reason for the way I feel. I know she wouldn't look at anyone else. But I can't feel it! All the knowing in the world doesn't do any good if you can't feel it."

"That's a hunk of truth if I ever heard one," wheezed the old man, leaning across his fat belly and poking a stubby finger at Crae. "Like getting turned around in directions. You can say 'That's East' all you want to, but if it don't feel like East then the sun goes on coming up in the North."

There was a brief pause and Crae lifted his face to the cool pine-heavy breeze that hummed through the trees, wondering again why he was spreading his own private lacerations out for this gross, wheezing, not-too-clean old stranger.

"Them there psy-chiatrists—some say they can help fellers like you."

Crae shook his head, "I've been going to a counselor for three months. I thought I had it licked. I was sure—" Crae's voice trailed off as he remembered why he had finally consented to go to a counselor.

"Bring a child into an atmosphere like this?" Ellena's voice was an agonized whisper, "How can we Crae, how can we? Anger and fear and mistrust. Never—not until—"

And his bitter rejoinder. "It's you and your slutting eyes that make 'this atmosphere.' If I don't watch out you'll be bringing me someone else's child—"

And then his head was ringing from the lightning quick blow to his face, before she turned, blazing-eyed and bitter, away from him.

"No go, huh?" The old shoulders shrugged and the old man wiped one hand across his stubby chin.

"No go, damn me, and our vacation is ruined before it begins."

"Too bad. Where you going? Big Lake?"

"No. South Fork of East Branch. Heard they've opened the closed part of the stream. Should be good fishing."

"South Fork?" The chair agitated wildly, then slowed. "Funny coincidence, that."

"Coincidence?" Crae glanced up.

"Yeah. I mean you, feeling like you do, going fishing on South Fork."

"What's my feelings got to do with it?" asked Crae, doubly sorry now that he had betrayed himself to the old feller. What good had it done? Nothing could help—ever—but still he sat.

"Well, son, there's quite a story about South Fork. Dunno when it started. Might be nothing to it." The faded eyes peered sharply through the glasses at him. "Then again, there might."

"What's the deal?" Crae's voice was absent and his eyes were on the His and Hers signs. "I've been coming up here for five years now and I never heard any special story."

"Seems there's a fish," said the old man. "A kinda special kinda fish. Not many see him and he ain't been seen nowhere around this part of the country 'ceptin on South Fork. Nobody's ever caught him, not to land anyway."

"Oh, one of those. Patriarch of the creek. Wily eluder of bait. Stuff like that?"

"Oh, not exactly." The rocking chair accelerated and slowed. "This here one is something special."

"I'll hear about it later, Pop." Crae stood up. Ellena was coming back down the path, outwardly serene and cool again. But she went in the side door into the store and Crae sat down slowly.

"They say it's a little longer than a man and maybe a man's reach around." The old man went on as though not interrupted.

"Pretty big—" Crae muttered absently, then snapped alert. "Hey! What are you trying to pull? A fish that size couldn't get in South Fork, let alone live there. Bet there aren't ten places from Baldy to Sheep's Crossing as deep as five feet even at flood stage. What kind of line you trying to hand me?"

"Told you it was kinda special." The old man creased his eyes with a gap-toothed grin. "This here fish don't live in the creek. He don't even swim in it. Just happens to rub his top fin along it once in a while. And not just this part of the country, neither. Heard about him all over the world, likely. This here fish is a Grunder—swims through dirt and rocks like they was water. Water feels to him like air. Air is a lot of nothing to him. Told a feller about him once. He told me might be this here Grunder's from a nother dy-mention." The old man worked his discolored lips silently for a moment. "He said it like it was supposed to explain something. Don't make sense to me."

Crae relaxed and laced his fingers around one knee. Oh, well, if it was that kind of story—might as well enjoy it.

"Anyway," went on the old man, "like I said, this here Grunder's a special fish. Magic, us old-timers would call it. Dunno what you empty, don't-believe-nothing-without-touch-it-taste-it-hear-it-proof younguns would call it. But here's where it hits you, young feller." The old finger was jabbing at Crae again. "This here Grunder is a sure cure for jealousy. All you gotta do is catch him, rub him

118

three times the wrong way and you'll never doubt your love again."

Crae laughed bitterly, stung by fear that he was being ridiculed. "Easy to say and hard to prove, Pop. Who could catch a magic fish as big as that on trout lines? Pretty smart, fixing it so no one can prove you're a ring-tailed liar."

"Laugh, son," grunted the old man, "while you can. But who said anything about a trout line? Special fish, special tackle. They say the Grunder won't even rise nowhere without special bait." The old man leaned forward, his breath sounding as though it came through a fine meshed screen. "Better listen, son. Laugh if you wanta, but listen good. Could be one of these fine days you'll wanta cast a line for the Grunder. Can't ever sometimes tell."

The tight sickness inside Crae gave a throb and he licked dry lips.

"There's a pome," the old man went on, leaning back in his chair, patting the front of his dirty checked shirt as he gasped for breath. "Old as the Grunder most likely. Tells you what kinda tackle."

> *"Make your line from her linen fair.*
> *Take your hook from her silken hair.*
> *A broken heart must be your share*
> *For the Grunder."*

The lines sang in Crae's mind, burning their way into his skeptical brain.

"What bait?" he asked, trying to keep his voice light and facetious. "Must be kind of scarce for a fish like that."

The faded old eyes peered at him. "Scarce? Well, now that depends," the old man said. "Listen."

> *"This is your bait, or your lure or flies,*
> *Take her sobs when your lady cries,*
> *Take the tears that fall from her eyes*
> *For the Grunder."*

Crae felt the sting of the words. The only time he'd seen Ellena cry over his tantrums was the first time he'd really blown his top. That was the time she'd tried to defend herself, tried to reason with him, tried to reassure him and finally had dissolved into tears of frustration,

119

sorrow and disillusionment. Since then, if there had been tears, he hadn't seen them—only felt her heart breaking inch by inch as she averted her white, still face from his rages and accusations.

"My wife doesn't cry," he said petulantly.

"Pore woman," said the old man, reaming one ear with his little finger. "Anyway, happen some day you'll want to go fishing for the Grunder, you won't forget."

The sound of Ellena's laughter inside the store drew Crae to his feet. Maybe they could patch this vacation together after all. Maybe Ellena could put up with him just once more. Crae's heart contracted as he realized that every "once more" was bringing them inevitably to the "never again" time for him and Ellena.

He went to the screen door of the store and opened it. Behind him, he could hear the creak of the old man's chair.

"Course you gotta believe in the Grunder. Nothing works, less'n you believe it. And be mighty certain, son, that you want him when you fish for him. Once you hook him, you gotta hold him 'til you stroke him. And every scale on his body is jagged edged on the down side. Rip hell outa your hand first stroke—but three it's gotta be. Three times—"

"Okay, Pop. Three times it is. Quite a story you've got there." Crae let the door slam behind him as he went into the shadowy store and took the groceries from an Ellena who smiled into his eyes and said, "Hello, honey."

A week later, the two of them lolled on the old army blanket on the spread-out tarp, half in the sun, half in the shade, watching the piling of dazzling bright summer thunderheads over Baldy. Stuffed with mountain trout, and drowsy with sun, Crae felt that the whole world was as bright as the sky above them. He was still aglow from catching his limit nearly every day since they arrived, and that, along with just plain vacation delight, filled him with such a feeling of contentment and well-being that it overflowed in a sudden rush of tenderness and he yanked Ellena over to him. She laughed against his chest and shifted her feet into the sun.

"They freeze in the shade and roast in the sun," she said, "Isn't it marvelous up here?"

"Plumb sightly, ma'am," drawled Crae.

"Just smell the spruce," said Ellena, sitting up and filling her lungs ecstatically.

"Yeah, and the fried fish," Crae sat up, too, and breathed in noisily. "And the swale, and," he sniffed again, "just a touch of skunk."

"Oh, Crae!" Ellena cried reproachfully, "Don't spoil it!" She pushed him flat on the blanket and collapsed, laughing, against him.

"Oof!" grunted Crae. "A few more weeks of six fish at a sitting and all the rest of the grub you're stashing away and I'll have to haul you home in a stock trailer!"

"Six fish!" Ellena pummeled him with both fists. "I'm darn lucky to salvage two out of the ten when you get started—and I saw you letting your belt out three notches. Now who's fat stuff!"

They scuffled, laughing helplessly, until they both rolled off the blanket onto the squishy black ground that was still wet from spring and the nearness of the creek. Ellena shrieked and Crae, scrambling to his feet yanked her up to him. For a long minute they stood locked in each other's arms, listening to the muted roar of the little falls just above camp and a bird crying, "See me? See me?" from the top of a spruce somewhere.

Then Ellena stirred and half-whispered, "Oh, Crae, it's so wonderful up here. Why can't it always—" Then she bit her lip and buried her face against him.

Crae's heart reluctantly took up it's burden again. "Please God, it will be," he promised. "Like this always." And she lifted her face to his kiss.

Then he pushed her away.

"Now, Frau, break out the corn meal and the frying pan again. I'm off to the races." He slipped the creel on and picked up his rod. "I'm going down where the old beaver dam used to be. That's where the big ones are, I'll betcha."

" 'By, honey," Ellena kissed the end of his sunburned nose. "Personally, I think I'll have a cheese sandwich for supper. A little fish goes a long way with me."

"Woman!" Crae was horrified. "What you said!"

He looked back from the top of the logging railroad embankment and saw Ellena squatting down by the creek, dipping water into the blackened five gallon can they used for a water heater. He yelled down at her and she waved at him, then turned back to her work. Crae filled his lungs with the crisp scented air and looked slowly around at the wooded hills, still cherishing drifts of snow in their shadowy folds, the high reaching mountains that lifted the spruce and scattered pines against an achingly blue sky, the creek, brawling its flooded way like an exuberant snake flinging its shining loops first one way and then another, and his tight little, tidy little camp tucked into one of the wider loops of the creek.

"This is it," he thought happily. "From perfection like this, we can't help getting straightened out. All I needed was a breathing spell."

Then he set out with swinging steps down the far side of the embankment.

Crae huddled deeper in his light Levi jacket as he topped the rise on the return trip. The clouds were no longer white shining towers of pearl and blue, but heavy rolling gray, blanketing the sky. The temperature had dropped with the loss of the sun, and he shivered in the sudden blare of wind that slapped him in the face with a dozen hail-hard raindrops and then died.

But his creel hung heavy on his hip and he stepped along lightly, still riding on his noontime delight. His eyes sought out the camp and he opened his mouth to yell for Ellena. His steps slowed and stopped and his face smoothed out blankly as he looked at the strange car pulled up behind theirs.

The sick throbbing inside him began again and the blinding flame began to flicker behind his eyes. With a desperate firmness he soothed himself and walked slowly down to camp. As he neared the tent, the flap was pushed open and Ellena and several men crowded out into the chill wind.

"See," cried Ellena, "Here's Crae now." She ran to him, face aglow—and eyes pleading. "How did you do, honey?"

"Pretty good." Somewhere he stood off and admired the naturalness of his answer. "Nearly got my limit, but of course the biggest one got away. No fooling!"

Ellena and the strange faces laughed with him and then they were all crowding around, admiring the catch and pressing the bottle into his cold hands.

"Come on in the tent," Ellena tugged at his arm. "We've got a fire going. It got too cold to sit outdoors."

Then she was introducing the men in the flare and hiss of the Coleman lantern while they warmed themselves at the little tin stove that was muttering over the pine knots just pushed in.

"This is Jess and Doc and Stubby and Dave." She looked up at Crae. "My husband, Crae."

"Howdy," said Crae.

"Hi, Crae." Jess stuck out a huge hand. "Fine wife you got there. Snatched us from death's door. Hot coffee and that ever lovin' old bottle. We were colder'n a dead Eskimo's—wup—ladies present."

Ellena laughed. "Well, lady or not, I know the rest of that one. But now that we've got fish again, why don't you men stay for supper?" She glanced over at Crae.

"Sure," said Crae, carefully cordial. "Why not?"

"Thanks," said Jess. "But we've stayed too long now. Fascinating woman, your wife, Crae. Couldn't tear ourselves away, but now the old man's home—" He roared with laughter. "Guess we better slope, huh, fellers? Gotta pitch camp before dark."

"Yeah. Can't make any time with the husband around," said Stubby. Then he leaned over and stage-whispered to Ellena, "I ain't so crazy 'bout fishing. How 'bout letting me know when he's gone again?"

After the laughter, Crae said, "Better have another jolt before you get out into the weather." So the bottle made the rounds slowly and finally everyone ducked out of the tent into the bleakly windy out-of-doors. The men piled into the car and Jess leaned out the window.

"Thought we'd camp up above you," he roared against the wind, "but it's flooded out. Guess we'll go on downstream to the other campground." He looked around admiringly. "Tight little setup you got here."

"Thanks," yelled Crae. "We think so too."

"Well, be seeing you!" And the car surged up the sharp drop from the road, the little trailer swishing along in back. Crae and Ellena watched them disappear over the railroad.

"Well," Crae turned and laid his fist against Ellena's cheek and pushed lightly. "How about chow, Frau? Might as well get supper over with. Looks like we're in for some weather."

"Okay, boss," Ellena's eyes were shining. "Right away, sir!" And she scurried away, calling back, "But you'd better get the innards out of those denizens of the deep so I can get them in the pan."

123

"Okay." Crae moved slowly and carefully as though something might break if he moved fast. He squatted by the edge of the stream and clumsily began to clean the fish. When he had finished, his hands were numb from the icy snow water and the persistent wind out of the west, but not nearly as numb as he felt inside. He carried the fish over to the cook bench where Ellena shivered over the two-burner stove.

"Here you are," he said slowly and Ellena's eyes flew to his face.

He smiled carefully. "Make them plenty crisp and step it up!"

Ellena's smile was relieved. "Crisp it is!"

"Where's a rag to wipe my shoes off with? Shoulda worn my waders. There's mud and water everywhere this year."

"My old petticoat's hanging over there on the tree—if you don't mind an embroidered shoe rag."

Crae took down the cotton half-slip with eyelet embroidery around the bottom.

"This is a rag?" he asked.

She laughed. "It's ripped almost full length and the elastic's worn out. Go ahead and use it."

Crae worked out of his wet shoes and socks and changed into dry. Then he lifted one shoe and the rag and sat hunched over himself on the log. With a horrible despair, he felt all the old words bubbling and the scab peeling off the hot sickness inside him. His fist tightened on the white rag until his knuckles cracked. Desperately, he tried to change his thoughts, but the bubbling putrescence crept through his mind and poured its bitterness into his mouth and he heard himself say bitterly,

"How long were they here before I showed up?"

Ellena turned slowly from the stove, her shoulders drooping, her face despairing.

"About a half hour." Then she straightened and looked desperately over at him. "No, Crae, please. Not here. Not now."

Crae looked blindly down at the shoe he still held in one hand. He clenched his teeth until his jaws ached, but the words pushed through anyway—biting and venomous.

"Thirty miles from anywhere. Just have to turn my back and they come flocking! You can't tell me you don't welcome them! You can't tell me you don't encourage them and entice them and—" He slammed his shoe down and dropped the rag beside it. In two strides he caught her by both shoulders and shook her viciously. "Hellamighty! You even built a fire in the tent for them! What's the matter, woman, are you slipping? You've got any number of ways to take their minds off the cold without building a fire!"

"Crae! Crae!" She whispered pleadingly.

"Don't 'Crae, Crae' me!" he backhanded her viciously across the face. She cried out and fell sideways against the tree. Her hair caught on the rough stub of a branch as she started to slide down against the trunk. Crae grabbed one of her arms and yanked her up. Her caught hair strained her head backwards as he lifted. And suddenly her smooth sun-tinted throat fitted Crae's two spasmed hands. For an eternity his thumbs felt the sick pounding of her pulse. Then a tear slid slowly down from one closed eye, trickling towards her ear.

Crae snatched his hand away before the tear could touch it. Ellena slid to her knees, leaving a dark strand of hair on the bark of the tree. She got slowly to her feet. She turned without a word or look and went into the tent.

Crae slumped down on the log, his hands limp between his knees, his head hanging. He lifted his hands and looked at them incredulously, then he flung them from him wildly, turned and shoved his face hard up against the rough tree trunk.

"Oh, God!" he thought wildly. "I must be going crazy! I never hit her before. I never tried to—" He beat his doubled fists against the tree until the knuckles crimsoned, then he crouched again above his all-enveloping misery until the sharp smell of burning food penetrated his daze. He walked blindly over to the camp stove and yanked the smoking skillet off. He turned off the fire and dumped the curled charred fish into the garbage can and dropped the skillet on the ground.

He stood uncertain, noticing for the first time the scattered sprinkling of rain patterning the top of the split-log table near the stove. He started automatically for the car to roll the windows up.

And then he saw Ellena standing just outside the tent. Afraid to move or speak, he stood watching her. She came slowly over to him. In the half-dusk he could see

125

the red imprint of his hand across her cheek. She looked up at him with empty, drained eyes.

"We will go home tomorrow." Her voice was expressionless and almost steady. "I'm leaving as soon as we get there."

"Ellena, don't!" Crae's voice shook with pleading and despair.

Ellena's mouth quivered and tears overflowed. She dropped her sodden, crumpled Kleenex and took a fresh one from her shirt pocket. She carefully wiped her eyes.

" 'It's better to snuff a candle . . .' " Her voice choked off and Crae felt his heart contract. They had read the book together and picked out their favorite quote and now she was using it to—

Crae held out his hands, "Please, Ellena, I promise—"

"Promise!" Her eyes blazed so violently that Crae stumbled back a step. "You've been trying to mend this sick thing between us with promises for too long!" Her voice was taut with anger. "Neither you nor I believe your promises any more. There's not one valid reason why I should try to keep our marriage going by myself. You don't believe in it any more. You don't believe in me any more—if you ever did. You don't even believe in yourself! Nothing will work if you don't believe—" Her voice wavered and broke. She mopped her eyes carefully again and her voice was measured and cold as she said, "We'll leave for home tomorrow—and God have mercy on us both."

She turned away blindly, burying her face in her two hands and stumbled into the tent.

Crae sat down slowly on the log beside his muddy shoes. He picked up one and fumbled for the cleaning rag. He huddled over himself, feeling as though life were draining from his arms and legs, leaving them limp.

"It's all finished," he thought hopelessly. "It's finished and I'm finished and this whole crazy damn life is finished. I've done everything I know. Nothing on this earth can ever make it right between us again."

You don't believe, you don't believe. And then a wheezy old voice whistled in his ear. *Nothing works, less'n you believe it.* Crae straightened up, following the faint thread of voice. *Happen some day you'll want to go fishing— you won't forget.*

"It's crazy and screwy and a lot of hogwash," thought Crae. "Things like that can't possibly exist."

126

You don't believe. Nothing works, less'n—

A strange compound feeling of hope and wonder began to well up in Crae. "Maybe, maybe," he thought breathlessly. Then— "It *will* work. It's got to work!"

Eagerly intent, he went back over the incident at the store. All he could remember at first was the rocking chair and the thick discolored lips of the old man, then a rhythm began in his mind, curling to a rhyme word at the end of each line. He heard the raspy old voice again—

Happen some day you'll want to go fishing, you won't forget. And the lines slowly took form.

> *"Make your line from her linen fair.*
> *Take your hook from her silken hair.*
> *A broken heart must be your share*
> *For the Grunder."*

"Why that's impossible on the face of it," thought Crae with a pang of despair. "The broken heart I've got—but the rest? Hook from her hair?" Hair? Hairpin—bobby pin. He fumbled in his shirt pocket. Where were they? Yesterday, upcreek when Ellena decided to put her hair in pigtails because the wind was so strong, she had given him the pins she took out. He held the slender piece of metal in his hand for a moment then straightened it carefully between his fingers. He slowly bent one end of it up in an approximation of a hook. He stared at it ruefully. What a fragile thing to hang hope on.

Now for a line—*her linen fair.* Linen? Ellena brought nothing linen to camp with her. He fumbled with the makeshift hook, peering intently into the dusk, tossing the line of verse back and forth in his mind. Linen's not just cloth. Linen can be clothes. Body linen. He lifted the shoe rag. An old slip—ripped.

In a sudden frenzy of haste, he ripped the white cloth into inch wide strips and knotted them together, carefully rolling the knobby, ravelly results into a ball. The material was so old and thin that one strip parted as he tested a knot and he had to tie it again. When the last strip was knotted, he struggled to fasten his improvised hook onto it. Finally, bending another hook at the opposite end, sticking it through the material, splitting the end, he knotted it as securely as he could. He peered at

127

the results and laughed bitterly at the precarious make-shift. "But it'll work," he told himself fiercely. "It'll work. I'll catch that damn Grunder and get rid once and for all of whatever it is that's eating me!"

And for bait? *Take the tears that fall from her eyes* . . .

Crae searched the ground under the tree beside him. There it was, the sodden, grayed blob of Kleenex Ellena had dropped. He picked it up gingerly and felt it tatter, tear-soaked and rain-soaked, in his fingers. Remembering her tears, his hand closed convulsively over the soaked tissue. When he loosed his fingers from it, he could see their impress in the pulp, almost as he had seen his hand print on her cheek. He baited the hook and nearly laughed again as he struggled to keep the wad of paper in place. Closing one hand tightly about the hook, the other around the ball of cotton, he went to the tent door. For a long, rain-emphasized moment he listened. There was no sound from inside, so with only his heart saying it, he shaped, "I love you," with his mouth and turned away, upstream.

The rain was slanting icy wires now that stabbed his face and cut through his wet jacket. He stood on the rough foot bridge across the creek and leaned over the handrail, feeling the ragged bark pressing against his stomach. He held his clenched fists up before his face and stared at them.

"This is it," he thought. "Our last chance—*My* last chance." Then he bent his head down over his hands, feeling the bite of his thumb joints into his forehead. "O God, make it true—make it true!"

The he loosed the hand that held the hook, tapped the soggy wad of Kleenex to make sure it was still there and lowered it cautiously toward the roaring, brawling creek, still swollen from the afternoon sun on hillside snow. He rotated the ball slowly, letting the line out. He gasped as the hook touched the water and he felt the current catch it and sweep it downstream. He yelled to the roaring, rain-drenched darkness, "I believe! I believe!" And the limp, tattered line in his hand snapped taut, pulling until it cut into the flesh of his palm. It strained downstream, and as he looked, it took on a weird fluorescent glow, and skipping on the black edge of the next downstream curve, the hook and bait were vivid with the same glowing.

Crae played out more of the line to ease the pressure on his palm. The line was as tight and strong as piano wire between his fingers.

Time stopped for Crae as he leaned against the rail watching the bobbing light on the end of the line—waiting and waiting wondering if the Grunder was coming, if it could taste Ellena's tears across the world. Rain dripped from the end of his nose and whispered down past his ears.

Then out of the darkness and waiting, lightning licked across the sky and thunder thudded in giant, bone-jarring steps down from the top of Baldy. Crae winced as sudden vivid light played around him again, perilously close. But no thunder followed and he opened his eyes to a blade of light slicing cleanly through the foot bridge from side to side. Crae bit his lower lip as the light resolved itself into a dazzling fin that split the waters, slit the willows and sliced through the boulders at the bend of the creek and disappeared.

"The Grunder!" he called out hoarsely and unreeled the last of his line, stumbling to the end of the bridge to follow in blind pursuit through the darkness. As his feet splashed in the icy waters, the Grunder lifted in a high arching leap beyond the far willows. Crae slid rattling down the creek bank onto one knee. The swift current swung him off balance and twisted him so that his back was to the stream, and he felt the line slip through his fingers. Desperately, he jerked around and lunged for the escaping line, the surge of the waters pushing him face down into the shallow stream. With a gurgling sob, he surfaced and snatched the last turn of the winding strip from where it had snagged on the stub of a water-soaked log.

He pulled himself up onto the soggy bank, strangling, spewing water, blinking to clear his eyes. Soaked through, numbed by the cold water and the icy wind, with shaking hands he fashioned a loop in the end of the line and secured it around his left wrist, his eyes flicking from loop to line, making sure the hook and bait were still there. He started cautiously downstream, slipping and sliding through the muck, jarring into holes, tripping on rises, intent on keeping his bait in sight. A willow branch lashed across his eyes and blinded him. While he blinked away involuntary tears, trying to clear the dazzle that blurred his sight, the Grunder swept back upstream, passing so close that Crae could see the stainless steel gleam of overlapping scales, serrated and jagged, that swept cleanly down its wide sides to a gossamer tail and up to a blind-looking head with its wide band of brilliant blue, glittering like glass beads, masking its face from side to side where eyes should have been. Below the glitters was its open maw, ringed about with flickering points of scarlet.

Crae squatted down in the mud, staring after the Grunder, lost, bewildered and scared. He clasped his hands to steady the bobbing steel-like ribbon of line that gouged into his wrist and jerked his whole arm. Was the Grunder gone? Had he lost his last chance? He ducked his head to shelter his face from the drenching downpour that seethed on the water loud enough to be heard above the roar of a dozen small falls.

Then suddenly, without warning, he was jerked downstream by his left arm, scraping full length along the soggy bank until his shoulder snagged on a stunted willow stump. He felt the muscles in his shoulder crack from the sudden stop. He wormed his way up until he could get hold of the line with his right hand, then, twisting forward, he braced both feet against the stump and heaved. The line gave slightly. And then he was cowering beneath lifted arms as the Grunder jumped silently, its tail flailing the water to mist, its head shaking against the frail hook that was imbedded in its lower jaw.

"Got it!" gasped Crae, "Got it!" That was the last rational thought Crae had for the next crashing eternity. Yanked by the leaping, twisting, fighting Grunder, upstream and downstream, sometimes on his feet, sometimes dragged full length through the tangled underbrush, sometimes with the Grunder charging him head on, all fire and gleam and terror, other times with only the thread of light tenuously pointing the way the creature had gone, Crae had no world but a whirling, breathless, pain-filled chaos that had no meaning or point beyond *Hold on hold on hold on.*

Crae saw the bridge coming, but he could no more stop or dodge than a railway tunnel can dodge a train. With a crack that splintered into a flare of light that shamed the Grunder in brilliance, Crae hit the bridge support.

Crae peeled his cheek from the bed of ooze where it

was cradled and looked around him blindly. His line was a limp curve over the edge of the bank. Heavy with despair, he lifted his hand and let it drop. The line tightened and tugged and went limp again. Crae scrambled to his feet. Was the Grunder gone? Or was it tired out, quiescent, waiting for him? He wound the line clumsily around his hand as he staggered to the creek and fell forward on the shelving bank.

Beneath him, rising and falling on the beat of the water, lay the Grunder, its white fire dimming and brightening as it sank and shallowed, the wide blue headband as glittering, its mouth fringe as crimson and alive as the first time he saw it. Crae leaned over the bank and put a finger to the silvery scales of the creature. It didn't move beyond its up and down surge.

"I have to stroke it," he thought. "Three times, three times the wrong way." He clamped his eyes tight against the sharply jagged gleam of every separate scale.

Rip hell outa your hand first stroke, but three it's gotta be.

"I could do it," he thought, "if it were still struggling. If I had to fight, I could do it. But in cold blood—!"

He lay in the mud, feeling the hot burning of the sick thing inside him, feeling the upsurge of anger, the sudden sting of his hand against Ellena's face, her soft throat under his thumbs again. An overwhelming wave of revulsion swept over him and he nearly gagged.

"Go ahead and rip hell out!" he thought, leaning down over the bank. "Rip out the hell that was in it when I hit her!"

With a full-armed sweep of his hand, he stroked the Grunder. He ground his teeth together tight enough to hold his scream down to an agonized gurgle as the blinding, burning pain swept up his arm and hazed his whole body. He could feel the fire and agony lancing and cauterizing the purulence that had been poisoning him so long. Twice again his hand retraced the torture—and all the accumulation of doubt and fear and uncertainty became one with the physical pain and shrieked out into the night.

When he lifted his hand for the third time, the Grunder leaped. High above him, flailing brilliance against the invisible sky, a dark stain marking it from tail to head, the Grunder lifted and lifted as though taking to the air. And then, straightening the bowed brightness of its body, it plunged straight down into the creek, churning the water to incandescence as it plunged, drenching Crae with sand-shot spray, raising a huge, impossible wave in the shallow creek. The wave poised and fell, flattening Crae, half senseless, into the mud, his crimson hand dangling over the bank, the slow, red drops falling into the quieting water, a big, empty cleanness aching inside him.

Dawn light was just beginning to dissolve the night when he staggered into camp, tripping over the water buckets as he neared the tent. He stood swaying as the tent flap was flung open hastily. Ellena, haggard, red-eyed and worn plunged out into the early morning cold. She stood and looked at him standing awkwardly, his stiffening, lacerated hands held out, muddy water dripping from his every angle. Then she cried out and ran to him, hands outstretched, love and compassion shining in her eyes.

"Crae! Honey! Where have you been? What happened to you?"

And Crae stained both her shoulders as his hands closed painfully over them as he half whispered, "I caught him. I caught the Grunder—everything's all right—everything—"

She stroked his tired and swollen face, anxiety in her eyes. "Oh, Crae—I nearly went crazy with fear. I thought—" she shook her head and tears of gladness formed in her eyes "—but you're safe. That's all that matters. Crae—"

He buried his face in the softness of her hair. He felt sure. For the first time he felt *really* sure. "Yes, dear?"

"Crae—about what I said—I'm sorry—I didn't mean it, oh, I couldn't live without you—"

Gladness swelled within him. He pushed her gently from him and looked into her tear-streaked face. "Ellena—let's go home—"

She nodded, smiling. "All right, Crae, we'll go home—But first we'll have a good breakfast."

He laughed, a healthy, hearty laugh. "We'll do even better than that! We'll stop by at the camp of our four visitors. They owe us both a good meal for the drinks!"

Her eyes glowed at his words. "Oh, Crae—you really mean it? You're not—"

He shook his head. "Never again, honey. Never."

The porch of the Murmuring Pines Store and Station was empty as Crae stopped the car there at noon. Crae turned to Ellena with a grin. "Be back in a minute, honey, gotta see a man about a fish."

Crae left the car, walked up the steps and pushed open the screen door. A skinny, teen-age girl in faded Levis put down her comic book and got off a high stool behind a counter. "Help you, mister?"

"I'm looking for Eli," he said. "The old feller that was out on the porch about two weeks ago when I stopped by here. Old Eli, he called himself."

"Oh, Eli," said the girl. "He's off again."

"Off? He's gone away?" asked Crae.

"Well, yes, but that isn't what I meant exactly," said the girl. "You see, Eli is kinda touched. Ever once in a while he goes clear off his rocker. You musta talked to him when this last spell was starting to work on him. They took him back to State Hospital a coupla days later. Something you wanted?"

"He told me about a fish," said Crae tentatively.

"Hoh!" the girl laughed shortly, "The Grunder. Yeah. That's one way we can tell he's getting bad again. He starts on that Grunder stuff."

Crae felt as though he'd taken a step that wasn't there. "Where'd he get the story?"

"Well, I don't know what story he told you," said the girl. "No telling where he got the Grunder idea, though. He's had it ever since I can remember. It's only when he gets to believing it that we know it's time to start watching him. If he didn't believe—"

If he didn't believe. Crae turned to the door. "Well, thanks," he said, "I hope he gets well soon." The screen door slammed shut behind him. He didn't hear it. He was hearing the sound of water smashing over rocks, surging against the creek banks. Then the sound faded, and the sun was bright around him.

"Crae! Is everything all right?"

It was Ellena calling to him from the car. He took a deep breath of the clean, crisp air. Then he waved to her. "Everything's fine!" he called, and in two steps, cleared the porch and was on his way to the car.

Things

Viat came back from the camp of the Strangers, his crest shorn, the devi ripped from his jacket, his mouth slack and drooling and his eyes empty. He sat for a day in the sun of the coveti center, not even noticing when the eager children gathered and asked questions in their piping little voices. When the evening shadow touched him, Viat staggered to his feet and took two steps and was dead.

The mother came then, since the body was from her and could never be alien, and since the emptiness that was not Viat had flown from his eyes. She signed him dead by pinning on his torn jacket the kiom—the kiom she had fashioned the day he was born, since to be born is to begin to die. He had not yet given his heart, so the kiom was still hers to bestow. She left the pelu softly alight in the middle of the kiom because Viat had died beloved. He who dies beloved walks straight and strong on the path to the Hidden Ones by the light of the pelu. Be the pelu removed, he must wander forever, groping in the darkness of the unlighted kiom.

So she pinned the kiom and wailed him dead.

There was a gathering together after Viat was given back to the earth. Backs were bent against the sun, and the coveti thought together for a morning. When the sun pointed itself into their eyes, they shaded them with their open palms and spoke together.

"The Strangers have wrought an evil thing with us." Dobi patted the dust before him. "Because of them, Viat is not. He came not back from the camp. Only his body came, breathing until it knew he would not return to it."

"And yet, it may be that the Strangers are not evil. They came to us in peace. Even, they brought their craft down on barrenness instead of scorching our fields." Deci's eyes were eager on the sky. His blood was hot with the wonder of a craft dropping out of the clouds, bearing

134

strangers. "Perhaps there was no need for us to move the coveti."

"True, true," nodded Dobi. "They may not be of themselves evil, but it may be that the breath of them is death to us, or perhaps the falling of their shadows or the silent things that walk invisible from their friendly hands. It is best that we go not to the camp again. Neither should we permit them to find the coveti."

"Cry them not forbidden, yet!" cried Deci, his crest rippling. "We know them not. To taboo them now would not be fair. They may come bearing gifts . . ."

"For gifts given, something always is taken. We have no wish to exchange our young men for a look at the Strangers." Dobi furrowed the dust with his fingers and smoothed away the furrows as Viat had been smoothed away.

"And yet," Veti's soft voice came clearly as her blue crest caught the breeze, "it may be that they will have knowledge for us that we have not. Never have we taken craft into the clouds and back."

"Yes, yes!" Deci's eyes embraced Veti, who held his heart. "They must have much knowledge, many gifts for us."

"The gift of knowledge is welcome," said Tefu in his low rumble. "But gifts in the hands have fangs and bonds."

"The old words!" cried Deci. "The old ways do not hold when new ways arrive!"

"True," nodded Dobi. "If the new is truly a way and not a whirlwind or a trail that goes no place. But to judge without facts is to judge in error. I will go to the strangers."

"And I." Tefu's voice stirred like soft thunder.

"And I? And I?" Deci's words tumbled on themselves and the dust stirred with his hurried rising.

"Young—" muttered Tefu.

"Young eyes to notice what old eyes might miss," said Dobi. "Our path is yours." His crest rippled as he nodded to Deci.

"Deci!" Veti's voice was shaken by the unknown. "Come not again as Viat came. The heart you bear with you is not your own."

"I will come again," cried Deci, "to fill your hands with wonders and delights." He gave each of her cupped palms a kiss to hold against his return.

135

Time is not hours and days, or the slanting and shortening of shadows. Time is a held breath and a listening ear.

Time incredible passed before the ripple through the grass, the rustle through reeds, the sudden sound of footsteps where it seemed no footsteps could be. The rocks seemed to part to let them through.

Dobi led, limping, slow of foot, flattened of crest, his eyes hidden in the shadow of his bent head. Then came Tefu, like one newly blind, groping, reaching, bumping, reeling until he huddled against the familiar rocks in the fading sunlight.

"Deci?" cried Veti, parting the crowd with her cry. "Deci?"

"He came not with us," said Dobi. "He watched us go."

"Willingly?" Veti's hands clenched over the memory of his mouth. "Willingly? Or was there force?"

"Willingly?" The eyes that Tefu turned to Veti saw her not. They looked within at hidden things. "Force? He stayed. There were no bonds about him." He touched a wondering finger to one eye and then the other. "Open," he rumbled. "Where is the light?"

"Tell me," cried Veti. "Oh, tell me!"

Dobi sat in the dust, his big hands marking it on either side of him.

"They truly have wonders. They would give us many strange things for our devi." His fingers tinkled the fringing of his jacket. "Fabrics beyond our dreams. Tools we could use. Weapons that could free the land of every flesh-hungry kutu."

"And Deci? And Deci?" Veti voiced her fear again.

"Deci saw all and desired all. His devi were ripped off before the sun slid an arm's reach. He was like a child in a meadow of flowers, clutching, grabbing, crumpling and finding always the next flower fairer."

Wind came in the silence and poured itself around bare shoulders.

"Then he will return," said Veti, loosening her clenched hand. "When the wonder is gone."

"As Viat returned?" Tefu's voice rumbled. "As I have returned?" He held his hand before his eyes and dropped his fingers one by one. "How many fingers before you? Six? Four? Two?"

"You saw the Strangers, before we withdrew the coveti. You saw the strange garments they wore, the shining roundness, the heavy glitter and thickness. Our air is not air for them. Without the garments, they would die."

"If they are so well wrapped against the world, how could they hurt?" cried Veti. "They cannot hurt Deci. He will return."

"I returned," murmured Tefu. "I did but walk among them and the misting of their finished breath has done this to me. Only time and the Hidden Ones know if sight is through for me.

"One was concerned for me. One peered at me when first my steps began to waver. He hurried me away from the others and sat away from me and watched with me as the lights went out. He was concerned for me—or was studying me. But I am blind."

"And you?" asked Veti of Dobi. "It harmed you not?"

"I took care," said Dobi. "I came not close after the first meeting. And yet . . ." he turned the length of his thigh. From hip to knee the split flesh glinted like the raking of a mighty claw. "I was among the trees when a kutu screamed on the hill above me. Fire lashed out from the Strangers and it screamed no more. Startled, I moved the branches about me and—s-s-s-s-st!" His finger streaked beside his thigh.

"But Deci—"

Dobi scattered his dust handprint with a swirl of his fingers. "Deci is like a scavenging mayu. He follows, hand outstretched. 'Wait, wait,' he cried when we turned to go. 'We can lead the world with these wonders.'"

"Why should we lead the world? Now there is no first and no last. Why should we reach beyond our brothers to grasp things that dust will claim?"

"Wail him dead, Veti," rumbled Tefu. "Death a thousand ways surrounds him now. And if his body comes again, his heart is no longer with us. Wail him dead."

"Yes," nodded Dobi. "Wail him dead and give thanks that our coveti is so securely hidden that the Strangers can never come to sow among us the seeds of more Viats and Tefus."

"The Strangers are taboo. The coveti path is closed."

So Veti wailed him dead, crouching in the dust of the coveti path, clutching in her hands the kiom Deci had given her with his heart.

Viat's mother sat with her an hour—until Veti broke her wail and cried, "Your grief is not mine. You pinned Viat's kiom. You folded his hands to rest. You gave him

137

back to earth. Wail not with me. I wail for an emptiness—for an unknowledge. For a wondering and a fearing. You know Viat is on the trail to the Hidden Ones. But I know not of Deci. Is he alive? Is he dying in the wilderness with no pelu to light him into the darkness? Is he crawling now, blind and maimed up the coveti trail? I wail a death with no hope. A hopelessness with no death. I wail alone."

And so she wailed past the point of tears, into the aching dryness of grief. The coveti went about its doing, knowing she would live again when grief was spent.

Then came the day when all faces swung to the head of the coveti trail. All ears flared to the sound of Veti's scream and all eyes rounded to see Deci stagger into the coveti.

Veti flew to him, her arms outstretched, her heart believing before her mind could confirm. But Deci winced away from her touch and his face half snarled as his hand, shorn of three fingers and barely beginning to regenerate, motioned her away.

"Deci!" cried Veti, "Deci?"

"Let—let—me breathe." Deci leaned against the rocks. Deci who could outrun a kutu, whose feet had lightness and swiftness beyond all others in the coveti. "The trail takes the breath."

"Deci!" Veti's hands still reached, one all unknowingly proffering the kiom. Seeing it, she laughed and cast it aside. The death mark with Deci alive before her? "Oh, Deci!" And then she fell silent as she saw his maimed hand, his ragged crest, his ravaged jacket, his seared legs —his eyes— His eyes! They were not the eyes of the Deci who had gone with eagerness to see the Strangers. He had brought the Strangers back in his eyes.

His breath at last came smoothly and he leaned to Veti, reaching as he did so, into the bundle by his side.

"I promised," he said, seeing Veti only. "I have come again to fill your hands with wonder and delight."

But Veti's hands were hidden behind her. Gifts from strangers are suspect.

"Here," said Deci, laying an ugly angled thing down in the dust before Veti. "Here is death to all kutus, be they six-legged or two. Let the Durlo coveti say again the Klori stream is theirs for fishing," he muttered. "Nothing is theirs now save by our sufferance. I give you power, Veti."

Veti moved back a pace.

"And here," he laid a flask of glass beside the weapon. "This is for dreams and laughter. This is what Viat drank of—but too much. They call it water. It is a drink the Hidden Ones could envy. One mouthful and all memory of pain and grief, loss and unreachable dreams is gone.

"I give you forgetfulness, Veti."

Veti's head moved denyingly from side to side.

"And here." He pulled forth, carelessly, arms-lengths of shining fabric that rippled and clung and caught the sun. His eyes were almost Deci's eyes again.

Veti's heart was moved, womanwise, to the fabric and her hands reached for it, since no woman can truly see a fabric unless her fingers taste its body, flow, and texture.

"For you, for beauty. And this, that you might behold yourself untwisted by moving waters." He laid beside the weapon and the water a square of reflecting brightness. "For you to see yourself as Lady over the world as I see myself Lord."

Veti's hands dropped again, the fabric almost untasted. Deci's eyes again were the eyes of a stranger.

"Deci, I waited not for *things,* these long days." Veti's hands cleansed themselves together from the cling of the fabric. Her eyes failed before Deci and sought the ground, jerking away from the strange things in the dust. "Come, let us attend to your hurts."

"But no! But see!" cried Deci. "With these strange things our coveti can rule all the valley and beyond and beyond!"

"Why?"

"Why?" echoed Deci. "To take all we want. To labor no more save to ask and receive. To have power . . ."

"Why?" Veti's eyes still questioned. "We have enough. We are not hungry. We are clothed against the changing seasons. We work when work is needed. We play when work is done. Why do we need more?"

"Deci finds quiet ways binding," said Dobi. "Rather would he have shouting and far, swift going. And sweat and effort and delicious fear pushing him into action. Soon come the kutu hunting days, Deci. Save your thirst for excitement until then."

"Sweat and effort and fear!" snarled Deci. "Why should I endure that when with this . . ." He snatched up the

139

weapon and with one wave of his hand sheared off the top of Tefu's house. He spoke into the dying thunder of the discharge. "No kutu alive could unsheath its fangs after that, except as death draws back the sheath to mock its finished strength.

"And if so against a kutu," he muttered. "How much more so against the Durlo coveti?"

"Come, Deci," cried Veti. "Let us bind your wounds. As time will heal them, so time will heal your mind of these Strangers."

"I want no healing," shouted Deci, anger twisting his haggard face. "Nor will you after the Strangers have been here and proffered you their wonders in exchange for this foolish fringing devi." Contempt tossed his head. "For the devi in our coveti, we could buy their sky craft, I doubt not."

"They will not come," said Dobi. "The way is hidden. No Stranger can ever find our coveti. We have but to wait until—"

"Until tomorrow!" Deci's crest tossed rebelliously, his voice louder than need be. Or perhaps it seemed so from the echoes it raised in every heart. "I told—"

"You told?" Stupidly, the echo took words.

"*You told?*" Disbelief sharpened the cry.

"You told!" Anger spurted into the words.

"I told!" cried Deci. "How else reap the benefits that the Strangers—"

"Benefits!" spat Dobi. "Death!" His foot spurned the weapon in the dust. "Madness!" The flask gurgled as it moved. "Vanity!" Dust clouded across the mirror and streaked the shining fabric. "For such you have betrayed us to death."

"But no!" cried Deci. "*I* lived. Death does not always come with the Strangers." Sudden anger roughened his voice. "It's the old ways! You want no change! But all things change. It is the way of living things. Progress—"

"All change is not progress," rumbled Tefu, his hands hiding his blindness.

"Like it or not," shouted Deci. "Tomorrow the Strangers come! You have your choice, all of you!" His arm circled the crowd. "Keep to your homes like Pegu or come forward with your devi and find with me a power, a richness—"

"Or move the coveti again," said Dobi. "Away from betrayal and foolish greed. We have a third choice."

Deci caught his breath.

"Veti?" his whisper pleaded. "Veti? We do not need the rest of the coveti. You and I together. We can wait for the Strangers. Together we can have the world. With this weapon not one person in this coveti or any other can withstand us. We can be the new people. We can have our own coveti, and take what we want—anything, anywhere. Come to me, Veti."

Veti looked long into his eyes. "Why did you come back?" she whispered with tears in her voice. Then anger leaped into her eyes. *"Why did you come back!"* There was the force of a scream in her harsh words. She darted suddenly to the rocks. She snatched the kiom from the dust where it had fallen. Before Devi knew what was happening, she whirled on him and pinned death upon his ragged jacket. Then with a swift, decisive twist, she tore away the pelu and dropped it to the dust.

Deci's eyes widened in terror, his hand clutched at the kiom but dared not touch it.

"No!" he screamed. "No!"

Then Veti's eyes widened and her hands reached also for the kiom, but no power she possessed could undo what she had done and her scream rose with Deci's.

Then knowing himself surely dead and dead unbeloved, already entering the eternity of darkness of the unlighted kiom, Deci crumpled to the ground. Under his cheek was the hardness of the weapon, under his outflung hand, the beauty of the fabric, and the sunlight, bending through the water, giggled crazily on his chin.

One dead unbeloved is not as much as a crushed flower by the path. For the flower at least there is regret for its ended beauty.

So knowing Deci dead, the coveti turned from him. There was for memory of him only an uncertainty to Veti's feet and a wondering shock in Veti's eyes as she turned with the others to prepare to move the coveti.

The wind came and poured over the dust and the things and Deci.

And Deci lay waiting for his own breath to stop.

Turn the Page

When I was in the first grade, my teacher was magic. Oh, I know! Everyone thinks that his first teacher is something special. It's practically a convention that all little boys fall in love with her and that all little girls imitate her and that both believe her the Alpha and Omega of wisdom—but *my* teacher was really magic.

We all felt it the first day when finally the last anxious parent was shooed reluctantly out the door and we sat stiff and uneasy in our hard, unfriendly chairs and stared across our tightly clasped hands at Miss Ebo, feeling truly that we were on the edge of something strange and wonderful, but more wonderful than strange. Tears dried on the face of our weeper as we waited in that moment that trembled like a raindrop before it splinters into rainbows.

"Let's *be* something!" Miss Ebo whispered. "Let's be birds."

And we were! We were! *Real birds!* We fluttered and sang and flitted from chair to chair all around the room. We prinked and preened and smoothed our heads along the brightness of feathers and learned in those moments the fierce throbbing restlessness of birds, the feathery hushing quietness of sleeping wings. *And there was one of us that beat endlessly at the closed windows, scattering feathers, shaking the glass, straining for the open sky.*

Then we were children again, wiggling with remembered delight, exchanging pleased smiles, feeling that maybe school wasn't all fright and strangeness after all. And with a precocious sort of knowledge, we wordlessly pledged our mutual silence about our miracle.

This first day set the pace for us. We were, at different times, almost every creature imaginable, learning of them and how they fitted into the world and how they touched onto our segment of the world, until we saw fellow creatures wherever we looked. *But there was one of us who set himself against the lessons* and ground his heel viciously down on the iridescence of a green June-bug that blundered into our room one afternoon. The rest of us looked at Miss Ebo, hoping in our horror for some sort of cosmic blast from her. Her eyes were big and knowing—and a little sad. We turned back to our work, tasting for the first time a little of the sorrow for those who stubbornly shut their eyes against the sun and still curse the darkness.

And soon the stories started. Other children *heard* about Red Riding Hood and the Wolf and maybe played the parts, but we took turns at *being* Red Riding Hood and the Wolf. Individually we tasted the terror of the pursued—the sometimes delightfully delicious terror of the pursued—and we knew the blood lust and endless drive of the pursuer—the hot pulses leaping in our veins, the irresistible compulsion of hunger-never-satiated that pulled us along the shadowy forest trails.

And when we were Red Riding Hood, we knew under our terror and despair that help would come—*had* to come when we turned the page, *because it was written that way*. If we were the Wolf, we knew that death waited at the end of our hunger; we leaped as compulsively to that death as we did to our feeding. As the mother and grandmother, we knew the sorrow of letting our children go, and the helpless waiting for them to find the dangers and die of them or live through them, but always, always, were we the pursuer or the pursued, the waiter or the active one, we knew we had only to turn the page and finally live happily ever after, *because it was written that way!* And we found out that after you have once been the pursuer, the pursued and the watcher, you can never again be only the pursuer or the pursued or the watcher. Ever after you are a little of each of them.

We learned and learned in our first grade, but sometimes we had to stop our real learning and learn what was expected of us. Those were the shallow days.

We knew the shallow days when they arrived because Miss Ebo met us at the door, brightly smiling, cheerily speaking, but with her lovely dark eyes quiet and uncommunicative. We left the door ajar and set ourselves to routine tasks. We read and wrote and worked with our numbers, covering all we had slighted in the magic days before—a model class, learning neat little lessons, carefully catching up with the other first grades. Sometimes we even had visitors to smile at our industry, or the supervisor to come in and sharply twitch a picture to more exact line on the bulletin board, fold her lips in frustration and make some short-tempered note in her little green book before she left us, turning her stiff white smile on briefly for our benefit. And, at day's end, we sighed with weariness of soul and burst out of class with all the unused enthusiasm of the day, hoping that tomorrow would be magic again. And it usually was.

The door would swing shut with a pleased little chuckling cluck and we would lift our questioning faces to Miss Ebo—or the Witch or the Princess or the Fairy Godmother—and plunge into another story as into a sparkling sea.

As Cinderella, we labored in the ashes of the fireplace and of lonely isolation and of labor without love. We wept tears of hopeless longing as we watched the semblance of joy and happiness leave us behind, weeping for it even though we knew too well the ugliness straining under it —the sharp bones of hatefulness jabbing at scarlet satin and misty tulle. Cinderella's miracle came to us and we made our loveliness from commonplace things and learned that happiness often has a midnight chiming so that it won't leak bleakly into a watery dawn, and finally, that no matter how fast we run, we leave a part of us behind, and by that part of us, joy comes when we turn the page and we finally live happily ever after, *because it is written that way*.

With Chicken Little, we cowered under the falling of our sky. We believed implicitly in our own little eye and our own little ear and the aching of our own little tail where the sky had bruised us. Not content with panicking ourselves with the small falling, we told the whole world repeatedly and at great length that the sky was falling for everyone because it fell for us. And when the Fox promised help and hope and strength, we followed him and let our bones be splintered in the noisome darkness of fear and ignorance.

And, as the Fox, we crunched with unholy glee the bones of little fools who shut themselves in their own tiny prisons and followed fear into death rather than take a larger look at the sky. And we found them delicious and insidious.

Mrs. Thompson came down to see Miss Ebo after Chicken Little. There must be some reason why Jackie was having nightmares—maybe something at school? And Miss Ebo had to soothe her with all sorts of little Educational Psychology platitudes because she couldn't tell her that Jackie just wouldn't come out of the Fox's den even after his bones were scrunched to powder. He was afraid of a wide sky and always would be.

So the next day we all went into the darkness of caves and were little blind fish. We were bats that used their ears for eyes. We were small shining things that seemed to have no life but grew into beauty and had the wisdom to stop when they reached the angles of perfection. So Jackie chose to be one of those and he didn't learn with us any more except on our shallow days. He loved shallow days. The other times he grew to limited perfection in his darkness.

And there was one of us who longed to follow the Fox forever. Every day his eyes would hesitate on Miss Ebo's face, but every day the quietness of her mouth told him that the Fox should not come back into our learning. And his eyes would drop and his fingers would pluck anxiously at one another.

The year went on and we were princesses leaning from towers drawing love to us on shining extensions of ourselves, feeling the weight and pain of love along with its shiningness as the prince climbed Rapunzel's golden hair. We, as Rapunzel, betrayed ourselves to evil. We were cast into the wilderness, we bought our way back into happiness by our tears of mingled joy and sorrow. And—as the witch—we were evil, hoarding treasures to ourselves, trying to hold unchanged things that had to change. We were the one who destroyed loveliness when it had to be shared, who blinded maliciously, only to find that all loveliness, all delight, went with the sight we destroyed.

And then we learned more. We were the greedy woman. We wanted a house, a castle, a palace—power beyond power, beyond power, until we wanted to meddle with the workings of the universe. And then we had to huddle back on the dilapidated steps of the old shack with nothing again, nothing in our lax hands, because we reached for too much.

But then we were her husband, too, who gave in and

gave in against his better judgment, against his desires, but always backing away from a *no* until he sat there, too, with empty hands, staring at the nothing he must share. And he had never had anything at all because he had never asked for it. It was a strange, hard lesson and we studied it again and again until one of us was stranded in greed, another in apathy, and one of us almost knew the right answer.

But magic can't last. That was our final, and my hardest, bitterest, lesson. One day Miss Ebo wasn't there. She'd gone away, they said. She wouldn't be back. I remember how my heart tightened and burned coldly inside me when I heard. And shallow day followed shallow day and I watched, terrified, the memory of Miss Ebo dying out of the other kids' eyes.

Then one afternoon I saw her again, thin and white, blown against the playground fence like a forgotten leaf of last autumn. Her russety dress fluttered in the cold wind and the flick of her pale fingers called me from clear across the playground. I pressed my face close against the wire mesh, trying to cry against her waist, my fingers reaching hungrily through to her.

My voice was hardly louder than the whisper of dry leaves across a path. "Miss Ebo! Miss Ebo! Come back!"

"You haven't forgotten." Her answer lost itself on the wind. "Remember. Always remember. Remember the whole of the truth. Truth has so many sides, evil and good, that if you cling to just one, it may make it a lie." The wind freshened and she fluttered with it, clinging to the wire. "Remember, turn the page. Everyone *will* finally live happily ever after, *because that's the way it's written!*"

My eyes blurred with tears and before I could knuckle them dry, she was gone.

"Crybaby!" The taunt stung me as we lined up to go back indoors.

"I saw her!" I cried. "I saw Miss Ebo!"

"Miss Ebo?" Blank eyes stared into mine. There was a sudden flicker way back behind seeing, but it died. "Crybaby!"

Oh, I know that no one believes in fairy tales any more. They're for children. Well, who better to teach than children that good must ultimately triumph? Fairy tale ending—they lived happily ever after! *But it is written that way!* The marriage of bravery and beauty—tasks accom-

146

plished, peril surmounted, evil put down, captives freed, enchantments broken, humanity emerging from the forms of beasts, giants slain, wrongs righted, joy coming in the morning after the night of weeping. The lessons are all there. They're told over and over and over, but we let them slip and we sigh for our childhood days, not seeing that we shed the truth as we shed our deciduous teeth.

I never saw Miss Ebo again, but I saw my first grade again, those who survived to our twenty-fifth anniversary. At first I thought I wouldn't go, but most sorrow can be set aside for an evening, even the sorrow attendant on finding how easily happiness is lost when it depends on a single factor. I looked around at those who had come, but I saw in them only the tattered remnants of Miss Ebo's teachings.

Here was the girl who so delighted in the terror of being pursued that she still fled along dark paths, though no danger followed. Here was our winged one still beating his wings against the invisible glass. Here was our pursuer, the blood lust in his eyes altered to a lust for power that was just as compulsive, just as inevitably fatal as the old pursuing evil.

Here was our terror-stricken Chicken Little, his drawn face, his restless, bitten nails, betraying his eternal running away from the terror he sowed behind himself, looking for the Fox, any Fox, with glib, comforting promises. And there, serene, was the one who learned to balance between asking too much and too little—who controlled his desires instead of letting them control him. There was the one, too, who had sorrowed and wept but who was now coming into her kingdom of children.

But these last two were strangers—as I was—in this wistful gathering of people who were trying to turn back twenty-five years. I sat through the evening, trying to trace in the masks around me the bright spirits that had run with me into Miss Ebo's enchantment. I looked for Jackie. I asked for Jackie. He was hidden away in some protected place, eternally being his dark shining things, afraid—too afraid—of even shallowness ever to walk in the light again.

There were speeches. There was laughter. There was clowning. But always the underlying strain, the rebellion, the silent crying out, the fear and mistrust.

They asked me to talk.

I stood, leaning against the teacher's desk, and looked down into the carefully empty faces.

"You have forgotten," I said. "You have all forgotten Miss Ebo."

"Miss Ebo?" The name was a pursing on all the lips, a furrow on the brows. Only one or two smiled even tentatively. *"Remember Miss Ebo?"*

"If you have forgotten," I said, "it's a long time ago. If you remember, it was only yesterday. But even if you have forgotten her, I can see that you haven't forgotten the lessons she taught you. Only you have remembered the wrong part. You only half learned the lessons. You've eaten the husks and thrown the grain away. She tried to tell you. She tried to teach you. But you've all forgotten. Not a one of you remembers that if you turn the page everyone will live happily ever after, *because it was written that way*. You're all stranded in the introduction to the story. You work yourselves all up to the climax of terror or fear or imminent disaster, but you never turn the page. You go back and live it again and again and again.

"Turn the page! Believe again! You have forgotten how to believe in anything beyond your chosen treadmill. You have grown out of the fairy tale age, you say. But what have you grown into? Do you like it? I leaned forward and tried to catch evasive eyes. "With your hopeless, scalding tears at night and your dry-eyed misery when you waken. Do you like it?

"What would you give to be able to walk once more into a morning that is a-tiptoe with expectancy, magical with possibilities, bright with a sure delight? Miss Ebo taught us how. She gave us the promise and hope. She taught us all that everyone will finally live happily ever after *because it is written that way*. All we have to do is let loose long enough to turn the page. Why don't you?"

They laughed politely when I finished. I was always the turner of phrases. Wasn't that clever? Fairy tales! Well—

The last car drove away from the school. I stood by the fence in the dark schoolyard and let the night wash over me.

Then I was a child again, crying against the cold mesh fence—hopeless, scalding tears in the night.

"Miss Ebo. Miss Ebo!" My words were only a twisted shaping of my mouth. "They have forgotten. Let me forget too. Surely it must be easier to forget that there is a

148

page to be turned than to know it's there and not be able to turn it! How long? How long must I remember?"

A sudden little wind scooted a paper sibilantly across the sidewalk . . . *forever after* . . . *forever after* . . .

Stevie and The Dark

The Dark lived in a hole in the bank of the sand wash where Stevie liked to play. The Dark wanted to come out, but Stevie had fixed it so it couldn't. He put a row of special little magic rocks in front of the hole. Stevie knew they were magic because he found them himself and they felt like magic. When you are as old as Stevie—five—a whole hand of years old—you know lots of things and you know what magic feels like.

Stevie had the rocks in his pocket when he first found The Dark. He had been digging a garage in the side of the wash when a piece of the bank came loose and slid down onto him. One rock hit him on the forehead hard enough to make him cry—if he had been only four. But Stevie was five, so he wiped the blood with the back of his hand and scraped away the dirt to find the big spoon Mommy let him take to dig with. Then he saw that the hole was great big and his spoon was just inside it. So he reached in for it and The Dark came out a little ways and touched Stevie. It covered up his hand clear to the wrist and when Stevie jerked away, his hand was cold and all skinned across the back. For a minute it was white and stiff, then the blood came out and it hurt and Stevie got mad. So he took out the magic rocks and put the little red one down in front of the hole. The Dark came out again with just a little finger-piece and touched the red rock, but it didn't like the magic so it started to push around it. Stevie put down the other little rocks—the round smooth white ones and the smooth yellow ones.

The Dark made a lot of little fingers that were trying to get past the magic. There was just one hole left, so Stevie put down the black-see-through rock he found that morning. Then The Dark pulled back all the little fingers and began to pour over the black rock. So, quick like a rabbit, Stevie drew a magic in the sand and The Dark pulled back into the hole again. Then Stevie marked King's X all around the hole and ran to get some more magic rocks. He found a white one with a band of blue around the middle and another yellow one. He went back and put the rocks in front of the hole and rubbed out the King's X. The Dark got mad and piled up behind the rocks until it was higher than Stevie's head.

Stevie was scared, but he stood still and held tight to his pocket piece. He knew that was the magicest of all. Juanito had told him so and Juanito knew. He was ten years old and the one who told Stevie about magic in the first place. He had helped Stevie make the magic. He was the one who did the writing on the pocket piece. Of course, Stevie would know how to write after he went to school, but that was a long time away.

The Dark couldn't ever hurt him while he held the magic, but it was kind of scary to see The Dark standing up like that in the bright hot sunshine. The Dark didn't have any head or arms or legs or body. It didn't have any eyes either, but it was looking at Stevie. It didn't have any mouth, but it was mumbling at Stevie. He could hear it inside his head and the mumbles were hate, so Stevie squatted down in the sand and drew a magic again—a big magic—and The Dark jerked back into the hole. Stevie turned and ran as fast as he could until the mumbles in his ears turned into fast wind and the sound of rattling rocks on the road.

Next day Arnold came with his mother to visit at Stevie's house. Stevie didn't like Arnold. He was a tattle-tale and a crybaby even if he was a whole hand and two more fingers old. Stevie took him down to the sand wash to play. They didn't go down where The Dark was, but while they were digging tunnels around the roots of the cottonwood tree, Stevie could feel The Dark, like a long deep thunder that only your bones could hear—not your ears. He knew the big magic he wrote in the sand was gone and The Dark was trying to get past the magic rocks.

Pretty soon Arnold began to brag.

"I got a space gun."

Stevie threw some more sand backwards. "So've I," he said.

"I got a two-wheel bike."

Stevie sat back on his heels. "Honest?"

"Sure!" Arnold talked real smarty. "You're too little to

151

have a two-wheel bike. You couldn't ride it if you had one."

"Could too." Stevie went back to his digging, feeling bad inside. He had fallen off Rusty's bike when he tried to ride it. Arnold didn't know it though.

"Could not," Arnold caved in his tunnel. "I've got a BB gun and a real saw and a cat with three-and-a-half legs."

Stevie sat down in the sand. What could you get better than a cat with three-and-a-half legs? He traced a magic in the sand.

"I've got something you haven't."

"Have not." Arnold caved in Stevie's tunnel.

"Have too. It's a Dark."

"A what?"

"A Dark. I've got it in a hole down there." He jerked his head down the wash.

"Aw, you're crazy. There ain't no dark. You're just talking baby stuff."

Stevie felt his face getting hot. "I am not. You just come and see."

He dragged Arnold by the hand down the wash with the sand crunching under foot like spilled sugar and sifting in and out of their barefoot sandals. They squatted in front of the hole. The Dark had pulled way back in so they couldn't see it.

"I don't see nothing." Arnold leaned forward to look into the hole. "There ain't no dark. You're just silly."

"I am not! And The Dark is so in that hole."

"Sure it's dark in the hole, but that ain't nothing. You can't have a dark, silly."

"Can too." Stevie reached in his pocket and took tight hold of his pocket piece. "You better cross your fingers. I'm going to let it out a little ways."

"Aw!" Arnold didn't believe him, but he crossed his fingers anyway.

Stevie took two of the magic rocks away from in front of the hole and moved back. The Dark came pouring out like a flood. It poured in a thin stream through the open place in the magic and shot up like a tower of smoke. Arnold was so surprised that he uncrossed his fingers and The Dark wrapped around his head and he began to scream and scream. The Dark sent a long arm out to Stevie, but Stevie pulled out his pocket piece and hit The Dark. Stevie could hear The Dark scream inside his head so

152

he hit it again and The Dark fell all together and got littler so Stevie pushed it back into the hole with his pocket piece. He put the magic rocks back and wrote two big magics in the sand so that The Dark cried again and hid way back in the hole.

Arnold was lying on the sand with his face all white and stiff, so Stevie shook him and called him. Arnold opened his eyes and his face turned red and began to bleed. He started to bawl, "Mama! Mama!" and ran for the house as fast as he could through the soft sand. Stevie followed him, yelling, "You uncrossed your fingers! It's your fault! You uncrossed your fingers!"

Arnold and his mother went home. Arnold was still bawling and his mother was real red around the nose when she yelled at Mommy. "You'd better learn to control that brat of yours or he'll grow up a murderer! Look what he did to my poor Arnold!" And she drove away so fast that she hit the chuckhole by the gate and nearly went off the road.

Mommy sat down on the front step and took Stevie between her knees. Stevie looked down and traced a little, soft magic with his finger on Mommy's slacks.

"What happened, Stevie?"

Stevie squirmed. "Nothing, Mommy. We were just playing in the wash."

"Why did you hurt Arnold?"

"I didn't. Honest. I didn't even touch him."

"But the whole side of his face was skinned." Mommy put on her no-fooling-now voice. "Tell me what happened, Stevie."

Stevie gulped. "Well, Arnold was bragging 'bout his two-wheel bike and—" Stevie got excited and looked up. "And Mommy, he has a cat with three-and-a-half legs!"

"Go on."

Stevie leaned against her again.

"Well, I've got a Dark in a hole in the wash so I—"

"A Dark? What is that?"

"It's, it's just a Dark. It isn't very nice. I keep it in its hole with magic. I let it out a little bit to show Arnold and it hurt him. But it was his fault. He uncrossed his fingers."

Mommy sighed. "What *really* happened, Stevie?"

"I told you, Mommy! Honest, that's what happened."

"For True, Stevie?" She looked right in his eyes.

153

Stevie looked right back. "Yes, Mommy, For True."

She sighed again. "Well, son, I guess this Dark business is the same as your Mr. Bop and Toody Troot."

"Uh, uh!" Stevie shook his head. "No sir. Mr. Bop and Toody Troot are nice. The Dark is bad."

"Well, don't play with it any more then."

"I *don't* play with it," protested Stevie. "I just keep it shut up with magic."

"All right, son." She stood up and brushed the dust off the back of her slacks. "Only for the love of Toody Troot, don't let Arnold get hurt again." She smiled at Stevie.

Stevie smiled back. "Okay, Mommy. But it was his fault. He uncrossed his fingers. He's a baby."

The next time Stevie was in the wash playing cowboy on Burro Eddie, he heard The Dark calling him. It called so sweet and soft that anybody would think it was something nice, but Stevie could feel the bad rumble way down under the nice, so he made sure his pocket piece was handy, shooed Eddie away, and went down to the hole and squatted down in front of it.

The Dark stood up behind the magic rocks and it had made itself look like Arnold only its eyes didn't match and it had forgotten one ear and it was freckled all over like Arnold's face.

"Hello," said The Dark with its Arnold-mouth. "Let's play."

"No," said Stevie. "You can't fool me. You're still The Dark."

"I won't hurt you." The Arnold-face stretched out sideways to make a smile, but it wasn't a very good one. "Let me out and I'll show you how to have lots of fun."

"No," said Stevie. "If you weren't bad, the magic couldn't hold you. I don't want to play with bad things."

"Why not?" asked The Dark. "Being bad is fun sometimes—lots of fun."

"I guess it is," said Stevie, "but only if it's a little bad. A big bad makes your stomach sick and you have to have a spanking or a sit-in-the-corner and then a big loving from Mommy or Daddy before it gets well again."

"Aw, come on," said The Dark. "I'm lonesome. Nobody ever comes to play with me. I like you. Let me out and I'll give you a two-wheel bike."

"Really?" Stevie felt all warm inside. "For True?"

"For True. And a cat with three-and-a-half legs."

"Oh!" Stevie felt like Christmas morning. "Honest?"

"Honest. All you have to do is take away the rocks and break up your pocket piece and I'll fix everything for you."

"My pocket piece?" The warmness was going away. "No sir, I won't either break it up. It's the magicest thing I've got and it was hard to make."

"But I can give you some better magic."

"Nothing can be more magic." Stevie tightened his hand around his pocket piece. "Anyway, Daddy said I might get a two-wheel bike for my birthday. I'll be six years old. How old are you?"

The Dark moved back and forth. "I'm as old as the world."

Stevie laughed. "Then you must know Auntie Phronie. Daddy says she's as old as the hills."

"The hills are young," said The Dark. "Come on, Stevie, let me out. Please—pretty please."

"Well," Stevie reached for the pretty red rock. "Promise you'll be good."

"I promise."

Stevie hesitated. He could feel a funniness in The Dark's voice. It sounded like Lili-cat when she purred to the mice she caught. It sounded like Pooch-pup when he growled softly to the gophers he ate sometimes. It made Stevie feel funny inside and, as he squatted there wondering what the feeling was, lightning flashed brightly above the treetops and a few big raindrops splashed down with the crash of thunder.

"Well," said Stevie, standing up, feeling relieved. "It's going to rain. I can't play with you now. I have to go. Maybe I can come see you tomorrow."

"No, now!" said The Dark. "Let me out right now!" and its Arnold-face was all twisted and one eye was slipping down one cheek.

Stevie started to back away, his eyes feeling big and scared. "Another time. I can't play in the wash when it storms. There might be a flood."

"Let me out!" The Dark was getting madder. The Arnold-face turned purple and its eyes ran down its face like sick fire and it melted back into blackness again. "Let me out!" The Dark hit the magic so hard that it shook the sand and one of the rocks started to roll. Quick like a rabbit, Stevie pressed the rock down hard and fixed all

155

the others too. Then The Dark twisted itself into a thing so awful looking that Stevie's stomach got sick and he wanted to upchuck. He took out his pocket piece and drew three hard magics in the sand and The Dark screamed so hard that Stevie screamed, too, and ran home to Mommy and was very sick.

Mommy put him to bed and gave him some medicine to comfort his stomach and told Daddy he'd better buy Stevie a hat. The sun was too hot for a towheaded, bare-headed boy in the middle of July.

Stevie stayed away from the wash for a while after that, but one day Burro Eddie opened the gate with his teeth again and wandered off down the road, headed for the wash. It had been storming again in the Whetstones. Mommy said, "You'd better go after Eddie. The flood will be coming down the wash this afternoon and if Eddie gets caught, he'll get washed right down into the river."

"Aw, Eddie can swim," said Stevie.

"Sure he can, but not in a flash flood. Remember what happened to Durkin's horse last year."

"Yeah," said Stevie, wide-eyed. "It got drownded. It even went over the dam. It was dead."

"Very dead," laughed Mommy. "So you scoot along and bring Eddie back. But remember, if there's any water at all in the wash, you stay out of it. And if any water starts down while you're in it, get out in a hurry."

"Okay Mommy."

So Stevie put on his sandals—there were too many stickers on the road to go barefoot—and went after Eddie. He tracked him carefully like Daddy showed him—all bent over—and only had to look twice to see where he was so he'd be sure to follow the right tracks. He finally tracked him down into the wash.

Burro Eddie was eating mesquite beans off a bush across the wash from The Dark. Stevie held out his hand and waggled his fingers at him.

"Come on, Eddie. Come on, old feller."

Eddie waggled his ears at Stevie and peeked out of the corner of his eyes, but he went on pulling at the long beans, sticking his teeth way out so the thorns wouldn't scratch his lips so bad. Stevie walked slow and careful toward Eddie, making soft talk real coaxing-like and was just sliding his hand up Eddie's shoulder to get hold of the ragged old rope around his neck when Eddie decided to be scared and jumped with all four feet. He skittered across to the other side of the wash, tumbling Stevie down on the rough, gravelly sand.

"Daggone you, Eddie!" he yelled, getting up. "You come on back here. We gotta get out of the wash. Mommy's gonna be mad at us. Don't be so mean!"

Stevie started after Eddie and Eddie kept on playing like he was scared. He flapped his stringy tail and tried to climb the almost straight-up-and-down bank of the wash. His front feet scrabbled at the bank and his hind feet kicked up the sand. Then he slid down on all fours and just stood there, his head pushed right up against the bank, not moving at all.

Stevie walked up to him real slow and started to take the old rope. Then he saw where Eddie was standing:

"Aw, Eddie," he said, squatting down in the sand. "Look what you went and did. You kicked all my magic away. You let The Dark get out. Now I haven't got anything Arnold hasn't got. Dern you, Eddie!" He stood up and smacked Eddie's flank with one hand. But Eddie just stood there and his flank felt funny—kinda stiff and cold.

"Eddie!" Stevie dragged on the rope and Eddie's head turned—jerky—like an old gate. Then Eddie's feet moved, but slow and funny, until Eddie was turned around.

"What's the matter, Eddie?" Stevie put his hand on Eddie's nose and looked at him close. Something was wrong with the burro's eyes. They were still big and dark, but now they didn't seem to see Stevie or anything—they looked empty. And while Stevie looked into them, there came a curling blackness into them, like smoke coming through a crack and all at once the eyes began to see again. Stevie started to back away, his hands going out in front of him.

"Eddie," he whispered. "Eddie, what's the matter?" And Eddie started after him—but not like Eddie—not with fast feet that kicked the sand in little spurts, but slow and awful, the two legs on one side together, then the two legs on the other side—like a sawhorse or something that wasn't used to four legs. Stevie's heart began to pound under his T-shirt and he backed away faster. "Eddie, Eddie," he pleaded. "Don't, Eddie. Don't act like that. Be good. We gotta go back to the house."

But Eddie kept on coming, faster and faster, his legs

157

getting looser so they worked better and his eyes staring at Stevie. Stevie backed away until he ran into a big old cottonwood trunk that high water brought down after the last storm. He ducked around in back of the trunk. Eddie just kept on dragging his feet through the sand until he ran into the trunk too, but his feet kept on moving, even when he couldn't go any farther. Stevie put out one shaky hand to pat Eddie's nose. But he jerked it back and stared and stared across the tree trunk at Eddie. And Eddie stared back with eyes that were wide and shiny like quiet lightning. Stevie swallowed dryness in his throat and then he knew.

"The Dark!" he whispered. "The Dark. It got out. It got in Eddie!"

He turned and started to run kitty-cornered across the wash. There was an awful scream from Eddie. Not a donkey scream at all, and Stevie looked back and saw Eddie—The Dark—coming after him, only his legs were working better now and his big mouth was wide open with the big yellow teeth all wet and shiny. The sand was sucking at Stevie's feet, making him stumble. He tripped over something and fell. He scrambled up again and his hands splashed as he scrambled. The runoff from the Whetstones was coming and Stevie was in the wash!

He could hear Eddie splashing behind him. Stevie looked back and screamed and ran for the bank. Eddie's face wasn't Eddie any more. Eddie's mouth looked full of twisting darkness and Eddie's legs had learned how a donkey runs and Eddie could outrun Stevie any day of the week. The water was coming higher and he could feel it grab his feet and suck sand out from under him every step he took.

Somewhere far away he heard Mommy shrieking at him, "Stevie! Get out of the wash!"

Then Stevie was scrambling up the steep bank, the stickers getting in his hands and the fine silty dirt getting in his eyes. He could hear Eddie coming and he heard Mommy scream, "Eddie!" and there was Eddie trying to come up the bank after him, his mouth wide and slobbering.

Then Stevie got mad. "Dern you, old Dark!" he screamed. "You leave Eddie alone!" He was hanging onto the bushes with one hand but he dug into his pocket with the other and pulled out his pocket piece. He looked down at it—his precious pocket piece—two pieces of popsicle

158

stick tied together so they looked a little bit like an airplane, and on the top, lopsided and scraggly, the magic
letters INRI. Stevie squeezed it tight, and then he
screamed and threw it right down Eddie's throat—right
into the swirling nasty blackness inside of Eddie.

There was an awful scream from Eddie and a big burst-
ing roar and Stevie lost hold of the bush and fell down
into the racing, roaring water. Then Mommy was there
gathering him up, crying his name over and over as she
waded to a low place in the bank, the water curling above
her knees, making her stagger. Stevie hung on tight and
cried, "Eddie! Eddie! That mean old Dark! He made me
throw my pocket piece away! Oh, Mommy, Mommy!
Where's Eddie?"

And he and Mommy cried together in the stickery sand
up on the bank of the wash while the flood waters roared
and rumbled down to the river, carrying Eddie away,
sweeping the wash clean, from bank to bank.

And a Little Child—

I have arrived at an age—well, an age that begins to burden my body sometimes, but I don't think I'd care to go back and live the years again. There're really only a few things I envy in the young—one thing, really, that I wish I had back—and that's the eyes of children. Eyes that see everything new, everything fresh, everything wonderful, before custom can stale or life has twisted awry. Maybe that's what Heaven will be—eyes forever new.

But there is sometimes among children another seeing-ness—a seeing that goes beyond the range of adult eyes, that sometimes seem to trespass even on other dimensions. Those who can see like that have the unexpected eyes—the eerie eyes—the Seeing eyes.

The child had Seeing eyes. I noticed them first when the Davidsons moved into the camping spot next to ours on the North Fork. The Davidsons we knew from previous years, but it was our first meeting with their son Jerry, and the wife and child he had brought home from overseas. One nice thing about camping out is that you don't have to be bashful about watching other people settle in. In fact, if you aren't careful, you end up fighting one of their tent ropes while someone else hammers a peg, or you get involved in where to toe-nail in a shelf on a tree, or in deciding the best place for someone else to dip wash-water out of the creek without scooping gravel or falling in. Even being a grandmother twice over doesn't exempt you.

It was while I was sitting on my favorite stump debating whether to change my shoes and socks or let them squelch themselves dry, that I noticed the child. She was hunched up on a slanting slab of rock in the late afternoon sunshine, watching me quietly. I grinned at her and wiggled a wet toe.

"I suppose I ought to change," I said. "It's beginning to get cold."

"Yes," she said. "The sun is going down." Her eyes were very wide.

"I've forgotten your name," I said. "I have to forget it four times before I remember." I peeled off one of my wet socks and rubbed a thumb across the red stain it had left on my toes.

"I'm Liesle," she said gravely. "Look at the funny hills." She gestured with her chin at the hills down the trail.

"Funny?" I looked at them. They were just rolling hills humping rather abruptly up from the trail in orderly rows until they merged with the aspen thicket. "Just hills," I said, toweling my foot on the leg of my jeans. "The grass on them is kind of thick this year. It's been a wet spring."

"Grass?" she said. "It looks almost like—like fur."

"Fur? Mmm, well, maybe." I hopped over to the tent and crawled in to find some dry socks. "If you squint your eyes tight and don't quite look at it." My voice was muffled in the darkness of the tent. I backed out again, clutching a rolled pair of socks in my hand. "Oh, geeps!" I said. "Those gruesome old purple ones. Well, a few more years of camping out and maybe they'll go the way of all flesh."

I settled back on my stump and turned to the child, then blinked at the four eyes gravely contemplating me. "Well, hi!" I said to Annie, the child's mother. "I'm just forgetting Liesle's name for the last time."

Liesle smiled shyly, leaning against her mother. "You're Gramma," she said.

"I sure am, bless Pat and Jinnie. And you're wonderful to remember me already."

Liesle pressed her face to her mother's arm in embarrassment.

"She has your eyes," I said to Annie.

"But hers are darker blue." Annie hugged Liesle's head briefly. Then "Come, child, we must start supper."

" 'By, Gramma," said Liesle, looking back over her shoulder. Then her eyes flickered and widened and an odd expression sagged her mouth open. Annie's tugging hand towed her a reluctant step, then she turned and hurriedly scooted in front of Annie, almost tripping her. "Mother!" I heard her breathless voice. "Mother!" as they disappeared around the tent.

I looked back over my own shoulder. Liesle's eyes had refocused themselves beyond me before her face had changed. Something back there—?

161

Back there the sun was setting in pale yellow splendor and purple shadows were filling up the hollows between the hills. I've climbed little hills like those innumerable times—and rolled down them and napped on them and batted gnats on them. They were gentle, smooth hills, their fine early·faded, grassy covering silver against the sun, crisply tickly under the cheek. Just hills. Nothing could be more serene and peaceful. I raised an eyebrow and shrugged. You meet all kinds.

That night the Davidsons came over to our campfire and we all sat around in the chilly, chilly dark, talking and listening—listening to the wind in the pines, to the Little Colorado brawling its way down from Baldy, the sounds of tiny comings and goings through the brush—all the sounds that spell summer to those of us who return year after year to the same camping grounds.

Finally the fire began to flicker low and the unaccustomed altitude was making us drowsy, so we hunted up our flashlights and started our before-bed trek across the creek to the Little Houses hidden against the hillside. Men to the left, girls to the right, we entertained briefly the vision of tiled bathrooms back home, but were somehow pleasured with the inconvenience because it spelled vacation. We females slithered and giggled over the wet log-and-plank bridge across the creek. It still had a grimy ghost of snow along its sheltered edge and until even as late as July there would be a ragged snowbank up against the hill near the girls' Little House, with violets and wild strawberries blooming at its edge. Things happen like that at nine- thousand feet of elevation. We edged past the snowbank—my Trisha leading the group, her flashlight pushing the darkness aside imperiously. She was followed by our Jinnie—Pat is a goat and goes to the left—then came Mrs. Davidson, Annie and Liesle, and I was the caboose, feeling the darkness nudging at my back as it crowded after our lights.

Since the Little House accommodates only two at a time, the rest of us usually wait against an outcropping of boulders that shelters a little from a southeast wind which can cut a notch in your shinbones in less time than it takes to tell it.

I was jerkily explaining this to Annie as I stumbled along the semiovergrown path—it hadn't received its summer beating-down yet. I was reaching out to trail my hand across the first boulder, when Liesle gasped and stumbled back against me, squashing my toe completely.

"What's the matter, child?" I gritted, waiting for the pain to stop shooting up my leg like a hot fountain. "There's nothing to be afraid of. Your Mommie and I are here."

"I wanna go back!" she suddenly sobbed, clinging to Annie. "I wanna go home!"

"Liesle, Liesle," crooned Annie, gathering her up in her arms. "Mother's here. Daddy's here. No one is home. You'll have fun tomorrow, you'll see." She looked over Liesle's burrowing head at our goblinesque flashlighted faces. "She's never camped before," she said apologetically. "She's homesick."

"I'm afraid! I can't go any farther!" sobbed Liesle. I clamped Jinnie's arm sharply. She was making noises like getting scared, too—and she a veteran of cradle-camping.

"There's nothing to be afraid of," I reiterated, wiggling my toe hopefully. Thank goodness, it could still wiggle. I thought it had been amputated. Liesle's answer was only a muffled wail. "Well, come on over here out of the wind," I said to Annie. "And I'll hold her while you go." I started to take Liesle, but she twisted away from my hand.

"No, no!" she cried. "I can't go any farther!" Then she slithered like an eel out of Annie's arms and hit off back down the trail. The dark swallowed her.

"Liesle!" Annie set off in pursuit and I followed, trying to stab some helpful light along the winding path. I caught up with the two of them on the creek bridge. They were murmuring to each other, forehead to forehead. Annie's voice was urgent, but Liesle was stubbornly shaking her head.

"She won't go back," said Annie.

"Oh, well," I said, suddenly feeling the altitude draining my blood out of my feathery head and burdening my tired feet with it. "Humor the child tonight. If she has to go, let her duck out in the bushes. She'll be okay tomorrow."

But she wasn't. The next day she still stubbornly refused to go that last little way to the Little House. Jerry, her father, lost patience with her. "It's utter nonsense!" he said. "Some fool notion. We're going to be up here for two weeks. If you think I'm going to dig a special—

"You stay here," he said to Annie. He grabbed Liesle's

arm and trotted her briskly down the path. I followed. I make no bones about being curious about people and things—and as long as I keep my mouth shut, I seldom get a door slammed in my face. Liesle went readily enough, whimpering a little, half running before his prodding finger, down the path, across the bridge, along the bank. And flatly refused to go any farther. Jerry pushed and she doubled down, backing against his legs. He shoved her forward and she fell to her hands and knees, scrambling back along the path, trying to force her way past him—all in deathly panting silence. His temper flared and he pushed her again. She slid flat on the path, digging her fingers into the weedy grass along the edge, her cheek pressed to the muddy path. I saw her face then, blanched, stricken—old in its fierce determination, pitifully young in its bare terror.

"Jerry—" I began.

Anger had deafened and blinded him. He picked her up bodily and started down the path. She writhed and screamed a wild, despairing scream, "Daddy! Daddy! No! It's open! It's open!"

He strode on, past the first boulder. He had taken one step beyond the aspen that leaned out between two boulders, when Liesle was snatched from his arms. Relieved of her weight, his momentum carried him staggering forward, almost to his knees. Blankly, he looked around. Liesle was plastered to the boulder, spread-eagled above the path like a paper doll pasted on a wall—except that this paper doll gurgled in speechless terror and was slowly being sucked into the rock. She was face to the rock, but as I gaped in shock, I could see her spine sinking in a concave curve, pushing her head and feet back sharper and sharper.

"Grab her!" I yelled. "Jerry! Grab her feet!" I got hold of her shoulders and pulled with all my strength. Jerry got his hands behind her knees and I heard his breath grunt out as he pulled. "O God in Heaven!" I sobbed. "O God in Heaven!"

There was a sucking, tearing sound and Liesle came loose from the rock. The three of us tumbled in a tangled heap in the marshy wetness beyond the trail. We sorted ourselves out and Jerry crouched in the muck rocking Liesle in his arms, his face buried against her hair.

I sat there speechless, feeling the cold wetness penetrating my jeans. What was there to say?

Finally Liesle stopped crying. She straightened up in Jerry's arms and looked at the rock. "Oh," she said. "It's shut now."

She wiggled out of Jerry's arms. "Gramma, I gotta go." Automatically I helped her unzip her jeans and sat there slack-jawed as she trotted down the path past the huge boulder and into the Little House.

"Don't ask me!" barked Jerry suddenly, rising dripping from the pathside. "Don't *ask* me!"

So I didn't.

Well, a summer starting like that could be quite a summer, but instead everything settled down to a pleasant even pace and we fished and hiked and picnicked and got rained on and climbed Baldy, sliding back down its snow slopes on the seats of our pants, much to their detriment.

Then came the afternoon some of us females were straggling down the trail to camp, feet soaked as usual and with the kids clutching grimy snowballs salvaged from the big drift on the sharp north slope below the Salt House. The last of the sun glinted from the white peak of Baldy where we had left the others hours ago still scrabbling around in the dust looking for more Indian bone beads. We seemed to be swimming through a valley of shadows that were almost tangible.

"I'm winded." Mrs. Davidson collapsed, panting, by the side of the trail, lying back on the smoothly rounded flank of one of the orderly little hills near the creek.

"We're almost there," I said. "If I get down, I won't get up again short of midnight."

"So let it be midnight," she said, easing her shoulders back against the soft crispness of the grass. "Maybe some robins will find us and cover us with strawberries instead of strawberry leaves. Then we wouldn't have to cook supper."

"That'd be fun," said Leslie, hugging her knees beside Mrs. Davidson.

"Oh, Liesle!" Jinnie was disgusted. "You don't think they really would, do you?"

"Why not?" Liesle's eyes were wide.

"Oh, groan!" said Jinnie, folding up on the ground. "You'd believe anything! When you get as old as I am—"

"What a thought!" I said, easing my aching feet in my hiking boots. "Do you suppose she'd *ever* be ten years old?" I looked longingly at the cluster of tents on the edge of the flat. "Oh, well," I said and subsided on the hill beside the others. I flopped over on my stomach and cradled my head on my arms. "Why! It's warm!" I said as my palm burrowed through the grass to the underlying soil.

"Sun," murmured Mrs. Davidson, her eyes hidden behind her folded arm. "It soaks it up all day and lets it out at night."

"Mmmm." I let relaxation wash over me.

"They're sleeping a long time," said Liesle.

"Who?" I was too lax for conversation.

"The beasts," she said. "These beasts we're on."

"What beasts?" It was like having a personal mosquito.

"These ones with the green fur," she said and giggled. "People think they're just hills, but they're beasts."

"If you say so." My fingers plucked at the grass. "And the green fur grew all around, all around——"

"That's why it feels warm," said Liesle. "Don't pull its fur, Gramma. It might hurt it. 'Nen it'd get up. And spill us on the ground. And open its big mouth—and stick out its great big teeth——" She clutched me wildly. "Gramma!" she cried, "Let's go home!"

"Oh, botheration!" I said, sitting up. The chill of the evening was like a splash of cold water. "Say, it *is* getting cold. We'll catch our death of live-forevers if we lie out here much longer."

"But it's so warm and nice down here," sighed Mrs. Davidson.

"Not up here," I shivered. "Come on, younguns, I'll race you to the tent."

The moonlight wakened me. It jabbed down through a tiny rip in the tent above me and made it impossible for me to go back to sleep. Even with my eyes shut and my back turned, I could feel the shaft of light twanging almost audibly against my huddled self. So I gave up, and shrugging into a fleece-lined jacket and wriggling my bare feet into my sneakers, I ducked through the tent flap. The night caught at my heart. All the shadow and silver of a full moon plus the tumble and swell, the ivory and ebony of clouds welling up over Baldy. No wonder the moonlight had twanged through the tent. It was that kind of night—taut, swift, far and unfettered.

I sighed and tucked my knees up under the jacket as I sat on the stump. There are times when having a body is a big nuisance. Well, I thought, I'll stay out long enough to

166

get thoroughly chilled, then I'll surely sleep when I crawl back into my nice warm sleeping bag. My eyes followed the dark serrated treetops along the far side of the creek to the velvety roll of the small hills in the moonlight upstream, the thick silver-furred beasts-who-slept-so-long. I smiled as I thought of Liesle.

Then there she was—Liesle—just beyond the tent, her whole body taut with staring, her arms stiffly flexed at the elbows, her fingers crooked, her whole self bent forward as though readying for any sudden need for pursuit—or flight.

She made an abortive movement as though to go back into the tent, and then she was off, running towards the hills, her bare white feet flashing in the moonlight. I wanted to call after her, but something about the stillness of the night crowded the noise back into my throat, so I took after her, glad of a good excuse to run, fleet-footed and free, through the crispness of the silver night. A little farther, a little faster, a little lighter and I wouldn't even have had to touch the ground.

I lost sight of Liesle, so I leaned against a tree and waited for my breath to catch up with me. Then I saw her, a wisp of darkness in her worn flannel pajamas, moving from one small hill to another, softly tiptoeing away across them until the shadow of the aspen grove on the slope above swallowed her up. There was a pause as I wondered if I should follow, then she reappeared with the same soft, careful step. She stopped just a few feet from me and plumped herself down between two rounded knolls. She shivered in the icy air and snuggled down tight in the curving corner. I could hear her talking.

"Move over, you. Keep me warm. There's eight of you. I counted. I like you in the night, but I'm scared of you in the day. You don't belong in the day." She yawned luxuriantly and I saw that she was sinking slowly between those two grassy hills. "You really don't belong in the night, either." Liesle went on. "You better go back next time it's open." Only her head was visible now. She was all but swallowed up in the—in the what?

"Liesle!" I hissed.

She gasped and looked around. Suddenly she was sprawling out in the open again on the sloping hillside, shivering. She glanced back quickly and then began to cry. I gathered her up in my arms. "What's going on here, Liesle?"

"I had a dream!" she wailed.

I carried her back to the camp, sagging a little under her weight. Just before I dumped her down in front of her tent, I swear she waved over my shoulder, a furtive, quick little wave, back at the little sleeping hills.

Next day I determinedly stayed in camp when everyone else galloped off into the far distance toward Katatki to look for arrowheads. I had to make a noise like elderly and weary, and I know my children suspected that I was up to some mischief, but they finally left me alone. The dust had hardly settled on the curve downcreek before I was picking my way among the beast-hills.

I caught myself tiptoeing and breathing cautiously through my mouth, startled by the crunch of gravel and the sudden shriek of a blue jay. I sat down, as nearly as I could tell, between the same two hills where Liesle had been. I pulled up a tuft of grass with a quick twinge of my thumb and fingers. Grass—that's all it was. Well, what had I expected? I unlimbered my short prospector's pick and began to excavate. The sod peeled back. The sandy soil underneath slithered a little. The pick clinked on small rocks. I unearthed a beer cap and a bent nail. I surveyed my handiwork, then shoved the dirt back with the head of the pick. Sometimes it's fun to have too much imagination. Other times it gets you dirt under your fingernails.

I trudged back toward camp. Halfway there I stopped in mid-stride. Had I heard something? Or felt something? A movement as of air displacing? I turned and walked slowly back to the hillside.

Nowhere, nowhere, could I find the spot where I'd been digging. I knelt down and picked up the only loose object around. A rusty beer cap.

The Davidsons' vacation was nearly over. We had another week after they were to leave. I don't know how it happened—things like that are always happening to us—but we ended up with Liesle and Jinnie jumping up and down ecstatically together as all grownups concerned slowly nodded their heads. And I had an extra grandchild for the next week.

Of course, Liesle was a little homesick the first night after her folks left. After Jinnie had fallen asleep, she looked over at me in the glow of the Coleman lantern, with such forlornness that I lifted the edge of my sleeping bag and she practically flung herself into it. It was a tight squeeze, but finally she was snuggled on my shoulder, the crisp spray of her hair tickling my chin.

"I like you, Gramma," she said. "You're warm."

"You're warm, too," I said, feeling heat radiating from the wiry little body. I don't know what prompted my next question. Maybe it was that I *wanted* there to be something in Liesle's play-pretend. "Am I as warm as the beasts?"

I felt her startled withdrawal. It was like having a spring suddenly coil beside me.

"What are they going to do when it starts snowing again?" I asked into the awkward silence.

"I don't know," said Liesle slowly. "I don't know any beasts. Besides their fur would keep them warm."

"It looks like just grass to me," I said. "Grass withers when cold weather comes."

"It's 'sposed to look like grass," said Liesle. "So's no one will notice them."

"What are they?" I asked. "Where did they come from?"

"I don't know any beasts," said Liesle. "I'm going to sleep."

And she did.

Liesle might as well have gone on home for all the outdoor activity she got that week with us. Bad weather came pouring through the pass in the mountains, and we had rain and fog and thunder and hail and a horrible time trying to keep the kids amused. My idle words had stuck in Liesle's mind and festered in the inactivity. She peered incessantly out of the tent flap asking, "How long will it rain? Is it cold out there? It won't snow will it? Will there be ice?"

And when we had a brief respite after a roaring hailstorm and went out to gather up the tapioca-sized stones by the buckets-full, Liesle filled both hands and, clutching the hail tightly, raced over to the small hills. I caught up with her as she skidded to a stop on the muddy trail.

She was staring at the beast-hills, frosted lightly with the hail. She turned her deep eyes to me. "It's ice," she said tragically.

"Yes," I said. "Little pieces of ice."

She opened her hands and stared at her wet palms. "It's gone," she said.

"Your hands are warm," I explained.

"Warmness melts the ice," she said, her eyes glowing. "They're warm."

"They could melt the little ice," I acknowledged. "But if it really froze—"

"I told them to go back," said Liesle. "The next time it's open."

"What's open?" I asked.

"Well," said Liesle. "It's down the path to the Little House. It's the rock—it's a empty—it's to go through—" She slapped her hand back and forth across her pants legs, ridding them of the melted hail. Her bottom lip was pouted, her eyes hidden. "It doesn't go into any place," she said. "It only goes through." Anger flared suddenly and she kicked the nearest hill. "Stupid beasts!" she cried. "Why didn't you stay home!"

We started packing the day before we were to leave. Liesle scurried around with Jinnie, getting under foot and messing things up generally. So I gave them a lot of left-over odds and ends of canned goods and a box to put them in and they spent hours packing and unpacking. I had dismissed them from my mind and submerged myself in the perennial problem of how to get back into the suitcases what they had originally contained. So I was startled to feel a cold hand on my elbow. I looked around into Liesle's worried face.

"What if they don't know the way back?" she asked.

"Of course they know the way back," I said. "They've driven it a dozen times."

"No, I mean the beasts." She clutched me again. "They'll die in the winter."

"Winter's a long way off," I said. "They'll be all right."

"They don't count like we do," said Liesle. "Winter's awful close."

"Oh, Liesle, child," I said, exasperated. "Let's not play that now. I'm much too busy."

"I'm not playing," she said, her cheeks flushing faintly, her eyes refusing to leave mine. "The beasts—"

"Please, honey lamb," I said. "You finish your packing and let me finish mine." And I slammed the suitcase on my hand.

"But the beasts—"

"Beasts!" I said indistinctly as I tried to suck the pain

170

out of my fingers. "They're big enough to take care of themselves."

"They're just baby ones!" she cried. "And they're lost, 'relse'n they'd have gone home when it was open."

"Then go tell them the way," I said, surveying dismally the sweat shirt and slacks that should have been in the case I had just closed. She was out of sight by the time I got to the tent door. I shook my head. That should teach me to stick to Little Red Riding Hood or the Gingerbread Boy. Beasts, indeed!

Late that evening came a whopper of a storm. It began with a sprinkle so light that it was almost a mist. And then, as though a lever were being steadily depressed, the downpour increased, minute by minute. In direct proportion, the light drained out of the world. Everyone was snugly under canvas by the time the rain had become a downpour—except Liesle.

"I know where she is," I said with a sigh, and snatched my fleece-lined jacket and ducked out into the rain. I'd taken about two steps before my shoes were squelching water and the rain was flooding my face like a hose. I had sploshed just beyond the tents when a dripping wet object launched itself against me and knocked me staggering back against a pine tree.

"They won't come!" sobbed Liesle, her hair straight and lank, streaming water down her neck. "I kept talking to them and talking to them, but they won't come. They say it isn't open and if it was they wouldn't know the way!" She was shaking with sobs and cold.

"Come in out of the wet," I said, patting her back soggily. "Everything will be okay." I stuck my head into the cook tent. "I got 'er. Have to wring her out first." And we ducked into the sleep tent.

"I told them right over this way and across the creek—" her voice was muffled as I stripped her T-shirt over her head. "They can't see right over this way and they don't know what a creek is. They see on top of us."

"On top?" I asked, fumbling for a dry towel.

"Yes!" sobbed Liesle. "We're in the middle. They see mostly on top of us and then there's us and then there's an underneath. They're afraid they might fall into us or the underneath. We're all full of holes around here."

"They're already in us," I said, guiding her icy feet into the flannel pajama legs. "We can see them."

171

"Only part," she said. "Only the Here part. The There part is so'st we can't see it." I took her on my lap and surrounded her with my arms and she leaned against me, slowly warming, but with the chill still shaking her at intervals.

"Oh, Gramma!" Her eyes were big and dark. "I saw some of the There part. It's like—like—like a Roman candle."

"Those big heavy hills like Roman candles?" I asked.

"Sure." Her voice was confident. "Roman candles have sticks on them, don't they?"

"Look, Liesle." I sat her up and looked deep into her eyes. "I know you think this is all for true, but it really isn't. It's fun to pretend as long as you know it's pretend, but when you begin to believe it, it isn't good. Look at you, all wet and cold and unhappy because of this pretend."

"But it isn't pretend!" protested Liesle. "When it was open—" She caught her breath and clutched me. I paused, feeling as though I had stepped off an unexpected curb, then swiftly I tucked that memory away with others, such as the rusty beer cap, the slow ingestion of Liesle by the hills—

"Forget about that," I said. "Believe me, Liesle, it's all pretend. You don't have to worry."

For a long rain-loud moment, Liesle searched my face, and then she relaxed. "Okay, Gramma." She became a heavy, sleepy weight in my lap. "If you say so."

We went to sleep that last night to the sound of rain. By then it had become a heavy, all-pervading roar on the tent roof that made conversation almost impossible. "Well," I thought drowsily, "this is a big, wet, close-quotes to our summer." Then, just as I slipped over into sleep, I was surprised to hear myself think, "Swim well, little beasts, swim well."

It may have been the silence that woke me, because I was suddenly wide awake in a rainless hush. It wasn't just an awakening, but an urgent push into awareness. I raised up on one elbow. Liesle cried out and then was silent. I lay back down again, but tensed as Liesle muttered and moved in the darkness. Then I heard her catch her breath and whimper a little. She crawled cautiously out of her sleeping bag and was fumbling at the tent flap. A pale

172

watery light came through the opening. The sky must have partially cleared. Liesle whispered something, then groped back across the tent. I heard a series of rustles and whispers, then she was hesitating at the opening, jacket over her pajamas, her feet in lace-trailing sneakers.

"It's open!" she whimpered, peering out. "It's open!" And was gone.

I caught my foot in the sleeping bag, tried to put my jacket on upsidedown, and got the wrong foot in the right shoe, before I finally got straightened up and staggered out through an ankle-deep puddle to follow Liesle. I groped my way in the wet grayness halfway to the Little House before I realized there was no one ahead of me in the path. I nearly died. Had she already been sucked into that treacherous gray rock! And inside me a voice mockingly chanted, "Not for true, only pretend—"

"Shut *up!*" I muttered fiercely, then, turning, I sploshed at full staggering speed back past the tents. I leaned against my breathing tree to stop my frantic gulping of the cold wet air, and, for the dozenteenth time in my life, reamed myself out good for going along with a gag too far. If I had only scotched Liesle's imagination the first—

I heard a tiny, piercingly high noise, a coaxing, luring bird-like sound, and I saw Liesle standing in the road, intent on the little hills, her right hand outstretched, fingers curling, as though she were calling a puppy.

Then I saw the little hills quiver and consolidate and Become. I saw them lift from the ground with a sucking sound. I heard the soft tear of turf and the almost inaudible twang of parting roots. I saw the hills flow into motion and follow Liesle's piping call. I strained to see in the half light. There were no legs under the hills—there were dozens of legs under—there were wheels—squares —flickering, firefly glitters—

I shut my eyes. The hills were *going*. How they were going, I couldn't say. Huge, awkward and lumbering, they followed Liesle like drowsy mastodons in close order formation. I could see the pale scar below the aspen thicket where the hills had pulled away. It seemed familiar, even to the scraggly roots poking out of the sandy crumble of the soil. Wasn't that the way it had always looked?

I stood and watched the beast-hills follow Liesle. How could such a troop go so noiselessly? Past the tents, through the underbrush, across the creek—Liesle used the bridge—and on up the trail toward the Little House. I lost sight of them as they rounded the bend in the trail. I permitted myself a brief sigh of relief before I started back toward the tents. Now to gather Liesle up, purged of her compulsion, get her into bed and persuaded that it had all been a dream. Mockingly, I needled myself. "A dream? A dream? They were there, weren't they? They are gone, aren't they? Without bending a blade or breaking a branch. Gone into what? Gone into what?"

"Gone into nothing," I retorted. "Gone through—"

"Through into what?" I goaded. "Gone into what?"

"Okay! *You* tell *me!*" I snapped. Both of us shut up and stumbled off down the darkened path. For the unnumberedth time I was catapulted into by Liesle. We met most unceremoniously at the bend in the trail.

"Oh, Gramma!" she gasped. "One didn't come! The littlest one didn't come! There were eight, but only seven went in. We gotta get the other one. It's gonna close! Gramma!" She was towing me back past the tents.

"Oh, yipes!" I thought dismally. "A few more of these shuttle runs and I *will* be an old woman!"

We found the truant huddled at the base of the aspens, curled up in a comparatively tiny, grass-bristly little hillock. Liesle stretched out her hands and started piping at the beast-hill.

"Where did you learn that sound?" I asked, my curiosity burning even in a mad moment like this one.

"That's the way you *call* a beast-hill!" she said, amazed at my ignorance, and piped again, coaxingly. I stood there in my clammy, wet sneakers, and presumably in my right mind, and watched the tight little hillock unroll and move slowly in Liesle's direction.

"Make him hurry, Gramma!" cried Liesle. "Push!"

So I pushed—and had the warm feeling of summer against my palms, the sharp faint fragrance of bruised grass in my nostrils, and a vast astonishment in my mind. I'll never get over it. Me! Pushing a beast-hill in the watery chill of a night hour that had no number and seemed to go on and on.

Well anyway, between Liesle's piping and my pushing, we got the Least-one past the tents (encore!) across the creek and down the trail. Liesle ran ahead. "Oh, Gramma! Gramma!" Her voice was tragedy. "It's closing! It's closing!"

I hunched my shoulders and dug in with my toes and fairly scooted that dumb beast down the path. I felt a protesting ripple under my hands and a recoil like a frightened child. I had a swift brief vision of me, scrabbling on the trail with a beast-hill as Jerry had with Liesle, but my sudden rush pushed us around the corner. There was Liesle, one arm tight around a tree trunk, the other outstretched across the big gray boulder. Her hand was lost somewhere in the Anything that coalesced and writhed, Became and dissolved in the middle of the gray granite.

"Hurry!" she gasped. "I'm holding it! Push!"

I pushed! And felt some strength inside me expend the very last of itself on the effort. I had spent the last of some youthful coinage that could never be replenished. There was a stubborn silent moment and then the beast-hill must have perceived the opening, because against my fingers was a sudden throb, a quick tingling and the beast-hill was gone—just like that. The boulder loomed, still and stolid as it had been since the Dawn, probably—just as it always had been except—Liesle's hand was caught fast in it, clear up past her wrist.

"It's stuck." She looked quietly over her shoulder at me. "It won't come out."

"Sure it will," I said, dropping to my haunches and holding her close. "Here, let me—" I grasped her elbow.

"No." She hid her face against my shoulder. I could feel the sag of her whole body. "It won't do any good to pull."

"What shall we do then?" I asked, abandoning myself to her young wisdom.

"We'll have to wait till it opens again," she said.

"How long?" I felt the tremble begin in her.

"I don't know. Maybe never. Maybe—maybe it only happens once."

"Oh, now!" I said and had nothing to add. What *can* you say to a child whose hand has disappeared into a granite boulder and won't come out?

"Liesle," I said. "Can you wiggle your fingers?"

Her whole face tightened as she tried. "Yes," she said. "It's just like having my hand in a hole but I can't get it out."

"Push it in, then," I said.

"In?" she asked faintly.

"Yes," I said. "Push it in and wiggle it hard. Maybe they'll see it and open up again."

So she did. Slowly she pushed until her elbow disappeared. "I'm waving hard!" We waited. Then— "Nobody comes," she said. And suddenly she was fighting and sobbing, wrenching against the rock, but her arm was as tight-caught as her hand had been. I hugged her to me, brushing my hand against the rock as I quieted her thrashing legs. "There, there, Liesle." Tears were wadding up in my throat. I rocked her consolingly.

"O God in Heaven," I breathed, my eyes closed against her hair. "O God in Heaven!"

A bird cried out in the silence that followed. The hour that had no number stretched and stretched. Suddenly Liesle stirred. "Gramma!" she whispered. "Something touched me! Gramma!" She straightened up and pressed her other hand against the boulder. "Gramma! Somebody put something in my hand! Look, Gramma!" And she withdrew her arm from the gray granite and held her hand out to me.

It overflowed with a Something that Was for a split second, and then flaked and sparked away like the brilliance of a Roman candle, showering vividly and all around to the ground.

Liesle looked at her hand, all glittering silver, and wiped it on her pajamas, leaving a shining smudge. "I'm tired, Gramma," she whimpered. She looked around her, half dazed. "I had a dream!" she cried. "I had a dream!"

I carried her back to the tent. She was too exhausted to cry. She only made a weary moaning sound that jerked into syllables with the throb of my steps. She was asleep before I got her jacket off. I knelt beside her for a while, looking at her—wondering. I lifted her right hand. A last few flakes of brilliance sifted off her fingers and flickered out on the way to the floor. Her nails glowed faintly around the edges, her palm, where it was creased, bore an irregular M of fading silver. What had she held? What gift had been put into her hand? I looked around, dazed. I was too tired to think. I felt an odd throb, as though time had gone back into gear again and it was suddenly very late. I was asleep before I finished pulling the covers up.

Well! It's episodes like that—though, thank Heaven, they're rather scarce—that make me feel the burden of age. I'm too set in the ways of the world to be able to accept such things as normal and casual, too sure of what *is* to be seen to really see what is. But events don't have to be this bizarre to make me realize that sometimes it's best just to take the hand of a child—a Seeing child—and let them do the leading.

The Last Step

I don't like children.

I suppose that's a horrible confession for a teacher to make, but there's nothing in the scheme of things that says you have to love the components of your work to do it well. And that's all children are to me—components of my work. My work is teaching and teaching is my life and I know, especially in a job handling people, that they say it helps to like people, but love never made bricks build a better wall—loving never weeded a garden and liking never made glue stick harder. Children to me are merely items to be handled in the course of earning my living and whether I like them or not has nothing to do with the matter. I loathe children outside of school. I avoid them, and they me. There's no need for school to lap over into other areas of living any more than a carpenter's tools should claim his emotions after he leaves work.

And the pampering and soft handling the children receive—well, I suppose those who indulge in it have their justifications or think they have, but all it accomplishes as far as I can see is to pad their minds against what they have to learn—a kind of bandage before the wound, because educating children is a pushing forcibly of the raw materials of intelligence into an artificial mold. Society itself is nothing but a vast artificiality and all a teacher is for is to warp the child into the pattern society dictates. Left alone, he'd be a happy savage for what few brief years he could manage to survive—and I'd be out of a job. At any rate, I believe firmly in making sure each child I handle gets a firm grip on the fundamental tools society demands of him. If I do it bluntly and nakedly, that's my affair. Leave the ruffles and lace edging to others. When I get through with a child he knows what he should know for his level and knows it thoroughly and no love lost on either side. And if he cries when he finds he is to be in my class, he doesn't cry long. Tears are not permitted in my room.

I've been reading back over this. My tense is wrong. I *used to* teach. I *used to* make sure. Because this is the fifth day.

Well, when the inescapable arrives— But how was I to know? A person is what he is. He acts as he acts because he acts that way. There's no profit in considering things out of the pattern because there's no armor against deviation. Or has there been a flaw in my philosophy all this time? *Are* there other values I should have considered?

Well, time, even to such an hour as today brings, has to be lived through, so I'm writing this down, letting the seconds be words and the minutes paragraphs. It will make a neat close-quote for the whole situation.

I was in a somewhat worse mood on Monday than I usually was because I had just been through another utterly useless meeting with Major Junius. You'd think, since he is military, that he wouldn't bother himself about such foolishness even if parents did complain.

"Imagination," he said, tapping his fingertips together, "is an invaluable asset. It is, I might say, one of the special blessings bestowed upon mankind. Not an unmixed blessing, however, since by imagination one plagues oneself with baseless worries and fears, but I feel that its importance for the children should not be minimized."

"I don't minimize it," I snapped. "I ignore it. When you hired me to come out here to Argave and paid my space fare to bring me here, you knew my feeling on the matter. I am not without reputation."

"True, true." He patted his fingers together again. "But you are robbing the children of their birthright by denying them such harmless flights of fancy, their fairy tales and such imaginative literature."

"Time for such nonsense later," I said. "While I have them, they will learn to read and write and do the mathematics expected of them on this level, but by *my* methods and with *my* materials or I resign."

He puffed and blew and sputtered a little, clearly hating me and toying with the idea of accepting my resignation, but also visualizing the 130 children with only three teachers and Earth a four-month journey away. When

I saw that, as usual, he would do nothing decisive, I got up and left.

I went out to my detested ground duty. The children were due to arrive momentarily, dropping in giggling clusters from the helitrans that brought them out to Base from their housing. Their individual helidrops would land them in the play yard, and after unstrapping themselves and stacking the helidrops in the racks, they would swarm all over the grounds and I was supposed to be at least a token of directed supervision, though what child needs to be shown how to waste his time?

The children came helling down—as slang would inevitably have it—and the day began. I usually made my tour of the grounds along the fences that boxed us securely against the Argavian countryside, the sterilites along their bases effectively preventing Argavian flora or fauna from entering. More nonsense. If we want Argave, we shouldn't try to make it a Little Earth. And those of us fool enough to people this outworld military installation should accept whatever Argave has to offer— the bad with the good. It's near enough Earth-type that not many would die.

But to get back to the playground. One corner of it is a sandbox area where the smaller children usually played. That morning, I noticed some of the older boys in that area and went over to see what playground rules they were breaking. As it happened, they weren't breaking any. They were playing near the sandbox, but closer to the fence where Argavian rains had washed out the topsoil and, combined with the apparent failure of one of the sterilites, had developed a small rough area complete with tiny Argavian plants—a landscape in miniature. The boys didn't notice me as I stood watching them. They had begun one of those interminable games—nonsense games—where they furnish a running commentary to explain the game to themselves as they go along. There were three boys. I don't know their names because they hadn't been in my class and I never bother with other children. They were older boys, maybe fourth level. They were huddled at one end of the rough area, inspecting a line of tiny metal vehicles such as boys usually have stuffed among the junk in their pockets.

"And this," said the brown-haired one, "has Captain Lewis' family in it. Mrs. Lewis and the three kids and LaVerne, the maid—"

"What about the new baby?" the redhead asked.

Brown rocked back on his heels and looked at the car, then at Red. "It isn't born yet," he said.

"It might be by then," said Red. "Better mention it or it'll be left out."

"Goes," said Brown. And he half chanted, "This is the car for Mrs. Captain Lewis and the three kids and La-Verne and the new baby—or babies." He looked over at Red without a smile. "It might be twins."

"Goes," said Red. "Now that's all except the teachers."

"There's only one car left," said the blond-haired boy. "A little one."

"You're sure?" asked Brown. "Can't it be a big one?"

"No, it's a little one." Red wasn't looking at anyone. He seemed to be peering through his lashes at nothing—or something?

"Goes," said Blond. "Miss Leaven, Mr. Kaprockanze, and Miss Robbin—"

Red glanced quickly over at Blond as his voice dropped. "And Her," he said.

"Do we *hafta* take Her?" asked Blond. "This would be an awful good time to get rid of Her."

"We can't," said Red. "It's total. Anyway, do good to those who despitefully use you and persecute you and do all manner of evil against you unjustly—"

"Goes," said Blond. "I learned that, too, but you said it wrong."

"Well, we hafta anyway," said Red. "Now. Ready?"

The three boys looked solemnly at one another. Then their eyes closed, their intent faces turned upward and their lips moved silently.

Blond spoke. His voice was shaken with desolation that seemed almost real. "Will there be time?" he choked.

"Yes," said Red. "We'll have five days. If we can fair-the-coorze by then, we'll make it. Ready?"

Again, that short pause and then Red put his forefinger on the roof of the vehicle that headed the column and nudged it forward slowly over an almost unnoticeable line that was apparently meant for a road. The two other boys began nudging the other vehicles along.

I turned and left them, caught by something in their foolish play: *Miss Leaven, Mr. Kaprockanze and Miss Robbin*—I felt a sudden sick twang inside me that I thought I had long outgrown. Such foolishness to be upset by children's nonsense. But the roll call echoed in my head again. *Miss Leaven, Mr. Kaprockanze and Miss Robbin.* My name is Esther Corvin. I must be Her.

As is my invariable practice, at dismissal I left school at school and retired immediately to my quarters. I spent the evening playing bridge in the Quarters Lounge with a number of the other civilian employees of the Base and, near midnight, stood in my gown at my window looking out on the Argavian night—which is truly splendid with three colored moons and a sky crowded with tight clusters of brilliant stars.

Quite uncharacteristically, I lingered at the window until I was shivering in the heavily scented Argavian breeze. Then I suddenly found myself leaning far out over the sill, trying to catch a glimpse of the corner of the school yard, madly wondering if those vehicles were toiling minutely forward through the Argavian night. Something must be wrong with me, I thought. And took an anti-vir before I went to bed.

I had no idea that the incident would be prolonged. Consequently I was astonished and mildly annoyed to see the three boys huddled in the corner the next morning. I determinedly stayed away from them, even going so far as to turn one end of jump rope for some of the girls to divert my attention. My helpfulness was more of a hindrance. The children were so startled by my offer that none of them could jump more than twice without missing. Finally, they stood dumbly looking at each other with red-splotched cheeks, so I relinquished the rope and left them. I drifted over to the corner to see—to find out—well, bluntly, I was irresistibly drawn to the corner.

Blond was knuckling tears out of his eyes. Tears in public? From a boy his age?

"You didn't *hafta*—" he choked.

"Did so," said Red, his face shadowed and unhappy. "It's the coorze, can't you see? Besides, I didn't do it. It just will be—"

The two sat staring at a vehicle that had been smashed under the fall of a plum-sized pebble that had rolled down the side of a miniature ravine. Brown was busy nudging another vehicle very slowly along the precarious rim of the road that edged around the pebble.

"Goes," said Blond. "But they were our best friends—"

"Goes," said Red, blinking and sniffling quickly. Then

briskly: "Get the rest of them around there now. We hafta get to The Knoll before night."

I don't know what possessed me then. I almost *ran* to the office and rang the bell five minutes early. "There!" I thought triumphantly as I jabbed the button. "It's night and you didn't get to The Knoll."

I was ashamed of myself all the rest of the day. I pride myself on being a practical, down-to-earth sort of person—and for me to be rocked by such utter nonsense! Actually to feel that I was participating in such foolishness!

That night in Quarters, I tried to analyze the situation. What were the boys doing? Did boys customarily make themselves so much a part of their play that they wept over their games? Why did I react so strongly that I was compelled to participate?

I lay in the dark staring up at the ceiling patterned by the glow of the moons and found my pulses insisting *The Knoll, The Knoll, The Knoll.* I probed deep into my memory. What did The Knoll connote to me? But try as I would, I could make it mean nothing more than a picnic spot we sometimes visited out in the obsidian hills behind the Base. There was a knob of solid volcanic glass there called The Knoll. A small spring spilled the orangy water of Argave into a shallow pool next to the picnic flat. It was reached by a road—Evac 2—that had such a reputation that any bad stretch of highway was (most regrettably) referred to as a knollful road.

Well, it was possible. The boys had probably been on picnics there. Apparently they were borrowing terminology freely.

Next day—the third day—was rainy, rainy with the needle-like, orangy downpour that has been known to draw blood. One glance at the sky told me it was to be an all-day affair. Argavian clouds never blow away. They spend themselves completely in rain. Grimly I put on my raineralls, which cover one from head to foot with even a plastic shield over the face, a curtain effect with the bottom loose for ventilation. I half sloshed, half waded to school. The children were helling in, their bright raineralls splotching the dull brown sky with color. Since they were completely shielded from the dampness by the raineralls, there was no need for them to go indoors if they didn't choose to, which meant that most of them stayed outdoors and I had to be on ground duty, rain or no rain.

I was extremely annoyed—especially since some rain had splashed my face and the loathsome taste of it was on my lips and I had no way to wipe it off until I could take off the raineralls. The children were excited and overstimulated by the weather and ran purposelessly all over the playground. Finally someone organized a game of "Who's Your Love?" and raced around, laughing, catching individuals in their circle and chanting: "Who's your lover? Tell his name. If you will not, Shame, shame, shame!" In their mad excitement, they even circled me, chanting and laughing until someone realized whom they had captured. Then they shrieked and ran, scattering like frightened quail, someone's words floating back to me: "Somebody loves Her?"

I was unaccountably stung by the words, however fitting they might be, and turned and sloshed across the playground to the corner. I felt a surge of fury as I saw the three boys bent over their game. I stepped closer, wishing furiously that I could topple them over with a well-placed shove of my foot. Why did they never sense my presence? I saw that they were concentrating on ferrying their vehicles across a tiny raging torrent that cut the vestigal road in two, the dirty threads they were using alternately slacking and tightening.

"If we coulda got past there yesterday," said Brown, "it woulda been goes. But that dang bell rang."

"Yes," said Red, his eyes hooded behind the plastic shield. "It musta been the coorze."

Blond nudged the miniature ferry, a rough bundle of twigs and bits of wood, with his finger. One tiny splinter broke away and swept down the torrent. "Maybe it won't last," he said. "Maybe we oughta wait until the rain stops."

"Can't," said Red. "This is the third day. Only got two days to rendezvous." He turned fiercely on Blond. "Unless you want to give up and let everyone die!"

"We could tell ahead," whimpered Blond. "Our dads—"

"Wouldn't believe us," whispered Red, his eyes shuttering. "They've never faired-the-coorze. How many more to go?"

"Four," said Brown. "And two have been drownded already."

"Anybody get out?" asked Blond.

184

"Only Butch," whimpered Brown. "I pushed him in with the Scotts."

"*We're* not across yet." Blond's voice shook. "Will we make it?"

"Start across," said Red.

I slopped over to the school building and started a rousing argument in the office that resulted in the bell ringing five minutes late. *There*, I thought. *There's your five minutes back.*

That afternoon as we watched the children helling up to the helitrans through the last of the downpour, Miss Robbin looked past me to Miss Leaven and said, "I can't imagine what happened to Leonard. He cried all day for his mother. Imagine, a boy his age crying for his mother."

"This putrid rain would make anyone cry," said Miss Leaven. "He's a cute kid, isn't he? All those blond curls."

Blond said my feet in the squishy orange mud. *Blond, blond, blond.*

The situation followed me home, a formless, baseless haunting. I caught myself pacing aimlessly and sat down with a book. I read four pages without retaining a word. I took an anti-vir and an aspirin and started cleaning out my desk drawer. I finally went back to the troublesome cable I was knitting in a sweater and grimly set myself to counting knits and purls. The evening went somehow and I went to sleep in an aura of foreboding.

I was unduly upset when I was awakened by the alert signal some time in the very early morning hours. As a civilian there was nothing for me to do during a practice alert except to try to go back to sleep. Actually, if ever a real alert was called and we had to evacuate, there was a plan that was supposed to be put into operation. I don't think any of us civilians and noncombatants had many illusions about what would actually happen under such circumstances. We'd be pointed down a road and told to "git," and we'd be on our own after that. We were expendable.

I lay awake, trying to rid myself of the vision of what a person looked like after an unprotected attack by the enemy. They have a nasty type of projectile that merely pricks the skin. But then the pricked place almost explodes into an orange-sized swelling that, when cut or punctured, which it must be immediately to ease the unendurable agony, sprays out hundreds of tiny creatures that scatter wildly, digging for hiding holes. And their tiny claws prick the skin. And then the pricked places—

I turned over and drowsed fitfully until the all clear sounded and then, for the first time on Argave, I overslept and arrived at school unfed and feeling that my clothes were flung on, which certainly didn't improve my disposition. It was one of those days that reminded me that sometimes I loathed myself as much as I loathed the children. During ground-duty time I walked briskly around the playground perimeter, feeling caged and trying to work it off. I saw the three boys bent over their interminable game in the corner, but I avoided them, sick to the bone of school and kids and—and myself. I was just holding on until the mood would pass.

But after school I began to wonder about the game, and contrary to my usual practice, I stayed after school. I was all by myself on the empty playground as I squatted in the corner. I looked uncomprehendingly at the scratches, the tiny heaps of gravel, the signs and symbols scrawled on the ground. They meant nothing to me. There was no interpreter to read me the day's journey.

Day's journey? To where? I squatted there, no doubt a grotesque object, with my head between my hands, my arms resting on my knees, and rocked back and forth. Surely my sanity was going. No adult in her right mind would worry over a tiny row of toy vehicles sprawled in the sticky mud of the playground. But I looked again. I finally found the lead vehicle. The whole column had detoured around a large rock and seemed to be helplessly bogged down in the mud. With a quick guilty glance around me, I carefully patted the mud smooth in front of the column, making a tiny safe highway to bring it back around the rock. I started to pick up the first vehicle to clear its wheels of the mud. But I couldn't lift it. Incredulous, I tried again. With all my strength I pulled at that tiny toy. It might have been part of the bones of the world. It moved not a fraction of an inch. I felt a fingernail snap and relinquished my hold. I felt fury bubble up inside me, and grabbing a double handful of mud, I slopped it down on the smooth road I had just made. My breath whistled between my clenched teeth. I felt like hammering the whole thing flat, smashing all the little vehicles out of sight in the muck—hammering, beating, tearing—!

I drew a quavering breath and stood up. Adults are

186

not supposed to have tantrums. I held my two muddy hands away from me as I went indoors to wash. I left a muddy thumbprint on the door latch as I went in. I wiped it off thoroughly with tissue as I left the building, my mind carefully blank of the whole situation. I couldn't understand or explain it. Hence it should be ignored. On this premise I have built my life. Built it—or lost it?

Friday, I paced the playground, trying to forget the far corner. My mind was seething with questions that kept frothing up like bubbles and popping unanswered, even unstated. But this was the fifth day. That's all they had talked about: five days. After this day I could let my bemused mind go back to its usual thoughts. Then, a little bleakly, I tried to remember what I used to think about. I couldn't remember.

A flame of resentment began burning inside me. These —these *brats* had upset my whole life. Logically or illogically I was caught in the web of their nonsense. I was being pried out of my pattern and I didn't like it. Years of training and restraint and denial had gone into making that pattern and those brats were shattering it. They were making me an ununderstandable and inexplicable thing—a thing to be ignored. I pressed my lips tightly together, my jaw muscles knotting, my heels gouging the soft turf of the playground as I patrolled. If this foolishness persisted one moment beyond this day, I'd report the three of them to the office for—for perversion. That would rock them good! Them and their families. Let *their* patterns be shattered. Let *their* nasty insides spill out like cracked, rotten eggs!

Sharply I caught myself up, my breath thick in my upper chest. How horrible can one person get? After all, the knife is not responsible for the gash it makes—or the blood that stains it. It's the hand behind the knife— The Hand. I felt a little dizzy at such odd, unaccustomed thoughts crowding into my mind—a billowing, shapeless turmoil.

When I felt I had myself under full control, I started casually for the corner. At that moment the bell rang. I saw three heads snap up at the sound and assumed that they were responding. Consequently, when I got to the door and had all the classes lined up to go in and looked over at the corner and saw the three still there, I was justifiably annoyed. I delegated Peter to see that the lines went in order and stalked out to the three truants. My firm step wavered and softened as I approached the trio. I leaned over them, not caring whether they saw me or not. I opened my mouth to speak, but it stayed open—and silent—as I took in the scene.

Something new had been added. A miniature spacecraft was balanced delicately on its fins on a small flat area. All the toy vehicles were pulled up in a circle around it—all but two: the last ones in the convoy. Red was nudging the next to the last over a flimsy bridge built of matted stems and grass across a miniature chasm that decisively ended the makeshift road. The bridge swayed and sagged. The vehicle slid and rocked and Red wiped the sweat from his forehead when Blond took over and started the vehicle over towards the spacecraft. Red reached his finger out to the last vehicle and made it toil through the dust up to the makeshift bridge. I suddenly became conscious of how absorbed I had become and my anger flared again. I reached out my foot and stepped heavily. I felt the twigs give under my shoe. reluctantly brittle, like living bones. I ground my foot down until the dust scuffed up over the sole. Then I said, "The bell rang."

My voice left no room for argument. After a slight pause, the three boys got up from the ground. Even then they didn't look at me. Brown looked at Red and said, "Tomorrow?"

"No," said Red. "This is the fifth day. There aren't any more days."

"But how will they ever make it—?"

"It's none of our business." Red hunched his shoulders. "We tried. We faired-the-coorze. It's finished."

"But what will they do?" Blond took a weary step, easing his tired knees with his hands.

Red shrugged. "*She* did it. Let Her figure it out."

"But I *like* my teacher," protested Blond.

"Goes," said Red. "But we can't help it. No one falls alone, even if we think they ought to."

"I don't like to play this game," wailed Blond. "I think it stinks!"

"Who's playing!" Red's face crumpled. "O Loving Father, who's playing?"

Brown and Blond put their arms around him and helped him, his face moving blindly, towards the school building.

I looked down at the mess I had made. The last car

was poised precariously on the rim of the ruin. All the rest around the spacecraft looked like little chicks gathering around a mother hen for warmth and shelter against the night. I snorted at the conceit, and flicking the dust off my shoe with a tissue, went into school.

That was Friday. Saturday a wave of uneasiness swept across the Base. There were restless knots of people gathered in the PX and the Commissary and the Club, chattering the same chatter as usual but with absent, worried looks. Sunday it was evident that many of the key personnel were not around. They had dispersed without a farewell. At two o'clock Monday morning, I found myself groping awake to the alert signal. This time was different. It felt different. It sounded different. I staggered out of bed, groping blindly for my clothes. I struggled with wrong-side-out hooks for interminable minutes before I awoke enough to turn the light on. I scrambled into my raineralls (our evac uniform) and went to the closet for my evac bag which, in the face of ridicule, I had packed when I first arrived—as we were supposed to do. By the time fists were hammering on our doors and loud feet were shaking our corridor and loud voices crying, "This is it! Out! Out! All Civvies out!" I was dressed and ready.

We were two days from Base before I caught on. I hadn't even been clued—except in a vague *déjà vu* way —by the shivering wait in the weird pre-dawn darkness as we were assigned to our cars.

"That's everyone except the teachers."

"There's only a small car left." Mrs. Lewis' face leaned, pale and anxious out of the window. "It'll be crowded. Maybe we could make room for one."

"No," the lieutenant in charge of us said decisively. "You'll need that room, especially if the baby decides to come."

Tears came to Mrs. Lewis' eyes. "Thanks," she said. "Has there been any news?"

"Only that the first skirmish is over. Ninety per cent casualties."

"O Loving Father!" Mrs. Lewis whispered to her cupped hands. "All the strong young men."

We were pointed down a road and told to "git," our only tie with the military the reluctant young lieutenant.

189

"Not on this knollful road!" I heard Miss Leaven wail. Then she laughed. Her laughter tightened into a sob.

Reluctantly that first day, I shared what few eatables I had in my evac kit. We had no lunch stop scheduled. None of the others had a complete kit as they should have had. They would have had their own food if they had complied with the regulations.

Early morning of the second day, we were startled out of our weary stupor by a sudden grinding crash and an abrupt bumper-to-bumper stop. We all got out of the cars and walked stiffly forward along the column. I took one look at the car lying crushed under the huge boulder that had fallen from the wall of the ravine, leaned heavily against the slope of the hill and hid my eyes. I rocked myself achingly in a sudden flood of apprehension. My whole being rebelled against the situation. It was impossible. There could be nothing but wildest coincidence to tie this event to three boys hunched in a corner of a playground. It was all my sick imagination that started to draw parallels. Imagination! That curse!

But we didn't make The Knoll that night. Darkness shut down unexpectedly early after we had edged around the boulder and it left us to creep slowly in the darkness across the splintery obsidian plain, never quite sure we were still on the fragmentary road.

Next morning the orangy rain began jabbing spitefully down and we found ourselves stopped by a vivid torrent that had cut the road in two. By now I was numb and trying to make myself more so. I couldn't watch the building of the makeshift ferry. I couldn't watch the crossings. I covered my ears so I couldn't hear the cries when the two cars were swept away. I blindly thrust my extra sweater out to wrap the limp, dripping Butch in before he was pushed into Scott's car. I didn't tense and gasp as we were ferried across. I knew—I knew—There was light long enough to get our—the last—car across and then the almost tangible darkness again.

Later when we stopped to rest, worn out by inching through hub-deep mud, I walked forward around the turn and saw the road stretching smoothly—almost paved-looking—away into the darkness. I waited quietly, until, with a low rumble and a moist sucking splat, mud slid from the hill above and bogged the road completely.

I went back to our car and stood stupidly near it, too disoriented even to sit down. I believe it was Miss Robbin who led me to the door and helped me in. Her face was puffed and splotchy. I remember watching with a detached sort of wonder as a tear slid down her cheek. I wondered dully how it would feel to have a small wet face pushed tight against your throat, and a tousled blond head hugged tight in your arms as a child cried for his mother. No one ever wept in my arms. I have never cried comforted, either. Blond had cried twice for his tragedy, but he had had something he thought worth the tears.

This is noon of the fifth day. We are eating our lunch now. By two o'clock they will have finished the rickety bridge that has been devised to get us across the last ravine. The dull gleam of the spacecraft is ahead of us. Voices around me are quick with relief and hope. Mrs. Lewis is reassuring Miss Leaven again that the pains will hold off until they can get across. The trek is over. We have rendezvoused. This is the last step. Step?

It's all I can do to keep from looking constantly up at the sky, wincing. If I could break through this stiff pattern of mine, I would urge them to start now! Don't waste any time! Finish the bridge! Start now so there'll be time! Let *us* go first instead of last! Watch out! Watch out! The foot will come plunging down out of the empty sky—

Instead, I sit and stare into my cooling coffee, almost too weary to lift my pencil again.

But how was I to know? A person is what he is. He acts as he acts because he acts that way. Isn't it so? *Isn't it so?*

O Loving Father—

SCIENCE FICTION AND FANTASY
FROM AVON ⬡ BOOKS